Path of the Wolf

Book 3
The War Trail Series

Charles A. McDonald

Copyright © 2016 Charles A. McDonald
All rights reserved.
ISBN: 9781790813544

DEDICATION

I dedicate this book *Path of the Wolf* to my precious wife, Louise Bertha, who guided me down the trail, and has been my constant inspiration from the first day we met. I love you.

ACKNOWLEDGMENTS

I would like to thank Arthur J. Moore Jr. for all of his hard work helping to make this book better. And especially, for my wife Louise for her love, endless hours of encouragement, research assistance, and comments.
I would also like to thank Robert Griffing for his artwork "In the Heat of Battle" used in the cover design.

The War Trail Series

The War Trail

Dark Moon

Path of the Wolf

The Trail North

The Last Viking

Also by Charles A. McDonald

IN THIS VALLEY THERE ARE TIGERS

Chapter 1

It was the year 1779, the month Wolfgang knew as May, near the middle of the time of When-The-Leaves-Are-Showing. It was spring on the most northern point of the Belle Fourche River. During the time of the Flower Growing Moon, the land always suffered one or two final snowstorms. There was still snow on the ground in the dark places and the nights were cold. The distant Big Horn Mountains, to the west, were still covered with snow. The wind would soon clear the land of snow in the low places. It was always windy on this land.
The Cottonwoods' new leaves were a startling green, and as the seedpods burst there was a constant motion of the blades and downy seeds loosed in great quantities upon the wind. Winter was over, and once again the land was fertile with the promise of life. The young trumpeter swans, called cygnets, were beginning to hatch. The butterflies of the bird world: the yellow-throated, orange-crowned, yellow-breasted, black-and-white, and American redstart warblers had returned to the territory. The birds sang with vigor.

The cow elk dropped their wiggling, moist calves to the earth. As the calves lay stretched out and hidden in their infantile vulnerability, grizzly, and black bears, mountain lions, wolves, coyotes and eagles hunted the calves, killing many in the first two weeks of life. Those that avoided the jaws and talons of the predators used their speed and endurance to follow their mothers, and survive until their first winter.

* * *

The Cheyenne warriors had patiently watched the luminous Crow village. Gradually, the lodges, glowing amber from the lodge fires burning within, went dark one by one. The Cheyenne watched the silvery, moon-splashed Crow village and its horse herd go completely silent. Even the dogs were now quiet.

According to the Cheyenne, it was the Moon When the Horses Got Fat. The weakened Crow horses had recovered from four months of eating cottonwood bark and cured grass. The Cheyenne had planned well for their night raid. The squaw-pony herd used for carrying burdens had been located and disregarded. Only the best stock would be taken, the Crow war-ponies, the fastest animals of high strength and endurance, sure-footed, reliable animals of good temperament that could be controlled easily.

During the spring, the Great-She-Bear sat high in the northwestern sky where all could see it. The Cheyenne were waiting until the seven stars, The Big Dipper, had turned around and the-star-that-does-not-move, the North Star, moved to its middle-of-the-night position. The seven stars depicted the Great She-Bear. Four stars formed the scoop, which represented a bear, and the three stars of its handle symbolized the three hunters stalking her. The appearance of a silvery-white moon, rising in the clear, windless skies, as the temperature cooled; and dew on the grass, told the watching Cheyenne warriors that they could expect fair weather the next day. They all had the same thought.

No rain!

During night raids, when an entire village was asleep, it was best to go in twos, to avoid detection. One raider watched for danger while the other stole the horses. The Cheyenne had waited downwind and had quietly taken into the Crow herd, freezing whenever a horse snorted. Because their initial approach hadn't been detected, they were counting on the surprise for an easy victory.

* * *

The young Crow warrior, Kicking Horse, was tired. All he heard were horses and an occasional night bird. He had spent the day practicing his horsemanship. This practice consisted of swinging down from the saddle and running alongside the horse, then swinging up and over to run along the other side, and finish by standing on the saddle at full gallop. After his exhausting day, he was on night guard with the horse herd. Kicking Horse rode slowly and softly along the tree line. Somewhere to the east, a distant coyote yipped. As he circled the herd, he had stopped his slow movement and listened, letting the silence fill his head. A night bird whistled in the woods. Kicking Horse held his horse. He listened hard. The bird whistled again. After a little bit, Kicking Horse nodded to himself and moved his horse forward.

"Bird."

Earlier in the night when he had made one of his frequent pauses to listen, he had heard a familiar sound, the prolonged "Whiew-ew-ew-ew," of a curious deer. He had seen the movement of the curious deer out of the corner of his eye. He had noticed the animal's sudden alert posture as the animal became uncomfortable. It had given a quick, loud blast of air through its nose, "Whphew," and was gone.

* * *

Some of the horses had begun to snort and shy. The horses then ran a short way and stopped, danced sideways throwing their heads, then continuing to graze. The horse's movement seemed uncharacteristic, and Kicking Horse anticipated danger. He wondered if it was real or imagined. He realized his mental images were allowing his imagination to spook him and tried to calm his nerves, knowing fear bred self-doubt. He kept reminding himself to remain confident and trust his own mind.

Kicking Horse remained stock-still, his face averted as he listened, with every fiber of his body, for any sound.

What could have frightened the horses? Wolves?

In an instant he felt a faint shiver of premonition; a flicker of heightened sense, but then it was gone. He shook off the cold feeling that had crept over his body and continued his slow rounds. There had been no sound, no scent, no hint of movement, but something was there; something was amiss. A big, slow-drifting cloudbank obscured the moon and darkness overshadowed the land. Kicking Horse shut his eyes for a minute and strained his ears listening to the night. Suddenly, he realized what it was. His sixth sense told him someone or something was there.

Who are they?

From the silence came the sound of the horses breaking away again, running and trotting. Then the moon reappeared, and in the distance he caught a glimpse of dark, dim forms moving slowly among the horses. The muscles of his back stiffened with anticipation and knotted so tightly that they ached. He instantly realized the terrible danger he was in, and he momentarily froze.

A war party!

The ground vibrated, and a close, ominous noise caused Kicking Horse to pause. He realized he could not speak or make a sound. Then he heard them coming. His breathing became more rapid as his fear froze him in place. He stood without moving because his legs were heavy and numb under him. His legs began to tremble as he fought to control his breathing, to relax and dissolve his fear. As he listened, he heard more footsteps approaching.

A black silhouette, with dark-circled eyes, lying in a shallow depression, rose, and with a swift rush, knocked the slow-moving Crow guard to the ground. For a brief moment, Kicking Horse saw the cruelty of the warrior's expression. His nostrils and lips twitched while Kicking Horse struggled to move his cold, stiff muscles. Alone, Kicking Horse found he was locked in a silent struggle with a warrior older and stronger. The more former warrior's arms were sinewy and well muscled. The two men struggled, gasping, using only the strength of their upper bodies. As the silent life and death struggle continued, the older warrior's teeth gleamed in the night as an evil smile spread over his face. He knew he had gained the upper hand against Kicking Horse.

The Cheyenne warrior's alert, dark, bloodshot eyes kindled with hatred and burning delight as he looked into the eyes of his victim. His lips drew back in a snarl as his left hand sought the area beneath his victim's chin to shut of any call of alarm. However, his hand found purchase on the lower face of Kicking Horse, who raised his right arm high in anticipation of a final blow. Kicking Horse's instincts had served him well as he saw the axe descending towards his head for the final blow. To avoid the strike, he seized and bit down on one of his attacker's bony fingers while instantaneously twisting his head. He took a quick breath and screwed up his face, making a convulsive effort to throw the weight off above him. As the Cheyenne lost his critical power, he cried out in extreme pain, realizing his balance was spoiled. He was shoved forward and cartwheeled over the young Crow's head. The Cheyenne warrior, for a sickening moment, had a panicked thought that he was about to die; that the younger, weaker Crow warrior had won.

I am going to die!

Chapter 2

Kicking Horse did not let go of his attacker and came up on top of him, clawing the knife from his hip. Taking the advantage with his curved, eight-inch trade knife, drawn, and reflecting the light, Kicking Horse was ready to kill. The Cheyenne warrior now faced the image of the long knife penetrating his flesh. Before Kicking Horse could finish his attacker, deeply burying his blade between the Cheyenne's ribs, just under the arm, he heard rustling behind him. He turned his head and glanced up, aware of a warrior poised, momentarily. Terror filled Kicking Horse of the dreadful inevitability of seeing an ax outlined against the night sky overhead. Kicking Horse stiffened in fear as he realized the swung axe would split his skull. The pain exploded in his head as the fatal, wicked blow of the tomahawk struck him. He bleated as it bit deep, splitting the top of his head in half, driving him to the ground. Kicking Horse stiffened as his world faded to black. His blood-splattered head stared blindly at the ground.

The Cheyenne warrior was helped from the ground by his comrade. He fought for his breath as he swayed from exhaustion, panting and shaking, dazed and weak as the frenzy left him. He stood staring down at the lifeless form of the young Crow.

AAAAAH! "He nearly killed me," he said.

He flexed his hand as blood dripped from it onto the ground. His hand ached terribly, and he tried to ignore it. His friend knelt briefly over the young Crow warrior and tugged and wrenched the tomahawk loose, then rose to say, "Now we take the horses. Avoid the light-colored horses; white, gray, dun or buckskin. They are more subject than their darker horses to flies and mosquitos, and seem to grow hot and die more often." His friend grinned, and his eyes gleamed as he held the fresh scalp. The raw smell of blood was in their nostrils.

* * *

Wolfgang and Stars Come Out were up early. Stars Come Out, his wife, had cooked the morning meal and he had eaten heartily. The sun was already two fingers above the horizon. Half-an-hour high. Each finger movement of the sun represented 15 minutes of time. Wolfgang liked the way the Indians kept track of time.

Wolfgang had just finished up cleaning his three rifles. He examined his two newer rifles that had rifle stocks that were thicker. The octagonal barrels were more massive, and shorter. Using his fingers, he determined that the barrels were about thirty-eight inches long. Each rifle had two triggers. The rear triggers were set triggers. Once pulled and set, it made the forward trigger a hair trigger for accurate shot placement. He merely had to apply slight pressure, and the rifle would fire. And they were of larger calibers, fifty-caliber, which was good. Examining the coned muzzles, and their slow rifling twist to stabilize the patched round ball, he was satisfied there was no pitting in the barrels.

His older, long, small-bored Kentucky rifle was heavy-barreled and extremely accurate. It was less effective on large game, also awkward to carry on horseback and ill-suited to mounted combat. His old long rifle had often suffered from the rigors in the saddle and combat. But it had come far with him, and he loved it best.

The stocks of the two newer rifles no longer had patch boxes. These were the rifles, which while in the trading post had been referred to as the "mountain" or "Tennessee" rifle. The talk had been that they required a powder charge up to a one-to-one load, equal weights of powder and ball. He had selected one rifle and test fired it at a distance of 200 yards earlier that morning. It delivered remarkable precision at that distance.

Wolfgang had then experimented with the loads as he tested each of the rifles. He found that a lead ball weighing 217 grains, and patched with fine linen so that it would fit tight, worked best. He could use 205 grains of powder, and the rifle would give a low trajectory and great smashing power with little recoil.

He sat, looking at his own long rifle. Most black powder rifles had to be cleaned every few shots because of the hard carbon buildup. If the rifle became fouled, a ball could not be rammed down the barrel, rendering the rifle useless. Wolfgang was thankful for the grooves in his barrel. The lubricant held there kept the fouling soft and allowed him multiple shots.

* * *

Wolfgang knew he must water and then saddle his buffalo runner. He was waiting for Black Shield. A brief, uneasy silence reigned over the village. Wolfgang and Stars Come Out attention was drawn to the distant sound of a crier riding through the village with an announcement about something that happened during the night. There was a noticeable nervous stir in the village, and among the older men who had been relaxing, sitting around small fires, chattering among themselves and laughing. Cries rose from the camp. People started angrily shouting as they emerged from their lodges, then came cries of alarm. The village people could be heard muttering excitedly. The neighing of horses carried faintly on the wind in the distance.

He is late!

Suddenly there was a tapping on the lodge; the door curtain was thrust aside. Black Shield stooped and entered and stood just inside the door. He was a tall, muscular warrior. His handsome beaked nose protruded far beyond his deeply sunken, dark eyes. Shoulder-length black hair hung around his lean face, with temple braids like Wolfgang.

He looked at Wolfgang wild-eyed and gasped out, "Iskoochiia. A Cheyenne war party was here during the night. Many of the horses are gone and two night guards are dead. The crier is delivering the message to the village now."

"The Cheyenne and the Crow had been at war for generations," mused Wolfgang.

Black Shield's jaw clenched. He stared without blinking at the imposing man, the one known as the Two-legged Man-Bear. He was tall, lean, a strong blond man with brawny arms, and the striking characteristic of wolf-like eyes. Wolfgang called "Okwaho"—the Wolf, by the Iroquois far to the east, who moved with a quiet sureness and power.

He was a white man, adopted by the tribe, whose scarred face had been burned dark by years spent in the sun with the Crow. His blond hair, cut at his shoulders and worn loose except for temple braids, stood looking at him, grimly.

"Who was killed?" asked Wolfgang. All expression died from his face, hearing a distant low wail. The sound was followed by a rising eerie moaning cry of a woman. Moments later, another pitiful screech rose as a family mourned their loss. It was the traditional Mourning Song of the People. The sound grated on the ears of Stars Come Out. After a heartbeat, Stars Come Out felt a sudden jolt of adrenaline, stunned trembling as nervous apprehension coursed through her body, she squinted askance at Black Shield.

My husband will be leaving!

"Red Deer and Kicking Horse," Black Shield said, staring at Wolfgang. They stared at each other momentarily, then Black Shield continued, "I found their trail. The thieves are driving the horses southeast, straight toward Bear Butte. Our chief will not split forces to follow them. He says this horse raid may be a ruse.

The enemy may attack the village. The chief says that you and I must follow them, find out who they are and where they are going, before the chief takes any action." Black Shield looked at Stars Come Out and saw her eyes briefly widen in astonishment and alarm.

As Black Shield and Stars Come Out looked at Wolfgang for advice, they observed a reluctance to go. Slowly they saw a change take place in his eyes and face, tortured by thoughts that he could not escape. Seeing his eyes, Stars Come Out froze in place. She watched helplessly, then turned away pursing her lips and rolling her eyes with an all-too-familiar feeling in the pit of her stomach. A look of shock and fear covered her face as tears welled up.

As if from a great distance, Wolfgang felt a voice and a spirit compelling him to go. Suddenly, he knew he was being urged to go, and he knew who was calling him to act.

Dark Moon!

At the very same moment, he thought of Dark Moon, Yellow Bird Singing, the tribal shaman, appeared with a catlike dignity, and with her large, deep-set eyes looked into his. She said, "I see the Great Bear inside you is no longer sleeping. The chief and his advisers have agreed that you and Black Shield will pursue the raiders. I had a vision of success. The dust of a war party will merely tell the raiders they are followed. Spirit Bird will watch over you both."

The Raven.

As Yellow Bird Singing watched Wolfgang, he suddenly remembered a long-ago elk hunt with Dark Moon and her words to him during the chase. To see one raven is lucky. The Raven will activate the energy of magic, linking it to your will and intention. He-With-The-Sun-In-His-Mouth. The symbol of dark prophecy—of death.

Yellow Bird Singing, staring intently into the windows of his soul, smiled at him and said, "I see you remember, he is called the Crooked Beak of Heaven, who devours human flesh, the one, who devours human eyes."

Wolfgang was amazed saying, "How do you know what I am thinking?"

"That's why I am the shaman," she replied. Momentarily, she was silent while looking at him, then, she continued. "You are a strong, brave man. You have laid down your independent spirit, realizing you need the people of this tribe. You are not an angry or selfish man and have accepted our chief as your leader. The people of this tribe need you, so be careful and come back to us."

Wolfgang just looked at Yellow Bird Singing. The change in the appearance of the apprentice, and the similarity to his dead wife, Dark Moon, was remarkable. Now as the shaman, she is great, Yellow Bird Singing is now tall and her lithe body, healthy and well formed. Her coal black hair with the hairpiece and an attached feather for honor is long and wild. Her striking eyes are dark and mysterious looking. She moves with the grace of the great cat. She is beautiful. Dangerous!

Wolfgang pulled his gaze away.

Black Shield was suddenly in awe of the adventure they were about to undertake.

Chapter 3

Wolfgang's favorite buffalo runner, Spirit Dog, was tied up outside the lodge. "Mouse!" Wolfgang called a young boy and gave him instructions to catch Mouse and bring him in immediately. He owned many horses and carefully considered their conformation as he determined their suitability. He needed a game and tenacious mount whose cannon bones were strong and whose disposition was without temper or flightiness. Mouse! He had schooled the horse and built his trust. Mouse had endurance, never suffered the trauma and stress of other horses and was athletic. He had a level head and was not prone to a trip that could cause a flip, and had good night eyes.

Wolfgang and the others inside the lodge heard the distant, frantic galloping of horse hooves growing louder, approaching at high speed. Then there was the sound of two horses sliding to a stop outside the lodge. The young boy had arrived with Mouse. The sound was so dull that they could see the animals sitting down on their haunches, their forelegs bracing and the hooves digging into the ground. Wolfgang heard a tentative sound of nostrils drawing air, weighing the scent. Wolfgang finished preparing for his journey, giving Mouse an opportunity to settle down. Then he got up and went outside.

Mouse, excited, rolling his white-ringed eyes, was bouncing up and down with eagerness to get going. He settled down upon seeing Wolfgang. Mouse had filled out and now moving with a quiet sureness and power as he welcomed Wolfgang with a whicker of recognition and a shake of his head. Mouse walked up, touched Wolfgang's shoulder, and sniffed his nose in greeting. Wolfgang blew into his nose and sniffed. Mouse's breath was sweet on his face.

"Good Morning Mouse," he said quietly, as his fingers gently scratched at Mouse's nose and then around his ears. "We're both going to have a long trail today. I hope you're ready." Mouse snuffled his hand for the little sweet that was sure to be there. That ritual finished, Mouse nuzzled him.

The gelding is more stable.

Wolfgang stepped back away from his horse. Mouse looked to be in superb form. His muscular development was better, and he stood taller and more substantial than the average Crow horse. His body was large, round and smooth. His chest was massive, broad and deep, supported by sound legs with healthy hoofs to match them. He was fast. He had an excellent disposition and had never been known to fall, or pitch, or balk at anything. Wolfgang studied his horse's action. His eyes inspected Mouse's legs, fixing on the horse's knees. He ran the flat of his hand slowly along the back of the cannon bone down to the fetlock tracing the "splint bones," checking the ligaments for inflammation or swelling. His fingers traced, then along the joints tendons of the back of the legs, feeling the soft tissue of the lower leg for any swelling and puffiness of an affected part. All he felt was a uniform cool-firmness indicating a healthy limb. He found them clean and cool. Mouse would have flinched to the touch, during his check, to any marked pain.

No sign of soreness!

He grabbed the tuft of hair just above the hoof at the animal's fetlock and then picked the foot up and checked the hollow of the pastern for cracks because they often occurred on the horses wintered on wet meadows.

Nothing!

Wolfgang's wife, Stars Come Out, her lips quivering, her face silently pleading as tears pooled in her dark eyes, and trying to calm her pounding heart, just looked at her husband. He is so beautiful and strong. He is now 44 winters old. His golden hair pulled back except for a handful of hair braided on both sides of his face, blue eyes, and his broad shoulders give him the appearance of youth. He should not be again going out to face great danger, against younger warriors. But, at least he has regained his interest in activities and coitus.

She said, "Travel well husband." Her voice lifting at the end, unable to speak more, she handed him his small, sacred tobacco pouch, made for him by Dark Moon, to protect him when he went off to war. She swallowed uneasily as terror gripped her.

She grabbed and pressed herself against him trembling, her lips twitching.

Wolfgang's eyes shone, they were alive and alert as he grabbed a tuft of Mouse's mane and swung himself up into the saddle. Mounted, Wolfgang sat for a moment facing south, scratching Mouse's mane. The two women, both watching Wolfgang, thought the same thing. Wolfgang and the horse are as one.

Wolfgang looked at Stars Come Out, and Yellow Bird Singing nodded his head and looked to another companion, the great wolf had appeared and stood to watch. The wolf was a magnificent animal, fathered by the second wolf that had been sired by an animal far to the east and raised by Wolfgang as part of his family. The long, dark-tipped, guard hairs on the gray wolf's shoulders, neck, and spine, stood up on end and waved with the wind. The black hair extended down along the top of the tail of the gray coat. The hair on the great male wolf's legs had a slightly tufted appearance.

The wolf stood firmly on his legs apart from everyone, wanting nothing to do with people, other than Wolfgang. Its head marked with dark hairs around its great yellow eyes and ears emphasized the features of its face. Its ears pointed toward Wolfgang, watching, raised wet nostrils, sniffing the air.

Wolfgang was well aware that the great wolf had appeared because all the village dogs had quietly disappeared. All the nearby people had noticed the sudden presence of the powerful spirit animal that was part of Wolfgang's family. Wolfgang momentarily watched the language of the wolf, in its facial expression and body movements, as the wind rippled the large animal's coat and saw the wolf shading its fur and making its signal to him. I'm ready!

The tribal shaman, Yellow Bird Singing, seeing the green-blue aura surrounding the wolf, stood thinking. This wolf is of a trustworthy and helpful nature. "Your power animal, the Pathfinder is here," remarked Yellow Bird Singing, smiling.

Wolfgang pointed, and the master hunter gave a quiet "woof," and suddenly and silently, without effort, trotted off in the tireless, fluid motion of a long-distance hunter.

He enjoys the chase!

Wolfgang focused on the direction he wanted to go. Mouse swiveled one ear backward, having picked up its riders silent cue to go. Wolfgang leaned forward. Mouse started away into a walk. He chirruped Mouse into a trot. The horse being able to understand moved in a southeastern direction. Wolfgang shifted his weight slightly, cueing Mouse to turn and stop. Wolfgang stared at his wife's frightened and saddened eyes, silently saying goodbye.

Stars Come Out felt discomfort in the center of her chest and shortness of breath as her eyes met Wolfgang's with the intimacy of a lingering touch. She raised her left arm, holding it aloft, praying that Wolfgang and Black Shield would hurry back safely to the village. Fear and frustration shot through her body like a hot fire and desperation showed in her eyes.

Looking at Stars Come Out, the tribal shaman, Yellow Bird Singing, trying to ease her pain, said, "His animal totems, his power medicine, the Great Bear and Wolf, has awakened in him. Your husband will meet his totem on this journey and call on its energy to inspire him. Now I must leave you, I must go find mushrooms for my visions."

Wolfgang looked far into the distance, glimpsing the disappearing wolf, affectionately said to Mouse, "Follow the path of the wolf."

Chapter 4

Early the next morning, Wolfgang and Black Shield had stood a long time. They listened to the wind, hearing what was moving, as the light came slowly in a covering of low-lying clouds. When it was full daylight, there was no sun, only a yellow wash across the overcast, leaden-colored eastern sky. They watched the flight of birds and were satisfied that the birds were unafraid and undisturbed. Colder, drier air was sweeping in from the Rockies. The wind was picking up and making a low moaning sound as it danced through the tall prairie grass. The early spring rains from the southwest were over; the weather was making the transition to summer heat. It was a time when severe thunderstorms could be expected at any time, without a moment's notice.

The wind was strong and blustery. They noticed in the distance to the west, the sound of thunder and lightning from a great snow-white cloud; its base a deep shade of blue. The sudden noise meant an accompanying afternoon downpour. It was a promise of life to the people, grasslands and its animals and bird life. Most of the moisture came to plains in this region during the Grass Growing Moon, Moon of Roses, and the Moon of Thunder. The clouds belly pulsed with fire. May, June and July mused Wolfgang. The two Crow warriors now noticed the sudden cool breeze out of the west, as they watched a distant stab of lightning and listened to the rumble of the storm rolling over the prairie.

* * *

It had been a long night on the trail, but the moon grew larger each night nearing the time of the full moon. The trail was plain enough. After the night of the full moon, the path will become smaller and smaller, with less light to travel by, mused Wolfgang, and will set just before sunrise.

Good! Less light to be seen by.

The stolen horses were being moved fast. They could see the prints were deep and far apart, with little rims of dirt pushed up in the back of each print. The stolen horses had been kept at a gallop most of the night and part of the early morning. Wolfgang and Black Shield studied the land. Their thoughts were the same.

The land is corrugated, and the Cheyenne are keeping the stolen herd in the long swales, coulee's and long shallow draws where they will be invisible even to someone nearby. Only the flight of birds in the far distance, mark their passing.

* * *

Wolfgang and Black Shield, using their natural knowledge, observed the most significant feature of the tracks; where the hind legs registered in relation to the forelegs. They could see from the tracks that the hind legs of the horses were planted near side-by-side, well in front of the fore hoofs. The forelegs were planted apart from, and one behind the other, to balance the body. The weaving trail they had been following was now more in a straight line, indicating that the horses had slowed their gait down and were now being kept at a trot.

* * *

Wolfgang and Black Shield were resting their horses below the crest of the ridge on the reverse slope. They had stalked up the slope of the hill and then crawled until only their heads peaked from cover so that anyone looking their way would see nothing. They saw just the movement of birds far ahead, then padded back down the slope. Wolfgang felt lucky to be with Black Shield, who wore three feathers for counting coup. Wolfgang knew the stories. The most honorable was when Black Shield had struck an armed enemy with his bow before killing him for his first coup feather. The other two feathers were for stealing horses; trained buffalo runners, tied to a lodge in an enemy village, on two separate occasions.

* * *

Black Shield edged his horse up alongside Wolfgang's; the nostrils of his mount flaring with effort. They sat their horses still at the top of a rise and looked south. They smelled the horse sweat as the animals snorted for breath. Their climb to the top of a large hill that rose out of the rolling plain that had tired the horses. The two just stared into the distance, examining the southern horizon--all their senses alert. They stared at the settling pall of dust that hung in the air, kicked up by the stolen horse herd. Both Wolfgang and Black Shield knew where the Cheyenne trail was leading.

Raising his voice against the wind, "They are going to cross the horses above the forks of La Belle Fourche. The Beautiful Fork, in the valley where the rivers meet and converge. The Redwater River and the two smaller creeks run into the Belle Fourche," said Wolfgang.

They saw a silent and ominous moving shadow on the ground, and then heard the soft rhythmic pushing of air; the beating of wings overhead. They looked up and saw the glistening ebony eye of the raven, gliding close by, looking at them, and then it was gone as it glided and soared upward on flat wings like a hawk. The mystical bird that foretells death kept a straight course into the distance, in the direction of the La Belle Fourche.

"He spoke to us," said Black Shield.

"The raven's magical energy is now linked to our will and intention," said Wolfgang, looking at Black Shield.

The chief of the Germanic gods, the learned one-eyed Odin, the inspiration for hard-bitten warriors; was known to shape-shift as a raven himself. It has to be true because my country and this new land and its wild people share the same beliefs.

* * *

The tracker's attention sharply focused, Wolfgang and Black Shield stared southeast into the distance through the grey haze, toward the lone mountain, known as Bear Butte. He saw a white-headed eagle soaring on long, broad wings, with its primary flight feathers splayed like fingers, watching for the opportunity to swoop on an unwary antelope fawn. The trackers had followed the stolen horses without difficulty. It was easy because horses have sharp, hard hooves leaving good tracks and a wide path of crushed flat grass. The trail looked lighter than the surrounding grass and could be seen for miles. Their vision remained sharp at the varying distances. Their eyes constantly shifted and searched to keep them focused. The vast emptiness of the endless green sea of tender grass moved in the wind like the ocean. Their eyes easily followed the clearly visible trail of crushed and bruised grass going away from them to the horizon.

Wolfgang glanced at the sun.

"Horses four fingers time ahead of us," Black Shield said.

Wolfgang looked at the horizon in all directions.

As they watched, they saw the white-headed eagle had located prey and was dropping down in a shallow glide toward a young antelope.

Black Shield looked at the position of the sun again.

"I figure they will not turn and fight. We should ride fast," said Wolfgang. They moved their horses into a fast canter, their long hair flying.

*   *   *

The dark, wet trampled grass contrasted with the surrounding silvery green that was bent and broken. The grass laid in the direction the horses had traveled. To get to the point on the horizon where the tracks disappeared, Wolfgang and Black Shield would often take shortcuts, which allowed them to remain out of sight. Upon reaching their destination, they would once again pick up the trail.

Following the trail was easy. At mid-afternoon Mouse ears up, kept looking off to the south, then nickered in communication, telling Wolfgang and Black Shield of the presence of another horse nearby. They quickly came across a limping horse, its head down in fatigue. They regularly checked for positive proof of the horse herd and the amount of time the horses spent at any given point in the prairie. They gathered this information from the discoloration of the grass by breaking off dead grass stems, comparing their color and moisture content to the stalks of live grass. They also checked the rough surface of the trail where the soil and displaced stones had been churned up by the passage of many hoofs. They knew from the tracks that the herd was in a loping pattern.

They identified individual horses they knew well by the uniqueness of their tracks. A horse track is a single semicircle with an unbroken front edge, and a triangular notch of the frog in the back. The oval horse hoof is difficult to confuse with any other animal. Many horses walk by placing their smaller hind feet exactly into the tracks made by their wider and rounder front feet. They checked the asymmetry in the hooves such as toe length, width, and depth. Cracks, chips, and broken hoofs provided information about which hoof had left the distinctive mark. Their people inspected the hooves often to detect any irregularities of their growth. They studied the gait and sharp edges of the tracks for time and the load the horses carried. Wolfgang realized that the unshod hoof of the Indian horse was healthier and could stand more neglect than a shod horse belonging to the Whiteman.

The state of the droppings was used as a time indicator and a sign of the animal's proximity. They broke open droppings to check moisture content, which confirmed how long ago the horses had been there. To identify the districts in which the thieves had already passed, they examined different species of gramma and buffalo grass content, present in the horses' droppings. The droppings, the size of a man's fist, were soft and still warm enough that they could smell them, indicating their close proximity. Identifying the different grasses growing in various districts, they were able to keep their minds active and aware. They determined the sex of the different horses by the attitude they assumed while urinating. The stallions and geldings stretched themselves and sent their stream forward of their hind legs, while the mares sent their flow of urine to the rear of their hind prints.

Chapter 5

The Cheyenne had unsuccessfully tried to hide the horse trail by moving like wolves at night, taking advantage of the fold after fold in the terrain's contours to observe but remain hidden. The Cheyenne also moved the herd out in front of buffalo and elk herds whenever possible. This allowed the moving elk and buffalo herds to cover their tracks. But the horse trail was clear enough even on hard ground because of the horse droppings. Since the Cheyenne were in a hurry to leave the Crow country behind, they maintained the same direction of travel.

They wasted little time moving through the Box Elder, Ash, Willow and Cottonwood trees that lined the river, except to stop briefly, go down to the water and offer their greenish-brown tobacco to the Water Spirit and their Creator. They asked the Water Spirit and their Creator for a safe journey and for guidance. Wolfgang and Black Shield then crossed the crystal clear waters of the Redwater River that flowed from the high granite spires in the center of the Black Hills. Wolfgang and Black Shield finally came to Whitewood Creek, where they decided to stop and rest the horses.

Black Shield said, "Soon water high." The spring runoff would soon raise the water level, but it is not yet time for the level of the creeks and streams to flood where they could not be crossed, thought Wolfgang. Wolfgang replied, "In the Moon of Roses, it will flood. Depending upon how fast the snow-pack melts in the mountains, it might prove difficult to cross the horses in the days ahead. The Cheyenne planned well." The Moon of Roses was the time that Wolfgang knew as June.

The soil along the creek was rich and the grass was good. The abundance of oaks meant an abundance of deer. The small creek had good water. Open bare hills surrounded them and they felt safe, while the horses grazed and rested. Having killed a small deer, they had eaten and rested, then rode straight to Spring Creek and crossed it to Nowahwas (Bear Butte), which was prominent on the skyline to the southeast.

*   *   *

Wolfgang and Black Shield climbed up through the steep rocks, loose stones and pines of Bear Butte. Sweat from the steep climb coated their bodies. Wolfgang stared into the distance as he climbed and saw a deep purple and bluish tint to the whole wet meadowland ahead. Camas! The flowering food plant was luxuriantly growing along the stream in the wet meadow. Elk and deer were contentedly grazing the plant. There is no danger!

Their faces perspiring from the climb, they checked the surrounding country. They wanted to be sure they did not ride into a Cheyenne ambush. Once Wolfgang and Black Shield reached the ridge, they lay prone upon the level, crescent shaped, high point amid the offerings of personal treasured items placed there to the Great Spirit. They looked across the level and smooth plain covered with streams. They observed Spring Creek to the north. Looking further north they could see the bluffs of the North Cheyenne River (Belle Fourche River). To the northeast, and east, the land was flat as far as they could see.

Nothing!

To the immediate south was the good water and plentiful grass and cottonwood trees along the Bear Butte Creek. In the far distance to the south and southwest, about ten miles away, were the towering black mass of cedar and pine-covered hills; lightened by stands of aspen and birch trees, weather-washed granite outcroppings, and sandstone cliffs where clear streams snaked their way down.

The Black Hills! A place of refuge from the bitter weather and raging blizzards of winter.

The fresh trail of the horses could be clearly seen heading southeast toward Alkali Creek, and the more distant Elk and Box Elder Creeks, that all ran into the Cheyenne River.

* * *

They were still following the run of their horses, stolen by Cheyenne raiders, and were carefully aware of their own movements. Against the growing light of the eastern sky the two warriors, sitting atop their horses, could just make out the silhouette of their enemies. They listened to a distant chorus of howls, which could only be ascribed to a pair of wolves. Their horses showed impatience to go by stomping their hooves and switching their tails. Wolfgang and Black Shield momentarily amused themselves by watching and listening to the staccato stamping of feet, then the low, deep cooing of a large group of birds, nearby, with a buffy appearance, and mottled feathers. The sharp-tailed grouse were on a low rise of sparse vegetation nearby. A number of displaying older males kept up a continuous noise. They jumped into the air and cackled as they fought with their claws, beaks, and wings.

"I have spent much time watching these birds. The strongest males fight to claim dominance and breeding rights with the females. The watching female selects the dominant male," said Black Shield. "I like to imitate how they dance."

* * *

The two riders had been quiet for a long time, each lost in their own thoughts. The horses picked their way carefully down a cut bank and waded halfway into a small stream and stopped to drink. Looking over at Black Shield, Wolfgang asked, "Where do the Cheyenne come from?"

"Our elders tell stories of the Cheyenne having been our enemies as far back as anyone can remember. The Cheyenne moved from the east to escape the Ojibwa and Lakota and then settled along the Fat River, (the Missouri). Now, the Cheyenne are moving again. This time they come further southwest for refuge from the epidemics brought by the French traders. These epidemics have decimated the Mandan and Hidatsa villages along the Missouri River. Because of this movement, tribal warfare has become more rampant upon the high plains," Black Shield responded, as the horses started to move up the cut bank into the grass and sage.

Our people are surrounded by enemies in all directions. The Blackfoot, to the north, the Shoshone to the west, the Lakota to the east and the Cheyenne to the south, mused Wolfgang.

Looking at Wolfgang, Black Shield referred to the Cheyenne and announced, "I know where the striped arrows are going."

Wolfgang looked at Black Shield and waited for him to continue. When Black Shield didn't offer a response, Wolfgang asked where they were headed.

"They are driving towards the head waters of the North Platte River where a wide valley is bordered by high bluffs. It is the western most village of the Cheyenne and a long way from here." As Black Shield spoke, the sun finally appeared and the sky began to clear. Then he added, "The old man with a furred cloak is numerous there."

Grizzlies!

Wolfgang felt a shiver go up his spine as he remembered the sound of the long rattling claws and the open mouthed roar of the grizzly, he had encountered so long ago. He was still for a moment and focused his thoughts. He then stated above the wind, "Today we must make good time and arrive at camp early.

Tonight it will be too dark to follow because there will be no moon." It was the time of the new moon. After some thought, Wolfgang continued thinking out loud and began to explain, "The waxing moon will continue to grow in size each night, until, in seven more days it enters its First Quarter. Tonight we must rest. If the clouds and weather permit, we will have good light for many days. The nights will begin to grow shorter and the days will grow longer."

Wolfgang and Black Shield both understood that showery and humid air would soon follow. They rode and talked, or lay hidden and watched the herds of wild game. From time to time, the sign of the trail was lost. The movement of the wild herds obscured the tracks and broke the monotony of the view. The vast space of the prairie in every direction was covered with buffalo, elk and antelope and the ground could not be seen. Because of the buffalo, numbering in the hundreds of thousands, they were always careful to keep the last directional sign of the horse herd they had tracked in the event they lost the tracks again. It was not uncommon to see Continuing, Wolfgang yelled, "Clouds are already building up." one to two hundred whitetail deer in a single herd. They killed just enough to feed themselves. Slowly they crawled up as far as they dared and peaked over the top and studied the plain as far as they could see.

Nothing!

Chapter 6

Both Wolfgang and Black Shield looked out over a sea of prairie grass. The rolling hills and draws could hide many men on horseback. They heard the familiar snorting, grunting-bellow, and smelled the unpleasant stink. The noise was a deep, sustained sound that was unlike any other. They edged up the hill a little further. There below them, was the staff of life. Buffalo! As they examined the small herd of mud-covered buffalo below, grazing in the wide, smooth coulee and richly grassed bottom, they noticed many lying down and some asleep. There were already many newly dropped, yellow calves. Because of the strong wind, the buffalo were able to tolerate the flies and swarms of buffalo gnats. Antelope were nearby.

Wolfgang and Black Shield watched the scattered groups of snuffling buffalo feed into the wind, their great jaws moving as they cropped the lush grass, while flicking their tails at the many flies. Without looking at Wolfgang, Black Shield made graceful and eloquent gestures with his hands to Wolfgang. "I will kill a young fat cow," said his hands.

They would raise too much dust to chase after cows with young calves.

Both men knew that the calves born in May were hunted for their meat, for their meat was best. The meat from a cow is at its best in the fall. Throughout most of the year, the meat of the bulls was tough and unpalatable compared with that of cows. The early summer months the meat of bulls is prime.

They watched the many buffalo birds gorging themselves on the animals backs, diligently feeding on the parasites and maggots of their hosts and other insects such as grasshoppers and beetles, kicked up by the moving animals. The birds moved from the backs to the head and around the ears, feeding on the swarms hovering about the animal's body as the buffalo fed and rested on the ground. Many of the birds were just resting in the fuzzy warmth, their appetites satisfied, now served as a sentinel for signs of danger.

Recognizing an opportunity, Black Shield said, "We must have food. Just follow me."

As Wolfgang watched, Black Shield drew his bow from his case and quiver along with three arrows. One he put crosswise in his mouth and the other he knocked to the bow. The third arrow was in his left hand, point down, feather's up, so that when the right hand reached out and drew the shaft, the left would not be cut. The horses threw their heads, anxious to run. Within an instant the horses took off with a clatter amid rattling stones over the rim and going down the hillside, quickly gaining speed down the rise. The expanding white rump of the antelope telegraphed a visual, long-range communication of warning to all the animals near and far and a loud, high-pitched musical singing sound of warning to those close by.

Hieu-u-u-u!

The graceful antelope, startled, took off with their heads held high, then stretched their heads and necks forward, laid back their ears and ran at a swift pace.

The buffalo alerted by the bird sentinels crying and fluttering on their backs and flying away abruptly with their chattering calls, erected their shaggy manes, their bloodshot eyes glared venomously. The nearest standing bull tested the air uneasily with wet nostrils, then snorted, rolled his eyes-balls and pawed the earth. With his ponderous humped shoulders thrusting forward, he began walking with a swinging gait, his long beard and great shaggy head waggling.

Those animals scattered here and there over the plain and

resting on the ground, got up, grunting, anger rolling from deep in their throats. The shaggy beasts cocked their tails and with an expression of fright, whirled and started running when they saw the hunters. The buffalo ran close together as if on command of a leader. The terrible sound of thudding and rattling of hooves filled the air like thunder. Wolfgang and Black Shield caught up to the sharp-horned, bobbing heads as the earth produced a deep rumbling.

The ears of Black Shield's horse flipped back and flattened briefly, then stood straightforward, intent upon its tender victim. The horse, lunging forward, quickly had him on the right side of a small cow. The young cow's broad, round hips indicated it was the fattest meat. The young cow was wild eyed with fear. Wolfgang could see that it was not necessary for Black Shield to urge his horse to get closer to the buffalo. The horse was soon by the side of the buffalo cow. Wolfgang prayed to God that his friend would not be lifted, horse and all, upon the horns of the buffalo. Black Shield leaned quite low on his horse's neck and released an arrow. It struck perfectly in back of the ribs with astonishing force, instantly disappearing forward and downward through the paunch and into the heart and lungs. The arrow was properly placed and driven down to the feathers, encountering no bones. Blood gushed from the cow's nostrils. It slowed, and dropped out of the herd. The cow's feet flew out from under her and she tumbled over and landed with a loud kerwhomp!, leaving hair and a bloody skid mark as it slid. At the smell of blood, the trailing herd of buffalo picked up speed.

The horses were hard to keep in check, becoming wild to continue the chase. They must not raise any more dust than necessary. Raised dust would signal to their enemies that they were on the move.

They dismounted and Wolfgang skinned down the cow's lower jaw, pulled the black tongue through the opening, and cut it off at the base; its blackness distinguished its delicacy. Black

Shield recovered his arrow, wiped off the blood and replaced it in his quiver. Together, they wrenched the head around, grounding the horns into the ground, close to the shoulder. Together they grasped a foreleg by the ankle, pulled and rolled the cow on its back, the body propped against the horn-grounded head, holding the body up, feet in the air. The carcass now held in place, Black Shield cut the hide from tail to neck, along the belly and down each leg. Within minutes the bare carcass lay on the spread-out hide. Thirsty, they drank the acidic water from the full paunch. Then took a break, selecting the raw liver, removed the gall from its place beneath the liver. Black Shield sprinkled the liver with the alkaline, yellow-green, bile fluid from the gall bladder, to improve the taste for them to munch on. They heard a rapid series; of guttural, harsh notes; from an excited magpie reach their ears. Black Shield and Wolfgang looked up and saw the beautiful, flashy, black and white family bird. Soon more of the cocky, long-tailed birds collected, working for the leftovers. Black Shield and Wolfgang sprinkled the salty bile from the gallbladder onto the liver and ate it raw and warm on the spot, dripping blood over their fingers and chins, as they watched the impudent, scavengers on the carcass.

The legs of the cow were cut off and they rolled the carcass onto its side. An incision was made along the base of the hump so they could break it off. They removed the tender muscle group, "loins," along each side of the backbone, from the neck to the pelvis. After they removed the ribs in two sections, they removed the tenderloin found inside the body under the ribs. The job was complete. The cow was butchered. Grass was used to clean their knives and ax. The portions were tied in the hide and packed on the horse.

Wolfgang started a small, smokeless fire of dry chokecherry wood and burned an offering of tobacco, showing respect for the animal's spirit.

Finally, they rode down a swale of high, rank waving grass

toward the nearest line of willows. The gray trunks and fluttering leaves of cottonwoods betrayed a creek bottom where they would first pick a cook site and then a more distant and safe campsite.

They kept an eye on the westering sun as they collected the heavy, hard firewood from a choke cherry thicket in a nearby ravine. The sun was still three fingers above the horizon as they roasted their meal; the liver and tongue, which were the best cuts. They ate their meal beneath the shade grove of huge, whispering cottonwood boughs. They sprinkled bile out of the spleen, to give their meat more flavor. As they ate, they watched the open woodland. Mule deer were feeding nearby among the bending branches in the thicket of the dark, red-brown trunks, of the small, old choke cherry trees. The trees were full of long clusters of foamy, full white flowers. They watched the looping flight of a flock of bright-yellow goldfinches with black trim and black caps and their olive-yellow females putting on a show as they fed. They listened to their long, high songs given in flight with each flap of their wings.

Per-chik-o-ree. Per-chik-o-ree.

"The choke cherry is favored by the deer," said Black Shield.

They finished their meal by cracking open the marrowbones that had been roasted in the fire, for the soft, rich, yellow marrow that could be found at the center of the bones. Finished with their meal, they put out the fire. They picked up and rode a good way to change their location for night camp, in case their cooking site had betrayed their location.

As Wolfgang and Black Shield rode out of the grassland and into the sagebrush, they could smell the bittersweet aroma of damp sage. The two Crow warriors first noticed the near invisible and silent flushing of sage grouse, whose wing and back plumage matched the sagebrush. Then, their sharp eyes saw the many glistening curls of green-and-white grouse droppings in the setting sun. Likeminded, Wolfgang and Black Shield chose a site where tall sagebrush grew next to the stream. From their campsite, they could see and watch the grayish-brown sage grouse wandering and feeding on the soft sage leaves and grasshoppers.

Wolfgang and Black Shield took time to groom and talk to their horses, an act that deepened their relationship. They kept their horses close at night and hobbled to prevent them from stomping the ground and being stolen, and would listen and watch the birds closely for any disturbance among them. This would serve as an early warning of enemies. As they neared the creek they noticed bear tracks in the creek sand and along the game trails. A solitary coyote barked and then howled.

Twilight came slowly, and the sunset lingered in its golden glory over the rolling hills, before day waned into dusk. They watched the shadows grow without spotting a thing, until the outline of the forest trunks and branches faded, softened and receded. A few wan stars had just begun to show and brighten. The birds had ceased their singing. In the light of the moon they watched the secretive creatures of the night stop, twist and turn, fluttering erratically and sharply turning silently in the darkened sky in pursuit of evasive insects. Some of the bats even seemed to hover.

Wolfgang remembered the legends of the clan animals told to him by his dead father and later his wife Dark Moon. He turned his head in the direction of Black Shield quietly saying, "The bat medicine is a symbol of change and promise, a new beginning. Our little helper has a strong and powerful medicine. They are telling us we are to be challenged on this journey, and that it is time for us to face our fears and prepare for change. What we do on this journey to new horizons, will have repercussions for years down our trail. We will awaken and see truth from a new perspective and increase our opportunity to meet with greater numbers of people."

Black Shield was silent, for a long time, in thought. Then, quietly he said, "You learned much from your wife the shaman. Like the bat, we must try to avoid obstacles and barriers."

Night was falling. They listened to the night sounds of insects, humming, chirping and thrumming a continuous song, low and monotonous. They heard the bark and eerie screams of foxes in the direction of their buffalo kill. In a short time the chuckling chortle of several coyotes was heard and then the yipping howl of a group of coyotes followed. The plains changed instantly, as a cacophony of coyotes sang and yelped back and forth. The night came alive with the call howl of wolves. The sound was pure, hornlike, and throaty.

Wolfgang's eyes and mind wandered to the seven stars that represented the Great She Bear that was nearly overhead. The four stars of the bowl, the bear, and the three stars of the handle, a trio of warriors stalking her. Wolfgang's eyes followed the line of stalking warriors and followed the arcing curve. His eyes searched along the same line and found the pale orange colored star in the northwest spring sky.

Arcturus!

He remembered being taught that it was the brightest star of the season in the spring sky. Both men observed the rapid flash of a shooting star as it plummeted downward. An Omen! Wolfgang and Black Shield both felt it was a sign of something about to happen.

After some time, the night became silent once again. Black Shield leaned over and glanced at Wolfgang.

"Something is there! " he whispered excitedly.

Chapter 7

Both Black Shield and Wolfgang realized that only the presence of a bear at the kill would bring about this silence. They smelled the water, grass and sage. As time went by, the loneliness of the night set in and the quiet was more noticeable. Wolfgang heard the drifting of a large bird cutting the air on near silent wings. He caught the ghostly form on soft-spread wings. The silhouette of a raptor, and its sweeping strokes glided passed. It angled between the trees and disappeared.

They watched the stars overhead, keeping track of the time, until the clouds obscured the moon. It was now, a dark, moonless night with no stars for light. Wolfgang and Black Shield heard the blood-curdling scream of a horned owl. They shivered. The sound was like an incantation, summoning up spirits. The sound had filled them with an evil essence. Like there was something else lying beyond their sight.

"Again an omen," said Black Shield quietly.

Wolfgang and Black Shield heard a plaintive, low, booming, hooting sound.

"Hoo-hoo-hoo-hoooo."

A great horned owl! It was perched nearby. The clean sound was abstract. Its last notes descending. The sound emanated from all points, it seemed like it could have come from anywhere, but Wolfgang and Black Shield knew it was on the forest edge. The sound was calm as a sigh. It was the mythic harbinger of death. Wolfgang crossed himself. Black Shield silently prayed.

The nocturnal predator listened intently from its vantage point on a limb. It peered patiently into the darkness, surveying its surroundings. Its bright yellow eyes studied its prey below.

The normally fearless, carnivorous animal was hunting during his favorite time, at night. Having just gone to the stream to drink, he had turned away before drinking his fill. Moving unsteadily away for some reason, he had been afraid of the water. Always he had demanded a healthy respect from the other animals, showing no quarter. Now he was slowly approaching a slow-moving form ahead of him. He did not know why he had begun to slobber at the mouth. His dark penetrating eyes stared at the alert form, wanting to bite it. A man creature!

Wolfgang and Black Shield were motionless. They were unaware of the movement of the night hunter. An animal feared by all, was approaching. It moved a few feet closer. The slight rhythm of noise made by the animal, indicated it was getting closer to the man creature.

The night hunter was bewildered and confused, moving unsteadily forward, 3 feet in a fake charge. Again it staggered forward several feet in another fake charge and came to an abrupt halt.

Wolfgang and Black Shield now felt the presence of another creature. Wolfgang felt a familiar rush of adrenaline pumping into his blood. His mouth was dry, feeling the cotton-alum taste in his mouth. Wolfgang and Black Shield both heard a light-footed approach through the leaves. They were now alert for the slightest movement, the faintest sound. Snake. A bad tempered bear. A lion! Indians! As Wolfgang and Black Shield's minds explored the realm of possibilities, they tried to sort out the night noises.

The night hunter was near-sighted and performed a foot-stomp warning by slamming its forefeet on the ground. He wanted to turn away and go, but for some unexplained reason, he started aggressively hissing and puffing himself up.

The man creatures had felt an intense expectancy, of something drawing nearer and nearer. They stiffened to attention. Sensing danger they hunkered down, listening with held breath. They hesitated, lost in the valley of decision, as their nerves wore thin. Powerful waves of emotions stretched them to the breaking point. The two warriors heard a "tap-tap-tap-tap," sound. Then they detected a small waddling creature. They smelled a faint, but familiar odor. Skunk! Relief flooded their bodies.

With intense concentration, the predator, above on the limb, moved its head from left to right, tracking its ground prey with supreme indifference. It swooped down from its vantage point, for the kill. There was no sound. The great horned owl struck the striped skunk with its long, sharp, three-pronged talons, as the skunk started to attack.

From the corner of their eyes, Wolfgang and Black Shield saw a flash of movement. They saw the feathered tufts of the Great Horned Owl as it lifted into the air with its favorite prey, a skunk. Then there was a welcomed silence. A smile registered on their faces. Skunk! A skunk had scared them. "Hmph!" Wolfgang emitted into the night.

Wolfgang jerked in momentary fright as he turned his head and saw Black Shield's tomahawk bearing silhouette upright. Black Shield whispered, "I was almost ready to kill it." Black Shield quietly squatted beside Wolfgang. He spoke again, saying, "The animal, maybe him sick." Both warriors had heard many stories about the black and white-striped animal harassing camps and fatally biting men in their sleep and later the men died. The night seemed long to the two warriors.

*   *   *

Now, the horses were quiet. Too quiet! The silence was brooding and ominous. Nothing moved! They suffered a chest constricting tension in the stillness. Something was still out there! Something large and frightening! Then they heard a steady, faint, rolling crackle, a muffled walking in the sand and the grating on the rocks of the creek bed. It sounded big and soft-footed as they plainly heard it sniffing the air. Hair stood up on Wolfgang's neck, and he expected something to come hurtling at them. It announced its presence.

Sssssss

Hau, hau, hau, hau.

The slight "S" sound that preceded the bear's announcement meant that there was no threat, they hoped. They could barely see its dark grotesque bulk, their nostrils widening at the smell. Any shift in the wind could result in an attack. The hair at the nape of Wolfgang's neck stood on end. Both men did not want to shoot a big bear from such a close distance in the dark. The pounding of the pulse in both men was the only sound they could hear. They had no trouble in staying awake. Their mouths had gone dry as they stood and talked to the horses, comforting them, being careful of the noise they made. Wolfgang concentrated and briefly saw a black silhouette standing against the night sky. It cocked its head as if watching curiously, its small eyes briefly catching the starlight and shimmering. The huge, round, lumbering bear silhouetted briefly against the sky, sniffing the wind, and withdrew. They could smell its hot fur and rank breath. It moved out of sight, but didn't go away. Terror made his hands tremble.

Wolfgang and Black Shield did not sleep the rest of the night as the bear continued to walk around, at a distance, during the night. He yawned, stretched and gazed at the eastern sky, there was a faint but definite pink tinge on the horizon. The coyotes were silent now, ready to turn the world over to the creatures of the day. It had been a long night.

Chapter 8

Daybreak brought a dull-gray, overcast sky that soon began breaking up and drifting away. The bear was gone. The melody of birds comforted them. Black Shield observed a scorpion burrow under the debris next to a rock.

The small creature that stings with a poison tail, and moves about at night and hides during the day.

They listened to the monotonous chatter of a pair of squirrels. Nearby, a squirrel scampered along a limb=hesitated once, twice, and then assumed a classic feeding position. He sat in a hunch with paws lifted to its mouth, nibbling. Occasionally, he would stop and listen. They watched as he then scampered along a limb toward the trunk and ran down the trunk of the tree, stopping periodically to watch for danger from below. Both warriors watched the small animal for signs of agitation from nearby danger, knowing that all squirrels becomes wary of the slightest disturbance and all their senses would lock onto something curious that they see, hear or smell. The squirrel ran around the trunk of the tree, and the next time they saw him he was on the ground.

The squirrel foraged around a little in the dry leaves, then sat up. Then he leaped onto a tree and flashed up and around the trunk of the tree. As they watched, the squirrel spread against the trunk and remain motionless. There was no bark of alarm or scolding of an intruder from other squirrels nearby. Playful squirrels were now scampering everywhere. Both warriors were sure it was safe.

* * *

Wolfgang and Black Shield separated, moving stealthily as shadows. Absolutely silent, they approached the creek and checked the tracks. Five long, non-retractable claws in a track wider than a hand span of spread fingers. They stood a long time unmoving, listening and watching, their keen eyes alert to every movement. Still reading the sign and watching, they slowly came together and looked at each other. Both warriors' eyes grew big as they smiled at each other and spoke at the same time.

"Big Bear!"

There was a sweetness in the air as they noted that the grouse were undisturbed. They washed, ate and talked of the courtship dancing rituals of these birds, with their spiky tail feathers, that inspired so many tribes to imitate them in dance and costume. When they were ready, they swiftly found the trail they were following, and set the horses in a long rocking gallop pace that they could hold a long time. As the antelope and elk sensed Black Shield and Wolfgang approaching, they dodged out of the warriors' way. The Sun was two hands from falling off the world. When it was time for the horses to blow, they broke stride and walked them. It was at this time that the freshness of the horse droppings revealed that they were close to the stolen herd.

They dogged the trail until the sun sank and the shadows stretched out longer and longer across the land. A deep rumbling sound in the earth made them aware of running buffalo further to the east. They watched the sky flare up in hues of orange and purple as the last glimmer of the sun disappeared over the horizon, and darkness slowly engulfed Wolfgang and Black Shield. As the shadows deepened around them, the two men lay in the darkness and listened to the noises around them. Where the horses were tethered, they could hear them blow softly now and then in the darkness. Without the moon to dull their brilliance, the stars shown like so many points of light above them.

As night set in, they, studied the stars and talked quietly about encounters with bears they and other Crows, had had over the years and about tribe members who had been killed by them. Black Shield told Wolfgang about a big wounded bear that he had once watched.

"I once saw a bear that had not been mortally wounded, packing a wound to stop the bleeding. He could reach the wound with a paw. He was packing damp leaves, moss and dirt that he had balled up and was packing it into the wound to plug up the hole," related Black Shield.

Wolfgang was silent for a while then answered saying, "Most bears have lots of fat and their blood clots up the wound. If they can reach the wound, and care for it themselves, their blood trails are lost quickly. My first wife told me that the bulk of knowledge concerning healing is kept secret. Medicine healers are respected for their plant knowledge. Plant medicines are often named for bears because the bear first discovers them in all our myths and tales. It is the bear who offers the knowledge to the people."

Ever alert as they talked in the faint ethereal blue glow of the night, their attentive eyes penetrated the shadows and watched for anything strange, missing nothing, looking for danger. They listened to the surroundings, heightened senses magnifying every sound, alert for any hint or shift of shadowed movement. They heard only the chuckling sound of the stream flowing over a shallow bed of pebbles, the light breeze rustling the grass and leaves. Then came another sound. A recognizable low, long, "whickering," tremulous sound came from the creek. Churrrr, churrr, churr.

"The bears little brother," whispered Wolfgang, "The Algonquin Indian calls the small, flat-footed, tree-climbing animal with the mystical mask and ring tail, 'arocoun or arckunem,' meaning hand scratcher. He teaches us how to change or transform ourselves by painting our face to become something we want to be or someone else, giving us mystery and magic."

They listened to the soft purring sound the animals made, as they faded into the distance down the creek, and Wolfgang and Black Shield knew they were safe for the time being.

Wolfgang stretched out his tall, muscular body, took one last look at the stars and closed his eyes. He quickly drifted off. The nightmare dream returned. Wolfgang dreamed, again, of his beloved first wife, Dark Moon. Again, he was back in the village on the Belle Fourche River, in the lodge sitting and listening to a tribal story, his browned face hard and tense with a stab of foreboding. He had a premonition of Dark Moon being in danger.

Wolfgang felt a choking and his throat closed. He was unable to breath. He saw himself running through the village, toward the willows lining the river. He felt the branches whipping his face. He saw himself running through the tall cottonwoods. He arrived at the bathing place, the small island in the river where Dark Moon bathed. "He didn't see her. Then he saw her as the sky began to darken. She was face down in the shallows." Her long dark hair spread out and waving in the current around her. "He froze. Anxiety seized his spine, as he looked around frantically." He felt cold. His heart beat rapidly and filled his ears. The sound around him was shut out. His eyes filled with tears as he ran to her. Her body was still, cold and relaxed. Wolfgang lifted his head to God and screamed, realizing she was dead.

Dead!

This dream was different from the others, Wolfgang, had always woke in a cold sweat from this nightmare that had tormented him since the death of his first wife, Dark Moon. The dream was not occurring as often anymore, and realized that the cold sweat was absent. But now, he seemed to always feel her strong presence with him during the day.

Black Shield sat beside his sleeping friend, who tossed and turned, watching and listening. Black Shield well remembered Wolfgang's agony over Dark Moon's death. For a long time Wolfgang had been disheveled, tired, hungry, suffering from an upset stomach due to the stress. Most distressing of all to his number two wife, Stars Come Out, was seeing and hearing him cry. There had been nothing anyone in the village could do to help him, but leave him alone.

Chapter 9

The Sun was still four fingers above the western horizon. The two concealed Crow warriors, listened and watched amid the roar and clatter, as the great brown current of the passing buffalo herd swept close enough for them to see the wicked gleam of wild black eyes set in shaggy hair, with horns waving menacingly. The sound was noisy, like thunder, as the hoofs thudded and rattled and the horns clashed. Wolfgang and Black Shield needed meat and decided to take a small cow from the tail end of the passing herd. The strong musky smell of buffalo rose to their noses. Luckily, both men were on the lee side of the herd, where the animals could not get "the wind" of them. A buffalo's sense of smell being acute, are able to detect hunters at a distance of up to a mile.

Wolfgang watched Black Shield address his impatient hunter, calling upon him to run well, keep close to the buffalo and don't get gored. Black Shield was armed with a short, thick, sinew-lined bow. The thicker the sinew layer, the more powerful the bow. Short shafts had broader arrowheads to increase the flow of blood. Wolfgang watched as Black Shield leapt up and directed his hunter out toward the nearest and fattest young cow, with a big round rump. The buffalo ran with tails waving high and heads bobbing. Black Shield spread himself flat over the withers, rode without reins, leaving both his hands free, guiding the horse with his knees alone, his eyes fixed on the terrain and animal ahead. His mount raced over the choppy ground as clumps of dirt smashed into his face. The hunter, identifying the selected animal, careened after the fleeing cow.

The savvy hunter slapped his horse on the rump and the animal jumped forward, dropped its head, flattened out and lengthened its stride. The horse pounced and separated the calf from the herd. Without further guidance, the well-balanced horse and rider, in a breakneck gallop, quickly covered the ground and sided up to the young, fat, buffalo cow. As the horse and rider approached, dung squirted out its bottom and shot backward, hitting horse and rider. When Black Shield was close enough to see her small brown eye cast back, he launched an arrow through the stomach, lungs, and into the heart. The cow began to froth blood through the mouth and nostrils. Black Shield, seeing the animal was mortally wounded, saw no need for another arrow. The arrow had completely disappeared and was sticking out the chest. The cow sank to one knee, rose, teetered and pitched forward, and quickly went down, flopping onto its side. Black Shield broke out of the dust to avoid any hazards.

The excited Wolfgang could see that killing the buffalo was no trouble, but that Black Shield was now having trouble keeping his hunter from chasing another. The horse finally stopped, stomped and flabbered its lips. They could not afford to raise too much dust for fear of it being noticed by unfriendly eyes. The two warriors were just getting ready to butcher the cow when they spotted movement in a timbered draw nearby that spun sideways into a broadside stance. The horses, their heads up, pitching just a little bit, with nostrils flaring, started wuffing. Their ears pinned back, and their eyes showed wild flashes of white all around. The horses started emitting a deep, staccato, coughing sound that meant serious trouble. Wolfgang turned quickly to Mouse, swelled himself up and looked him straight in the eye. He waved his arm and pointed away, firmly saying 'go!' Mouse obeyed immediately, and was followed by the other horse.

The horses spun on their hindquarters and frantically ran off, bucking and running into each other. Both warriors knew that only the dank, musky odor of the great bear was the cause.

"AIEEEE!"

Too late! Their movement was seen and their kill was detected by scent of the bear's exceptionally great nose. They saw it standing with its front legs hanging like arms. It was the beast that walks like man, and it was testing the breeze. "We have stumbled into the worst of situations; a grizzly with the smell of fresh meat in its nose," said Black Shield.

Of all the animals, the grizzly was the hardest to kill, protected by its exceptionally thick skull and thick muscle covering the sides of the forehead. The lord of the plains and mountains, one who could lick anything that walked and knew it. "The old man in a furred cloak," they both spoke at the same time, never taking their eyes off it. They were terrified and in awe, but stood their ground bravely. They could see the large grizzly, in a plunging gallop with an open-mouthed roar escaping its mouth, bounding toward them at great speed, its talons rattling as it ran. The sound of the terrible roars from the angry bear, were loud in their ears. Wolfgang touched the large scar on his cheek, remembering his near death experience from long ago. He found that he was trembling and was aware that his knee was twitching in a frantic rhythm, as he marveled at the smooth flow of massive muscles coming toward them. The sight of the bear struck fear into his heart. Wolfgang forced himself to stop the nervous tic as he fought to control his memories of being mauled, and the crushing pressure of the great bear. He remembered seeing a grizzly kill an adult buffalo bull with one smack of a paw and a bite to the neck. A warning entered his head.

Do not turn your back and run and initiate a chase.

The great, agile, yellowish-brown, surly animal, with massive shoulders, and a prominent hump that set grizzlies apart from black bears, stopped and popped its jaws. It exhaled forcefully through its nostrils and mouth, sneezing, and grunting, and then coughed. They heard the woofing sounds. Again the quick-tempered bear swaggered forward, its enormous wide head swinging from side to side as if perplexed. It lumbered forward with its terrible claws over four inches long, rattling. A single swipe of a paw could kill a moose. The great bear acted as if it owned the world, and stared with haughty arrogance with its small, piercing, pig-like, black eyes, then opened its great maw and gave a tremendous roar of challenge.

One fore leg, with its prodigiously long claws, swiped at the earth sending up a cloud of dust, as it puffed noisily. The shaggy hair on his neck and shoulders bristled, it's murderous little pig-like eyes stared and the brief exposure of its upper and lower yellow fangs was terrifying. Both warriors stood still, knowing the great bears for their poor eyesight. The great bear often thirsted for human blood and would attack without provocation with a great, blind fury. When a grizzly stakes its claim to a kill, all other creatures, including man, keep their distance. Wolfgang and Black Shield felt their mouths go dry, knowing the startling speed of the animal and the mortal danger they were in.

Black Shield believed the great bear had the supernatural understanding of human language. As Wolfgang watched, Black Shield stood with upstretched arms, eyes closed and spoke loudly, chanting a prayer for their safety, "Cousin, you have great spiritual power and wisdom. Our spirits go to the same Happy Hunting Grounds. We feel kinship with bears. This "two-legged man-bear" is your brother and wears your sign; lend us your strength for our journey. We mean you no harm. Forgive us. We offer you this meat. Let us go in peace." An ashen-faced Wolfgang could feel the bear's beady eyes, studying him.

The bear did not move a muscle, growl or pop its teeth. Black Shield watched as the bear turned its attention onto Wolfgang. The bear continued to stare at Wolfgang. Wolfgang heard an inner voice, the voice of his dead wife, the Algonquian Sorceress, Dark Moon.

"Speak to him again."

The fearful Black Shield listened to his companion talk to the Great Bear.

"Greetings Great Bear. You are my power animal as you can see," said Wolfgang pointing to his scars, "You have appeared to me many times. You are the provider and protector of my abilities. On this journey I need your energy, strength, self-confidence and inspiration to meet the challenge facing me."

Black Shield knew that Wolfgang's power animal could grant him the physical and emotional energy and spiritual alertness for his needs on their journey. Black Shield and Wolfgang heard the bear grunt as if in answer. Wolfgang felt great energy flow within him and knew that he had the potential energy granted.

"I now possess it!"

* * *

Wolfgang could smell the bear's barn-like odor and hear its throaty breath, as they backed away. The great bear just stared after them. Wolfgang told Black Shield of the voice and the flow of power in him as they continued their journey. As the sun eased itself down towards the horizon, Black Shield thought to himself about what had just happened. He had never seen, or heard of anyone who had talked to their power animal.

Wolfgang had been startled at his actions. I am thinking like the people, an Indian. He turned his head and saw that Black Shield had been staring at him, and Wolfgang realized that his entire mental outlook had changed. How long, he wondered, have I been doing this without realizing what I have been doing?

* * *

They had a long walk following the trail of their horses. As they walked and watched in silence, they could tell they would soon catch up with the horses. Their tracks indicated they had slowed down to a walk and would soon stop. Black Shield was greatly relieved after the encounter, but now felt a little uneasy around Wolfgang.

My friend is identified with a potent, mysterious and sacred animal spirit. Wolfgang, like the bear, is a powerful and unpredictable night fighter. Like the bear, he will travel across the land like the wind and appear and disappear like a ghost. The Grandfather bear is his animal guardian spirit helper and has given him power.

Wolfgang and Black Shield topped a small hill, and saw that they had caught up with their horses. In the distance, below them, they saw them huddled next to each other, head to tail, swishing flies out of each other's faces. The horses ears locked on them, seeing their leaders nickered to them and came to them trotting up the rise, only stopping when they were nose to nose with the two warriors. The horses lowered their heads in friendly submission. In greeting, Wolfgang and Black Shield rubbed their foreheads and talked to their horses for a bit. They sniffed noses, exchanging warm puffs of moist air. The horses lip-nibbled their shoulders as Wolfgang and Black Shield brushed and cleaned their feet. The horses stood quiet, waiting.

They checked all their gear and found they had lost nothing. Both men checked their animal's legs for small cuts. The hair lay flat. There were no breaks in the skin. They ran their hands carefully over the backs of the horse's forelegs checking their tendons to be sure there were no strains. Their legs felt uniformly clean and cool. Both warriors, talking to the horses, out of love and respect for their animals, asked them for permission to mount. Their journey continued.

Chapter 10

Wolfgang and Black Shield's eyes constantly moved in search of danger, surveying the skylines of the hills and gullies. They saw many antelope. They observed one individual antelope, nearest the distant fold in the hills that detected danger and flared its bright white rump patch signaling the others to flee. As the herd moved away, they continued to watch.

"White man," said Black Shield.

They had come upon a roving Spanish trader heading northwest toward the Missouri River, with mules loaded with arrow points, axes, knives, beads, jewelry, lead, powder, and blankets. The Spanish trader told Wolfgang and Black Shield, that he was accompanied by Ute Indians for protection. Wolfgang traded for lead, powder, salt, coffee and sugar. The Spanish trader told Wolfgang that the Americans, far to the east, had been at war with the British for three years now. France had made an alliance with the Americans and declared war on the British and that Spain had also declared war on the British. Wolfgang's eyes furrowed, as he asked, "What are the American's fighting the British for? The Spaniard replied, "Independence! Freedom!" The Spaniard watching Wolfgang closely, mentioned in parting, "The British Governor in Detroit, Henry Hamilton, the "Hair Buyer," is offering bounties for American scalps."

*   *   *

Only once during their journey had they been warned of an

intruder in the cool night, well after midnight. The night was sprinkled with stars providing enough light to see by. A nearly full moon loomed low on the horizon bathing their surroundings in a faint, ethereal, blue glow and casting faint shadows.

Both men were fully asleep and yet fully alert, simultaneously, listening to every sound. They stirred and their eyes flickered open. Startled they blinked to focus awake, and clear the lingering tendrils of sleep from their minds, slowly looking around with a primitive fear. Coming fully awake, they paid close attention to the senses of their bodies. Remaining motionless, they let the silence fill their heads, listening for the smallest discordant note that would signal a message. They listened a long time.

Wolfgang and Black Shield eased themselves up into a sitting position from the cold, hard ground. Their hard eyes were wide open. The little muscles around the mouth twitched, then their lips tightened stubbornly. They were instantly aware of a change in the night. There was no longer any commotion, snorting or tramping noise from the direction of the horses. No interaction of one crowding a neighbor too close and getting a nip and issuing a squeal and a kick. No sound of grass being torn and munched, or the stamping of hooves.

The horses were quiet! Too quiet! The horse's sense when things aren't right.

Suddenly, there was a simple bark. They listened to what the coyote had to say. The lone bark meant danger was lurking. Then came a series of short, aggressive choppy barks. Wolfgang and Black Shield knew high-pitched sounds served as an alarm signal, saying that the coyotes are on to your presence.

Whose presence!

Black Shield and Wolfgang's eyes were furtive and immediately wary. They both heard the bird singing sound of disturbed antelope warning each other, further away. Wolfgang and Black Shield instantly sat bolt upright.

*   *   *

The lion had been hidden among the juniper hunting bedded antelope, when he smelled horses. He was fond of colt meat. Horses were easy to catch. The great cat was enormous and his color was made up of a shimmering blend of four earth tones. The far-wanderer was well camouflaged for the semi-open area he was hunting. His color was a beautiful tawny brown with a buff belly and a white throat and chest that blended well with his surroundings. His face had brown-black stripes ringing his muzzle and the back of his ears. The tip of his tail was blackish brown. He was big for his kind and reached 8 feet long and weighed nearly 200 pounds. The smell of the horses was becoming stronger. It had grown dark when his snake-like head emerged into the open. Then his deep, narrow body came, evilly slinking, out of the shadows, into the haze of moonlight brilliance flooding the open ground.

His short, powerful legs were full of malevolent power as he placed one paw just in front of the other, stalking. It had been almost a week since he had killed and eaten. His last kill had been at dusk. He had knocked a young cow elk off her feet using his powerful shoulders and outstretched forelegs. With curved claws extended, the lion smashed the young cow to the ground. The lion, had gripped the cow's neck across the shoulders. With the other paw, the lion grabbed the nose and head of the cow, pulling it around and biting into the neck, breaking the spine with its great canine teeth. He had sucked all the blood it could before eating the lungs, heart and viscera. Now, as he remembered that kill, he padded silently, like smoke, in the direction of the scent of horses on padded feet. He cocked his ears inquisitively and stared fixedly toward the horses, moving carefully, using every bit of cover because people hunted him for his meat and hide. Being cautious and secretive, he decided to remain hidden where he was, watching and listening, close enough for a blinding rush, his tail twitching.

* * *

The horses were first to sense the danger. There was the smell, the pungent, acrid odor, and the slight rustle that could have been the wind that had made them aware for sometime. An almost imperceptible warning sound, quietly, circling out there, stalking them. Their frightened eyes now focused, simultaneously, upon a lion a little distance to their front, their ears automatically pricked toward the movement in the open sagebrush. The horses stood, snorting through flaring nostrils, at the stealthy approach of the big predator.

* * *

The great wolf that accompanied Wolfgang on most of his trips, lay next to him, its eyes and ears alert. Suddenly it lifted its head and tensed. It had heard nothing suspicious, but sensed a presence. Black Shield's wolf emitted a low, intense growl starting in its throat. Wolfgang tried to swallow past the thickening in his throat, at the faint sibilance of something brushing the gramma grass and the barely perceptible crunching of small rocks and twigs. The wolves stood and watched, baring their fangs. Their hackles rose on their necks and backs, standing upright. The wolves lowered their heads and bodies and moved forward deliberately.

The fierce growl of the two wolves told Wolfgang and Black Shield all they needed to know. There was an intruder close to their camp and the wolves head pointed in its direction. It seemed to be nearer now. Black Shield and Wolfgang commanded the two wolves to remain by their side.

"Stay!"

Time seemed to slow to a crawl, as they lay still, aware of

every instant that passed. No telling how long they had crouched there, waiting. It seemed an eternity to Wolfgang. He realized he was breathing hoarsely, and tried to stifle it.

Wolfgang tilted his head to one side, "Well, what is it?"

"I don't know!" responded Black Shield.

The active noises of the night became quiet for a time and, straining to hear, Wolfgang and Black Shield became immediately aware of another presence. For a fleeting moment there was a slight sound. Their breathing came more quickly, causing their hearts to start beating faster, as a chill ran up their spines causing them to slightly tremble.

The two men rose to a squat, straining to hear even the slightest noise. Listening to the night birds, again they heard a high-pitched alarm signal. A solitary bark, "Wuff," like a dog from an unseen coyote, warning of a dangerous presence lurking nearby. Now, the horses seemed uneasy. Wolfgang and Black Shield's brows knitted together in a deep frown. Both were making the same mental judgment. They took a deep breath, both responding silently, peering uneasily into the surrounding gloom. Their lips compressed into a thin line, Wolfgang and Black Shield felt a cold chill of anxiety as they crept toward the horses, their hearts pounding in their ears as they glanced nervously around.

The horses were starting to stir and stamp their hooves, roll their eyes nervously, while pitching their heads. The horses gently snickering turned their heads to welcome them, sniffing the air with soft noses as both men tried quieting and soothing the horses. Wolfgang and Black Shield touched their horse's necks while rubbing the animal's ear's. "I'm here, it's all right," speaking quietly and gently to them with their low hissing and whistling through their teeth while caressing them.

Their horses calmed down somewhat, huffing their hot, fragrant breath into the chill air, but their hides continued to ripple and their nostrils quivered and flared, registering their fear. They breathed warm air into their aural passages, rubbing and crooning to them until their ears quit twitching back and forth. They finally managed to calm the fidgeting and trembling horses, watching the horse's ears and letting them smell the wind for them. They both hoped it wasn't Cheyenne war ponies.

As Black Shield joined Wolfgang, he whispered, "Whatever it is, it is close because their pricked ears indicate they see it. I do not smell a bear." Black Shield pointed in the quarter from which the horses were looking. Then the wind changed slightly and the elusive, all-pervading odor came to them. They both smelled the terrible odor of the meat eater, looking about into the darkness.

Lion!

From a distance, they both heard an ominous cough, huff and angry snarl. The sound of a lion on the prowl.

Then for a while it was silent, but the horses were getting more nervous.

Then from the darkness nearby came a familiar, but rarely heard sound. "MROWRRRRR."

Black Shield and Wolfgang exchanged quick, knowing glances.

"Lion!" whispered Wolfgang under his breath, yet not so low that his companion, Black Shield, did not hear it. Both men were aware that lions typically attack for food and that they hunt using stealth and mobility. Their senses were heightened. Both men cocked their rifles. From the surrounding darkness, they heard, "HEESSS." The sound was followed by a spit. "FFFT."

The lone hunter had moved at intervals, without the slightest sound, freezing for long minutes. The lion now crouched low, eyes burning, with its head down flat between extended forepaws. The cat's black-tipped ears listened carefully. The lion's shoulders, were a mound of muscle as it froze, immobile, its long tail twitching. The lion remained down, lying motionless: with keen amber eyes, cold and concentrating on watching Wolfgang and Black Shield with seemingly supreme indifference. All at once, sensing danger, the lion made its decision. The lion, shifted, turned and trotted off. Through the screen of brush there was a blur of stealthy movement, as the lithe lion sifted, like smoke through the sage and away on its stealthy cushioned paws. The soft-padded, sound of the predator retreating into the distance, was welcomed with relief by the two warriors. Then in the distance, they heard the startling yowl of the frustrated mountain lion, as it faded into the night. It was a chilling, woman-like scream that sent chills up their spine.

Wolfgang said, "He has seen we are not alone. If it were just one of us it would be different." They examined the "impressed tracks" almost invisible on the soft ground in the dark. He traced the whole outline of tracks in the dark with his finger. The tracks were deep and well defined. The lion always retracts his claws to preserve their sharpness. They both knew that lions in open country make their day beds in thickets or under the roots of a fallen tree.

"The great cat has a taste for horses," said Black Shield, as he raised his arms and prayed to it to bestow its hunting ability upon them.

Chapter 11

It had turned cold early in the night. The clouds had passed over leaving the rest of the night cold and clear. They awoke while the stars were still bright and they lay listening to the sounds. Soon the only light, the ambient bluish glow from the stars, was gone as the horizon was beginning to pale. Dawn would soon stain the sky above the eastern horizon. Black Shield and Wolfgang lay on the reverse slope of a high ridge. Black Shield had just shook Wolfgang awake, saving him from the nightmare of reliving the pain of the past.

They watched the gray, then pink and yellow horizon brighten, as a glow set upon the ground. As the light grew stronger, the heavy frost began to sparkle. They looked across an endless, empty landscape, as a gentle cold wind began to whisper through the grass. The low places remained blue with shadows. They both noted that a few small birds were perched nearby. Birds always face into the wind. It confirmed what their wet finger told them-the cooler and drier wind was coming from the northwest. Both warriors knew that rain was unlikely.

The two warriors looked up to the top of the rise hearing a thin whistle slurred downward from above. They noticed a broad-winged hawk soaring over the wide-open landscape. They both watched the hawk for a time as it wheeled, swooped, soared and circled upward on the strong wind and thermal currents. Wolfgang turned and watched his friend, amazed at the wonder of nature and man's intimate connection with it.

Black Shield raised his arms to his totem, the hawk, and spoke; "I give thanks for making yourself known to me and watching over me when I travel. I honor you. Give us your protection. You are my spirit guide, my power medicine, my totem. Speak to me. Let me hear your thoughts about those I hunt. Help us to see that which is far away."

Black Shield believed his soul was linked to the hawk. He danced, with outstretched arms mimicking the hawks in soaring flight, honoring it. Both men paid attention to what they saw, heard and felt, as the sun began to slowly heat the air and earth. Thermals began to rise in columns. The dark-breasted raptor, with a heavy barred tail, glided with wings slightly uptilted in a wide circle. As it drifted lazily on the rising air, the bird's direction of flight passed directly overhead and the hawk continued in the direction that the two men were going.

An Omen!

Black Shield and Wolfgang looked briefly into each other's eyes. Both men understood the other's thoughts. Wolfgang was always amazed when he experienced this kind of phenomena: two men simultaneously receiving a sign from the Great Spirit. Wolfgang and Black Shield lifted their arms in supplication toward Great Spirit, to give thanks for this manifestation of his all-pervading presence and power.

Black Shield suggested, "Let's climb this ridge. We'll leave the horses at the bottom and climb to the top."

'We can spot the trail of the horses from up there,' replied Wolfgang.

The men quickly hobbled their horses, patted their horses on the neck while speaking softly to them, and set off up the ridge. The horse's heads were down and tails to the wind, swishing flies, happily began grazing. Wolfgang and Black Shield could hear the harsh tearing, as their mounts cropped the new, lush grass. As a precaution, they both liberally coated their faces with a mixture of a salve Yellow Bird Singing, their Shaman, had given them. The salve was made from Dog's Tongue, Larkspur, and Sweet Flag. It kept them from being bothered by a constant tickling inquiry of the ears, eyes, mouth and nose by clouds of bloodthirsty mosquitoes, gnats and carnivorous midges that they knew would hang in the sun-tinged shadows of the brush.

They carefully picked their way around outcroppings and tumbled slabs of rock, and made their way through a dense juniper thicket. As they jarred the foliage they perceived an exquisite fragrance that mixed with that of the prairie. They moved slow and tried their best to keep from sweating and blowing hard. Nearing the summit, the two men found a place with shade where they could break up their outline and remain hidden in the wind. Black Shield and Wolfgang lay down low to the ground and remained still while peering from behind a veil of grass that concealed their position. They both knew that if they kept their breathing slow and kept still, so they would not be bothered too much by mosquitoes.

The mosquitoes thrived in the musty thickness, but the two warriors thought they would be hard to find in the strong wind. Unfortunately, they heard the sinister whine and eerie, thin, high-pitched sound in the bowl of their ears, as a few of the pests found them. Wolfgang and Black Shield blamed the evil spirits for this, as they warily peeked through the thick foliage. The rich and luxuriant empty prairie stretched away as far as they could see.

Nothing!

They watched a few antelope does unaccompanied by their fawns, as they cleaned their rifles. Corrosive buildup in the barrel affected accuracy and a dangerous buildup of barrel pressure. On a vantage point, a nearby doe, with its super-keen eyes, was staring in the direction of its hidden offspring. A coyote, waiting for its meal of the day, was sitting in the distance watching the antelope doe and narrowing down the area where the fawn was laying flat, hiding in the cover of low vegetation. Due to the presence of the hunting coyote, the short white hairs on the antelope's butt flashed to others of its kind. This meant be prepared to run.

"Death is always waiting," stated Wolfgang.

The tall grass waved under a northeast wind, sweeping waves of undulating light and shade over the sea of buffalo grass. The prairie was alive and beautiful. The renewal brought by each season reminded Wolfgang of his beautiful wife, Dark Moon, now long gone. He realized that keeping active, like this pursuit of the Cheyenne raiders, would help heal the trauma he was suffering. This change of environment, away from the village, was good medicine.

Tears flooded, rolling down Wolfgang's well-tanned cheeks, as he felt the pain and loss of Dark Moon, who had traveled to the spirit world. His throat became strangled. Love is a madness that I cannot fight. I miss you so much. You were the light of my life. In his mind's eye he could see her deep, mysterious, hooded eyes, her smile, and remember the smell of her body.

Wolfgang sighed. His mouth was grim, as he felt a fresh spasm of grief well up in him.

I cannot bear it.

Keenly observant, Black Shield was aware that his friend was over-wrought and still coming to terms with his grief over Dark Moon.

A longing, verging on depression.

Black Shield watched Wolfgang's quivering body and trembling hands. He knew Wolfgang was drowning in a river of yearning sadness. As he watched the powerful waves of emotion wash over Wolfgang's face, Black Shield felt his friend's desperation. Black Shield pretended not to notice, forcing his face to stony stoicism. The Algonquin woman, Dark Moon, had come from the River of Sorcerers that fed Lake Huron far to the east. The French called it the French River.

Black Shield remembered. One winter ago, during the Moon of Roses, we had been at a story telling.

Wolfgang's wife, Dark Moon, had gone to the stream to bathe and had a heart attack and fell into the water, the day the sun had died and the stars came out and then the sun came back to life. The whole village had been awestruck.

* * *

The passage of time had worked subtle changes on Wolfgang. He was no longer troubled for days and nights with pangs of guilt. However, like now, he experienced sharp but short episodes of grief accompanied by a dull ache for his loss. He felt responsibility and guilt for not being with her at the time of her death. He still felt a persistent empty feeling over the loss of Dark Moon. Strangely, however Wolfgang could always feel Dark Moon's presence and love for him.

Why have you urged me on this journey?

There had been an explosion of wildflowers with the rain. He remembered many things that Dark Moon had taught him about the land and its beauty. He remembered that the prairie could cause both healing and death. There were the brilliant reds, dull reds, and various shades of yellow, pink, white and orange paintbrush. There was the yellow of cinquefoil. Blue penstemon flowers, and yellow groundsel. At this moment, the prairie conveyed a sense of love and safety. He watched. He listened. He thought.

Dark Moon's medicinal cinquefoil, dried leaves could be made into a pleasant tea. The bark of the root relieved pain, fevers, toothaches, and an astringent on wounds that stopped internal bleeding.

The small, colorful array of blush-purple blossoms of penstemon, with its irregular seeds feed the songbirds, ground squirrels and antelope.

Wolfgang worried whenever he saw the yellow groundsel.

The groundsel was poisonous to the horses if consumed in

quantity.

He saw white and yellow evening primrose flowers that open mainly in the twilight. The roots are used as cooked vegetables and its leaves used as salad. The roots, boiled in honey, are used as a soothing cough syrup. Its seed oil is good for the skin, lowering blood pressure, and arthritis.

In the low places there were patches of violet-blue wild iris.

The iris is a good indicator that water is close to the surface of the ground. A hole dug there will soon fill with water. The ground up roots and seeds, when mixed with animal bile, and put in the gall bladder then warmed by the fire for several days is a slow, but reliable poison. Arrows dipped in the mixture will kill a slightly wounded enemy within 3 to 7 days.

The violet-blue iris was abundant in the shallow-water marshy areas, where the spotted frogs made creaky-sounding music that was followed by a chuckle. He heard a distant throaty call, "Fraaakkk," and saw a great blue bird with an s-curved neck. The bird walked slowly through the distant wetland on arrow thin legs. It stood almost four feet tall and, as he watched it, stabbed its orange-yellow bill then held it aloft and quickly consumed a meal.

* * *

Wolfgang could see Dark Moon telling him all these things. He never thought he could survive her leaving him so suddenly. Wolfgang had never known such joy from the time he had met Dark Moon. That she had chosen him, so long ago, back in the Ohio country. He concentrated on breathing to control his emotions.

She is no longer here; yet, I see the image of her. No sound, no touch, yet I hear her and feel her. I can still smell her. My mind makes its own sense of things, translating the numinous phenomena of time into concretions. She is always there.

Then, where the grass dwindled on the distant horizon, something moved. Wolfgang squinted and saw a faint flicker of movement on the prairie horizon, no more than a thin scattering of dots.

Horses!

Chapter 12

Wolfgang and Black Shield had caught up to their horses. They were emerging from a depression in the prairie. Black Shield was already pointing. "I see them." The sight made their blood sing through their body. Black Shield drew his right index finger rapidly across to the left several times—indicating their penchant for using 'striped turkey feathers to fletch their arrows,' then he turned his head in Wolfgang's direction, fixing him with a hawk-like stare, as if to gauge his reaction.

Wolfgang nodded, understanding.

Cheyenne!

Black Shield said, "They refer to themselves as the T sis tsis' tas. The tribal sign signifies cut or gashed people, like the turkey feathers they use. The Cheyenne Soldier Societies are the Elkhorn Scrapers, Bow Strings, Kit-fox soldiers, Dog Soldiers, Crazy Dogs and the Crooked Lance Soldiers. There are two more, the Red Shields and Chief Soldiers, but they are made up of old warriors. The Cheyenne live at the headwaters of the upper Shell River (Platte River). They are allied with the Dakota and Arapahoes."

The group of Striped-feathered-arrows (Cheyenne) looked familiar. Then it hit him; they are the famous Wolf Soldiers. Wolfgang knew that this group was made up of the most formidable warriors on the plains. The Wolf soldiers' main purpose was to protect their people from attack and eliminate the power of their enemies by attacking them. Wolfgang knew that the fighting spirit is encouraged among the Wolf Soldiers and dying gloriously at the hands of the enemy was not a thing to be avoided.

The day was sunny and humid, but promised a cooling shower. Wolfgang and Black Shield were tired, but they knew the raiders would continue to push the herd south. The gibbous moon was now seven days old and would get brighter each night, unless a storm set in. They counted the Cheyenne. Seven!

"We must be like the hawk. Never show fear. We must use our keen eyes, speed, and strike with strong talons when time presents us with opportunity," said Wolfgang without looking at Black Shield. Wolfgang rubbed the geldings muzzle with the palm of his hand, blew into his nose before mounting, patted his neck—then sprang into the saddle. Their horses sprang forward and the riders stretched low along the necks, as their mounts stride lengthened. The thudding of hoofs pounding on soft ground was the only sound, as they trailed after the Cheyenne at a prodigious pace.

* * *

It was the season known to the Apache as, the Moon when the leaves are green. A young, lone, Kiowa-Apache warrior had been moving north in search of horses. He had seen his enemy, the Cheyenne, pushing a horse herd hard and knew that they were stolen Crow horses. His people had an alliance with the Crow and he decided that this was his opportunity to acquire wealth and honor among his small, isolated band. He had decided to follow the Cheyenne and cut out horses in the dark and drive them south, avoiding contact with the enemy. He would have no trouble following the herd, for they left many tracks and he could follow the sweet-smelling piles of horse droppings easily in the dark.

* * *

The lone Apache had followed the Striped-feathered-arrow warriors until they had finally stopped when the first stars came into the sky. His heart began to sing as he again located the mature mare, the herd matriarch. He watched the unsettled animal toss its head, bristled its mane, its mouth chomping, shifting its feet, while sniffing the air. The foolish Cheyenne had permitted themselves to believe they were safe because they were in the outer limits of their own country. He followed the acrid scent of an unseen cooking fire, past antelope ghostly white in the moonlight, moving slowly, stopping and listening. The sharp musty stench of the horses grazing nearby, and their still warm, soft droppings, filled his nostrils. As he slowly approached, he heard them. In the dark, he was painfully aware of every snap, crack and snort among the horses.

When the moon goes down I will start moving.

The eyes of the matriarch were squarely on his. Her ears were pinned and her back was rigid. The Apache turned his eyes away and stared down at the ground, then shut his eyes and took a deep breath and let all the tension flow out of himself, into the ground. The Apache knew he must reach out with his heart to the horse. Horses are masters at reading energy and body language, and even from a distance, pick up on the slightest human emotion. Now staring at the animal he allowed his good thoughts and energy to glide into the animal, telegraphing his intentions.

The horses jostled each other nervously. With nostrils flaring and their powerful flanks heaving, they stomped warily watching him. He had lain perfectly motionless as the dew formed. It was getting colder. The Apache waited for the herd matriarch to relax.

Frost will form soon. Movement through the dew or frost covered grass will flatten the stems and point the direction of travel and the dark change of color will reflect the sun better leaving a dark line through the prairie.

The Apache saw that the body language of the matriarch

revealed she was no longer frightened. The Apache's mind, now sharply in focus, telegraphed to the horse that he must soon move and not to be frightened. He meant her no harm.

The mare's inside ear was turned and locked on him in curiosity. Soon she began to lick and chew, a sign that she was relaxing, that all was well. The matriarch yawned, showing a release of emotion. The herd began to graze again.

She will not take flight! It was almost time to move!

He had a bush tied to the front of his head as he watched the moon touch the hills. For a long time he observed, his eyes flicking back and forth, picking up the shapes in the gloom. Finally, he found what he was looking for, a large gap between the Cheyenne raiders guarding the horses. He watched the moon, listening to the coyotes squabbling over a kill. Then the moon went down and he rose stiffly to his elbows. Using a fold in the ground, he lay on his belly with his short Buffalo Horn Bow strapped to his back. He put all his weight on his elbows, and pulled his body silently forward with the wind in his face. He moved slowly, scanning the ground for the quietest path. He stopped often to quiet his breathing and to keep his heart rate down.

Though he was suffering from exposure and pangs of hunger, he used great caution and careful consideration in all his movements. He moved with painful slowness only when he was sure he was unobserved and could take advantage of the existing murmuring from the herd, the wind, the flutter and calls of night birds, yipping of coyotes and howling of wolves. His eyes were always alert for an unseen guard.

There was no sound or movement except for those sounds carried through the ground. Now and then he heard a stamp of a hoof or a low squeal or nervous nickering, as one horse would nip at a neighbor that crowded too close. He frequently placed his ear to the end of a stick that touched the ground to listen. He identified every object in the dark and listened to every sound, learning their meaning.

Many of the horses seemed to be sleeping in their usual way, locking their forelegs in the upright extended position. Heads were lowered to a horizontal position with eyes closed, half-open or open, their lower lip lazily extended, ears slightly back, and one back leg cocked. Some horses were lying down. The Apache lay silent, waiting, smiling grimly. Stealth required patience and care, he thought.

One ear was placed to the ground. Blocking the other ear turned up with a small piece of buckskin, he could sense, and then hear, the sound of the Cheyenne night guard's horse long before it neared him. Whenever the Cheyenne guard was coming around, the Apache was able to anticipate his arrival by feeling the vibrations of the hooves through the hard ground beneath him. Soon, he would sense the movement and shape of the night guard's silhouette in his peripheral vision. The Apache remained stationary, with his head up, studying and memorizing the placement of the guard's hands, knees, feet and body as he prepared for his silent approach.

The Apache warrior, with his face and hands close to the ground, breathed into his jacket and scarf to prevent an obvious breath cloud above him. He cleared his route carefully and made frequent listening halts, adopting a pose that reflected the character of the surrounding bushes and rocks. He cocked his head in the direction he was listening, with his mouth slightly open, to aid his hearing.

His gaze was in constant motion, continually sweeping far and near, right and left and up and down. He also looked forward through the brush. Only once, he had to freeze because of a nervous horse that had turned its head toward him. The animal's jaws paused momentarily, and snorted, then continued grazing casually. It soon lost interest, and turned away and chewing contentedly. The nightrider stopped briefly and relieved himself and then moved on. The Apache's nose smarted at the pungent smell that identified a clear hole and crusty mark where the night guard urinated. The warrior knew he should now secure a horse and wait in that location for the first guard to return. Then, he would strike.

The young warrior rose to his feet. He kept his mind clear and stepped slowly, each foot placed with care, as he made his way to the nearest horse. It stomped once, shuddered, and flabbered its lips. The Apache answered. Hunh, un-hunh, as he put his hand over its nose, to prevent it from nickering. The Apache calmed the horse, then blew in her nose and sniffed in greeting. He looked deep into her eyes and gave her a good rub on her forehead and shoulders while using the animal's outline to hide his own. The mare he selected stood still for him; a good sign. The mare dropped her head nicely as he put a leather halter over her head. The Apache's roving hand told him the mare had plenty of depth through the chest and good shoulders. He made a loop and rotated it one turn and placed the nose loop on the mare so that when the lead end was pulled the pressure was transferred to the neck loop. I am ready! He kept very still, as the nightrider came along in the distance, huffing its hot breath into the chill air.

The Apache used his beautiful, black horn bow to silently kill the two night guards, as they individually rode by him. Both had merely spasmed, and tumbled to the ground. Grabbing a handful of the animal's hair above the withers, he mounted in one easy, effortless motion. He focused his direction for the horse and used a quiet non-verbal command-a telegraphed intention, a focused flow of energy, to put the horse from a standstill into a walk.

The animal walked.

She answered well. He liked this horse, it responded immediately.

With the first pale promise of dawn in the sky, he had the mare and the rest of the horses moving. He moved the herd slowly at first to lessen the sound of the horses' hooves in the brittle, frost covered grass. His mount began to throw her head, hopeful for a gallop, as the breath of man and horse puffed into the half-light. Easy! He thought. The horse settled down. The Apache and horse were one.

* * *

The Apache had moved the horses well away from the area of the night pasture. He then squeezed his legs just a fraction. The horse sensing what the rider wanted, responded to the pressure from the Apaches knees. The Apache now leaned forward, and dug his heels into the animal's side. The animal responded and bolted into a gallop. The wind rushed into his face and blew his dark, shoulder-length hair back.

Chapter 13

Wolfgang and Black Shield were alerted to the pricking up of the horses' ears. The animal's looked off to the northeast, their feet lightly dancing as they nickered in communication. Both warriors shared the same thoughts. Horses easily became aware of slight ground vibrations through their hooves. The horses turning their heads to look at something, confirmed their suspicions. Wolfgang and Black Shield felt their chest clutch as they vaguely detected a low murmuring sound of hoofbeats. Black Shield, looking at Wolfgang, saw the skin tighten on his face, as a thought pressed into his mind, we, are not alone! Now, they heard and felt the ground reverberate. It was followed by the muffled, deep, muffled bass drumming sound, of clattering hooves. The air was heavy with thoughts that neither of them expressed.

* * *

The stolen horses were being driven directly towards them by a lone warrior. A lone Indian was slapping the loose end of his reins across the neck of his horse and driving the herd hard. As the herd approached, the muffled drum of hooves gradually grew in intensity. The pounding and drumming of hooves reached their ears, rising sharply, then crescendoing, as they thundered toward them.

The lone warrior galloped behind the herd of horses, head low on his mare's neck, feeling the smooth strumming, hammering of the ground beneath him. The horse having smelled the fear of its rider, was responding to his mood, with a bobbing head and neck. The animal was covering the ground with great momentum.

Its muscles roiling over its shoulders, back, and rump, as its legs gathered up and unfolded. The horse, near winded, showed patches of sweat and lather on its flanks and froth from its wide mouth spattered back along its shoulders and rider. Wolfgang and Black Shield saw flashing glimpses of white eyes, exposed yellow teeth, billowing nostrils, and flying manes and tails.

As the lone rider drew closer, shrill cries could be heard.

"Aiii-yi-yi-yi!"

"Ai-yi-yi-yieee!!"

The high-pitched and threatening sounds could be heard above the din. Wolfgang and Black Shield could see the lone warrior was not alone and that the Cheyenne were in vigorous pursuit, urging their horses to lengthen their strides. The lone mans horse, in response to its rider had flattened his ears and kept his eyes forward. The animal's body was elongated in total effort, dropping his body down flat to lie under the wind of the herd ahead. The horses head was bobbing in time to its stride, accelerating and quickly pulling away from his pursuers at top speed. Its back muscles, flanks and belly bulged, as its legs reached out with the effort of eating up the ground and building its speed.

Wolfgang's brow furrowed into the inevitable question. He heard his friend say, "Gataka."

Wolfgang knew what Black Shield was referring to.

The Kiowa-Apache. The northern most band of Apaches, allied to our tribe.

Wolfgang's eyes narrowed suspicion, but did not reply at once.

"Then it is our enemies who follow close behind," he replied, as he felt his stomach knotted up and found it hard to swallow because his throat and chest tightened.

I can't get enough air.

He felt the familiar chill of tension tighten around his spine as he eyed the approaching horsemen anxiously. He swallowed nervously as his eyes widened. His nostrils flared as he felt his heart beat quicken. Wolfgang's heart was pounding so loudly that it was difficult to clearly make out the approaching sound of drumming hooves. Wolfgang took in several deep breaths, to get control.

"We've got ourselves into a tight situation here," Wolfgang mused, when he was sure that Black Shield was through talking.

* * *

The Apache was smiling inwardly to himself, feeling the coarse mane of the mare on his face, the acrid smell of her skin and feeling and hearing the deep roll of her breathing. Then he felt a pause in the stride, followed by a predatory lunge beneath him, her lips pulled back and his teeth clenched as he felt the animal's stride come up under him, shortening. A terrible thought came to the Apache warrior: Something is wrong with my horse.

The horse was beginning to weaken and labor. The mare's eyes were rolling in their sockets. The horse had lost its momentum. The lack of former smoothness and a jerking stride showed he was almost done. A quick turn of his head revealed his animal was wounded and he knew that he had to be prepared for the animal to go down in mid-stride. The horse, its head flattened out with its ears back, was giving its all. Then he felt the horse sag and waver, and knew it was time as the horses tongue shot out the side of his mouth. He had to prepare for a running dismount.

* * *

Wolfgang and Black Shield stood transfixed. The lone warrior cast a nervous glance over his shoulder prepared for a running dismount. The Apache, with his hands full of the animal's mane, swung his body across the animals back and slid down, loose-kneed, until his feet were just above the ground, to ride the shock of his feet hitting the ground. The Apache was initially jarred with the force of the impact, as his feet hit the ground. His body was flung forward from the momentum of the mare. He kept his balance, from the jarring force of hitting the ground, and kept his feet moving, running next to the horse. The Apache's horse, with arrows jutting from its haunches began to fall. The Apache veered away, slightly running like a startled antelope, while his mount went down in a cloud of dust. The Apache, still on his feet, increased his running speed.

* * *

Behind the Apache the voices of the Cheyenne raised in a sudden triumph like a song, as the beating of hooves grew louder and louder.

"The Apache have powerful muscular bodies that give them superb endurance," said Black Shield.

The Apache had lost no momentum and quickly settled into a long, stride that was fast and easy. It was evident to both Wolfgang and Black Shield that the Cheyenne would soon have him. The Apache horse, enraged by pain managed to get up, screaming as it plunged up and down and labored for breath. Blood dripped from its belly as its front legs collapsed. The horse whimpered, its eyes white and teeth bared.

Wolfgang said "Stay and watch. I will get our rifles, pouches and powder horns to help him."

Chapter 14

By the time Wolfgang returned, the Apache was still running close behind the stolen horses, around the ridge, fifty yards to their south. The Apache was trying to catch the herd and mount a fresh horse on the run. The way the Apache moved indicated that he would not easily tire. He seemed imbued with supernatural powers.

Wolfgang and Black Shield measured and poured 80 grains powder and tapped their barrel to settle the powder in the breech. On the right side of the stock, they removed a greased patch from the hinged, brass patch box. The sperm oil lube patch made loading easier and shot tight groups, thought Wolfgang. Wolfgang had been thankful many times for the waxy, aromatic lubricant with the earthy aroma he obtained at the Hidatsa village of Mittuta-Hanka, on the Missouri River, from the Basque trader.

The two Crow warriors seated the lubricated, patched ball in the coned muzzle and drove it down on top of the powder with the ramrod. Both men checked the scribed mark around the ramrod, ensuring it was flush with the muzzle. Wolfgang and Black Shield were satisfied that their balls were correctly seated. An air space, between the powder and ball, could cause the barrel to explode.

"Check your flint, Black Shield, and make sure its sharp. Be sure to keep the priming powder away from the touchhole for faster ignition. Use your touch hole pick to ensure you get a free pass for the flash." Wolfgang paused, above the growing, broken beat of the hooves,

"We don't need any hang-fires," he added.

They both inserted their touchhole pick into the tiny entry hole of the barrel ensuring it wasn't clogged and that the powder granules were pushed back inside the barrel. This would allow ignition of the main powder train, dependent on the free pass of the priming powder's hot flash. Using their small powder horns, they primed a half pan level of dry, fine-grained priming powder and banked it away from the touchhole so the flash of fire had instant ignition. Instant ignition would keep their sights from drifting off target.

At 100 yards the lead ball will register a 3-inch drop.

Wolfgang estimated the range to be 60 yards.

Shooting at this range the ball should strike the target dead on.

Looking at Black Shield, Wolfgang said "You take the front rider with the long-quilled 'buffalo bulls tail' fastened to his scalp lock in the back. I'll take the last rider, the one with the Medicine Hat and the buffalo-scalp bonnet with fur attached." Wolfgang felt confident that Black Shield trusted his ability to judge the range, shoot accurately and quickly reload.

"The one with the buffalo-scalp bonnet is a leader of a lower order, awarded by those around him. They are his friends who feel he is worthy. He feels he has to prove himself of being a leader. He is most dangerous to us," stated Black Shield.

Wolfgang's eye was quickly stimulated by the color of his rifle sight. A gust of wind made him blink. He quickly lined up the dab of blue on his front sight and the edge of yellow on the rear sight, making the sight picture jump out clearly, on an accurate, dead center, hold. Wolfgang remained perfectly still, eyes on his target. He gained control of his nerves to deliver effective fire upon his targets. He took a deep breath, and then, slowly emptying his lungs, started a steady squeeze on the trigger. He felt the satisfaction and excitement of the hunter.

Now lets see if that hat gives you protective powers and assures success. Wolfgang completed the squeeze with a surprise. The clacking sound of flint on steel, drawing sparks; a flash of fire on the side of the rifle came to him, as he held steady. Faster than the blink of an eye-the flash of priming powder shot through the touchhole.

Klatch!

The fine powder in the pan flashed and . . .

Poof!

The main charge exploded . . .

Boom!

The two Crow warrior's ears were filled with the loud music of a resounding, thundering boom. Wolfgang felt the recoil of his rifle, as the target was obliterated from his view by the dirty, blue-white, sulfurous smoke beginning to rise. His eyes were stunned, his nostrils filled with the smell of sulfur, and his ears heard the musical sensation of the round ball, sent on its way.

* * *

The Cheyenne warrior was intent upon the lone Apache. There was a brief angry sound, then, came the rushing sound, of air parting, followed by a distant explosion. The lead ball passed under the right arm, hitting the man in the chest and exited from his back. The color drained from his surprised face.

* * *

Thwack! From the sound, Wolfgang knew the rider was down.

The rumble of hooves grew louder and louder.

Wolfgang repeated the flintlock mantra to himself, "Powder, patch, and ball," as he started to reload. Loading, took time and concentration, of which, he had little of either. But, by now it came naturally. He yanked the wood plug from his powder horn with his teeth. To shortcut his loading time, Wolfgang used his powder measurer, the hollowed out tip of a cow horn tethered above his powder horn by a rawhide lace. He poured powder down the barrel. Then, Wolfgang dumped a half-inch pinch of crushed wasp nest material directly over the powder to insure the ball would fly true.

Using his wooden fast loader, of patched lead balls that hung around his neck, he centered his circular fast loader over his coned muzzle and pressed the greased patched ball, with a thinner patch material, into the barrel, and pressed it in with his speed-loader. The thinner, greased patch material, made loading easier for a second shot and kept him from bending or applying too much pressure on the ramrod. Using short strokes with his ramrod, he pushed the ball down the barrel and felt it crunch against the powder, and checked the mark on his wooden ramrod, indicating the ball was properly seated. The wooden ramrod was the weakest link in speeding up the reloading process. Thumbing the hammer to half cock, he thumbed the flint to test the edge for sharpness. He felt a knife-sharp edge. He took the vent pick and placed it in the flash hole until it penetrated the powder. This would insure that the flash hole was open. The powder felt firmly packed. He snapped the steel frizzen shut over priming pan.

He brought the hammer to full cock and concentrated. He steadied the front blade into the rear "V" sight, and gently squeezed the trigger.

Klatch!

The striking flint, struck the steel frizzen, and cut sparks. White-hot sparks sizzled in the flash pan, and the primer powder shot a flame through the hole, in a lightning-fast ignition.

Poof!

The jet of flame ignited the main barrel charge. The lead round ball flew down the rifled barrel.

Bang!

A cloud of sulfurous smoke filled the air.
Thwack!

Chapter 15

The last rider and the front rider went down and landed with solid impact. They lay flat on their backs, staring up at the glare of the sky with unseeing eyes. The sight of smoke and the sound of rifles caused the Cheyenne to break off the pursuit, dragging their ponies from a full run to a sliding stop on their haunches. The momentarily, panic-stricken, Cheyenne horses squealed and whinnied. They reared back, then crabbed and plunged, while their eyes rolled and nostrils flaring. As their horses wheeled, the Cheyenne warriors struggled to bring them under control. One Cheyenne pointed to the two dark clouds of smoke, and then, with his hands, made the sign-name for the Crows by imitating the moving wings of a bird.

The Cheyenne, after realizing there were only two men, calculated the distance. The Cheyenne warriors blew their whistles, raised their war cry, a mighty volume of fierce, high-keyed voices, and quickly broke into a gallop. They headed straight towards the ridge, where Wolfgang and Black Shield were. The Cheyenne knew that whoever it was, could not reload quickly. Wolfgang and Black Shield worried, the Cheyenne ponies were rapidly closing the distance. They centered their lead balls, surrounded by thin and flexible leather smeared with fat to make their shot lethally accurate. Wolfgang rammed the patched ball down, feeling it crunch against the powder. Wolfgang's eyes had checked the mark on his ramrod to be sure the ball had been seated against the gunpowder. Wolfgang stuck his touch-hole wire pick into the touch-hole to unclog it of any metal-salt crystals growing there and to keep the powder back away from the channel, to increase his chances of a good flash for ignition. The touchhole is open! Watching the oncoming warriors, knowing that they had only time for one more shot, he primed the lock pan with a half level of fine powder from his small horn.

In less than half a minute, Wolfgang had reloaded.

Wolfgang took out the ramrod and slipped it into the hoops under the barrel.

Black Shield, still reloading, the grooves resisting the ramrod, wondering if the leather patch was too thick. He grunted, forcing the patched ball down the powder-fouled barrel and muttered, "They must attack us to qualify as men." Wolfgang's expression grew serious, "These warriors attacking are uncertain but willing, knowing they are riding to meet death half-way."

The closer the two Cheyenne came, with their long lance heads, the lower they dropped and the more forward the riders lay behind the neck of their horses, driving their ponies with their heels. Their mounts nostrils flaring with effort, flowed toward Wolfgang and Black Shield, their heads bobbing up and down, manes and tails streaming out behind them.

"Don't miss," said Wolfgang, as he reached up with his right hand and brought the hammer to full cock. A drop of sweat trickled past Wolfgang's right eye as he concentrated. He steadied the front sight blade into the rear sighting "V," and settled it on the target.

Flint struck frizzen…

Klatch!

The fine powder in the pan flashed and…

Poof!

The puff of powder made Wolfgang's right eye smart and specks of powder stung his right cheek.

The main charge exploded…

Boom!

The rifle hammered back into Wolfgang's shoulder.

Smoke billowed; music to their ears.

White smoke filled the air and their nostrils, with a sulfurous smell, hiding their targets. The sound of their shots echoed across the vast prairie.

Two riders were toppled from their horses with the explosive sound of the rifles, as the lead balls found their targets. Both weapons had barely come to steady, when, with orange fire and white smoke, their rifles went off with a resounding bang.

The remaining two Cheyenne warriors, armed with short bows, continued unabated, bent forward along the sides of their horses' necks. "Ki-yi! Ky-ky-ky-ky!" The Cheyenne yipped. Wolfgang and Black Shield heard the steady, deep rumble, growing louder and louder, with it came the crackling of brittle sagebrush and greasewood, the thwack of quirts, and the spluttering cough of hard-breathing horses. Wolfgang, feeling his own adrenaline flow, now answered with his own high-pitched war cry: "Yee-yee-iii-haaaa!" He held his empty rifle across his front. Black Shield dropped his rifle and drew his tomahawk. Both men waited amid the sound of the rumbling thunder of approaching hooves at full gallop, as the warriors gave their shrill, staccato, long-drawn, war cry. Wolfgang and Black Shield stood their ground, their fear suddenly gone.

Like wolves coming in for the kill, the oncoming Cheyenne centered their attention on Wolfgang, the larger of the two Crow. Wolfgang saw a brief, triumphant glint in their dark, burning eyes, as he watched the nearest warrior bend his bow. The thrum of the bow releasing its tension was sharp. The arrow came towards him, followed by the flicker of the glittering arrow cleaving the air. The soft sound of death barely audible, hissing as the fletching passed closely by. The song of the arrow was angry, hissing, as the fluttering rush of feathers caught the air. A sound he had heard many times. He saw and heard the whining flight of the shaft from the first arrow and deftly sidestepped.

The second horse archer nocked, aimed and loosed his shaft. The unseen, whispering release of the second arrow leapt off the string and flew true. The arrow punched into and passed completely through Wolfgang's left leg. Black Shield heard the wet thwack and glimpsed Wolfgang's expression. The impact of the dark shaft, made his friend stagger and gasp in fearful surprise.

A spray of blood shot out of the wound. Wolfgang screamed in frustration and defiance of the wound, swinging his rifle by the barrel at the Cheyenne as he clattered by. Wolfgang hit him in the head with the butt of his rifle and knocked him from his horse. The brained rider dropped his bow, it went clattering in the brush, as his eyes bulged from their sockets and blood shot from his nostrils. The dead body hit the ground with a heavy thud and lay still.

Teeth bared, Black Shield threw himself up at the passing Cheyenne and struck him on the side of the neck with a killing blow, cutting deeply into the soft flesh and striking the collarbone with a dull thud. The rider, with an explosive grunt, spasmed, doubled over in the saddle and slumped forward. The Cheyenne rider started toppling from the horse, feebly clutching at the animals neck, blood spraying everywhere. He tumbled toward the ground. The warrior slammed into the ground, rolled, spasmed, jerked, and then lay still, as his horse let out a panicked neigh, and continued on, riderless. Knocked and thrown aside by the horse, Black Shield's heart was racing and his blood was pounding through his head, as he shakily recovered from the ground, and stood checking his limbs.

Black Shield looked to his friend. Wolfgang was clutching and attending his leg, with a look more astonished than pained. Wolfgang was suddenly aware how quiet and still his surroundings were. There was only the whispering of the wind. For the moment, the Apache was forgotten. Then, Black Shield walked over and checked to be sure the Cheyenne warriors were dead. He turned and moved to Wolfgang to treat and wrap his wound. Wolfgang's wound was bleeding freely, from a faintly puckered wound, like a small mouth, where the arrow had passed through the back of his leg, without hitting the bone or severing any major blood vessel. They decided to let the wound bleed for the moment to cleanse itself. Despite the pain, Wolfgang found he could put his weight on it.

Black Shield, looking at Wolfgang's bloody leg and feeling anxious, blurted out, "Are you all right?"

"I'll be all right," replied Wolfgang, as he felt his left leg weakening. Wolfgang was grateful that the arrow had passed all the way through. His wound stung. The pitch, binding the sinew wrapped arrow head to the shaft, could dissolve after 20 or 30 minutes, forcing a man or medicine woman to dig for it. Indians sometimes applied snake venom to the tips of their shafts and if such an arrow remained in the body for any time, it could cause death.

* * *

The lifeless Cheyenne lying on the ground wore belts with quillwork and brass bracelets. Their fringed leggings were fastened with decorated narrow straps that hung down the side of each leg. Both had necklaces made from the fingers of their slain enemies. They wore shell nose rings and their ears were pierced with shell ornaments attached. Their hair was dressed with red earth and their faces painted with red, blue, and yellow markings. Their moccasins were decorated with beaded triangles and had side seams and soft soles, with rawhide soles sewed on.

Black Shield pointed at the young warrior that Wolfgang had brained with his rifle stock and said, "Him, maybe 15-years-old on first horse raid." Then he motioned to the one he had killed and said, "Him, maybe twenty. Seasoned warrior. Him, have scars from strips cut from arms as sacrifice to the spirits.

Never sing wolf song again."

Wolfgang stared at the Cheyenne lying where they had fallen. The Cheyenne's hands were curling in death, lips barely parted, bodies twisted into attitudes grotesque and horrible, the blood of their wounds slowly hardening and turning black, now food for the blowflies, vultures, crows and wolves. Already Wolfgang and Black Shield listened and watched the high-pitched droning storm of carrion-feeding insects. Drawn by the scent of death and decay, the insects landed, crawling across their face and eyeballs and their wounds to feed, disappearing inside their mouths and noses, to lay their eggs. The two men knew the aroma that would permeate the air well. The smell of death!

The air will become thick and heady with a putrid stench that will hang in a cloud, clinging to the inside of ones nose and roof of the mouth and in the back of the throat. Wolfgang opened his mouth wide, already trying to clean himself.

If the animals don't find them, their faces and bodies will swell up, turning greenish-black and burst. In four days, the maggots will become a moving mass under their clothes, devouring the rotting bodies, until only their animal scattered bones and leather clothing will be left.

Chapter 16

The empty prairie stretched away among the undulating hills, to a distant meeting with the pale, empty sky. The horses were tired and had turned their tails to the cold, dry wind that was sweeping across the land from the distant Front Range of the Rocky Mountains. The horses were busy cropping the newly emerging grass, as the astonished Apache warrior remained at a distance, staring at Wolfgang and Black Shield, while allowing his breathing to slow. They could see he was tall but smaller than they. The Apache came across the open ground, boldly, as Wolfgang and Black Shield warily watched his approach, until he was less than twenty feet away and held his one arm up in greeting.

The near nude Apache, with a seemingly unconcerned air, stood proudly, studying Black Shield and Wolfgang. He wore only a headband and the characteristic breechcloth that hung almost to the knees. His feet were covered with front seamed, leather moccasins and leggings that combined to form a boot.

As they observed the lone warrior, Black Shield said, "The Gataka are great warriors and thieves, and are taught as children not to trust other tribes. Deceit is a virtue among their tribe. The Apache are unequaled in animal instinct. Like all of us, successfully stealing horses brings honor comparable to killing an enemy. His village women will admire him for his ability. The Apache hate the Spanish and their Christian Indian allies. They are great hunters of the jaguar."

The Apache warrior was a broad-shouldered man about five feet ten inches in height. His chest moved in and out as he breathed deeply, but easily, and his muscled body was shiny with sweat. He had a broad forehead and slightly rounded face with a distinguished nose. His large mouth and white teeth showed, as he appeared to grit his teeth, when the two wolves suddenly appeared at the side of the two Crow warriors.

The Apache had the appearance of a runner, and he clearly possessed more than ordinary powers of endurance. His broad shoulders, deep chest and sinewy arms and legs were toned and fit. His face remained stoic. The Apache's hawk-like brilliant eyes sparkled with excitement and his nostrils pulsated with the emotion of being saved from certain death by the two warriors. The Apache had identified these two warriors, easily, as Crow, from their dress and markings, and then, momentarily, his eyes grew wide. The Crow were allies of his tribe's many bands. The lone warrior was fierce-faced. He saluted them with his right hand by raising it, open palm forward. When he saw they were reading his sign, he clasped his hands together, the left under the right.

A sign for peace.

His stern, hard eyes bore into them as he spoke with his hands to maintain silence and secrecy, in case more Cheyenne or other enemies were nearby. With his right hand talking, he pointed his thumb at his chest, then his index finger at them, followed by the nail of his right index finger pressing against his thumb, he made a motion from his mouth outward a few inches and snapped his index finger straight forward, repeating the motion.

I and you make little talk.

Although Wolfgang and Black Shield were too far away for their ears to hear, due to the wind, their eyes studied the movements and meanings clearly. He made graceful and eloquent gestures. Black Shield held his right hand far out in front and then drew it toward his chest.

Come closer.

The Apache moved closer. His body remained rigid and unmoving, proud. His manner was composed with dignified demeanor as he signed from the distance in the universal language of the high plains. His hands moved quickly. The movements of his hands were rounded and sweeping in their rendition and easy to follow.

"Me Curly Bear," the Apache's hands gestured, "My small band lives at the confluence of the North and South Platte. The majority of the bands that make up my people live further south. We are being pushed west by many tribes coming from the east. The Spanish, to the south, use my people as slaves to mine silver in Chihuahua and in the Durango iron mines. They trade whiskey and arms for women and child slaves. They trade one horse for a captured slave and two horses if they are delivered directly to Santa Fe."

Then Curly Bear noticed the tall warrior's unhealthy-looking color, his wound and unsteady stance, as he began to wobble and shake uncontrollably. The adrenaline rush of the fight had subsided and Wolfgang's wounded leg felt stiff. The wound began to throb in waves of pain radiating outward, with his weight on it. Clenching his teeth, Wolfgang felt faint, and saw shadows on the periphery of his vision. He swayed from side to side, fighting back the agony in his leg. Feeling a wave of nausea, and losing focus of his surroundings, everything began to spin crazily. Wolfgang staggered. His legs buckled beneath him, and fell to his knees. The sound of his pain in bending his leg was cut off by the sound of his retching. The Apache's voice faded as Wolfgang slipped over the edge of consciousness into the blackness that enveloped him. His nostrils were filled with the acidic odor of his vomit. Darkness took Wolfgang.

* * *

The Apache warrior saw the dark, red blood was a constant

flow. The wound was not life-threatening, so as long as they kept the bleeding controlled they could move this man a long distance. He quickly looked around and saw what he was looking for in a nearby, wet, meadow. The gray-blue tinted stems of a medicine plant.

Chapter 17

It was the season known to the Western Indians as the Strawberry Moon. It was the month Wolfgang knew as June. In his homeland, June was known as the Rose Moon. Here in this land, it was the time when the grouse were drumming, the bighorn sheep were lambing and the magpies were laying their eggs. The bears were busy feeding in the dry valleys and hills on the Arrowleaf Balsamroot, being especially fond of the leaves and their flowering heads.

Wolfgang and Black Shield had been on the Cheyenne trail for over sixteen sleeps. During the chilly night in the light of the Full Moon, the 7th sleep of the Strawberry Moon, the Apache had assisted Black Shield in bringing the wounded Wolfgang to his small, well-hidden village. The only light showed through the open doorways from the embers of the fireplaces, as people emerged.

The presence of the three warriors was announced by the disturbance among the vicious camp dogs, from their snarling and bristling hair. The stiff-legged, strutting of the dogs guarding the camp, were seen by the people, every hair bristling, lips drawn back showing their teeth, crouching to spring. The surprised and unwary dogs alternately sniffed the ground and air around the new arrivals for their scent. The two, outnumbered, black wolves, stalked among the village dogs, with careless ease, wary of being attacked first stood shoulder-to-shoulder just staring. After the wolf's custom of giving no warning of their intentions, together attacked the snapping dogs, knocking them from their feet and driving in with their teeth, lacerating their soft throats with a righteous wrath.

The aggressive camp watchdogs had been quickly whipped by the wolves. The cowering dogs slashed opened, torn and bleeding, yelping with pain and fright, took refuge from the attack of the two, great, wolves that accompanied Wolfgang and Black Shield. The cringing camp dogs, snarling and bickering, clustered and crawled among the people's legs in fear. The vicious, heavily muscled wolves, with their bristly fur standing on end, had already killed two of the dogs, by ripping slashes to the veins of their throats and savaged others without mercy, into a red ruin of oozing wounds. To the people watching, the swiftness of it had been bewildering. The slinking wolves continued ranging along, protectively, by Wolfgang's horse. The wolves, moved with their peculiar sidelong movement with their red tongues hanging from wide, powerful jaws, eyes gleaming.

* * *

Word and sound of the new arrivals spread fast, old squaws and men came out of their lodges, shifting restlessly, venting guttural sounds, and quickly gathered the carcasses of the dead dogs for their cooking pot, others shouted Curly Bear's name and raised their hands to him, watching him enter the village with his guests and the two wolves. A strange calm fell over the village, as small children craned their necks to see.

The dwellings known as "wikiups," were conical frames cloaked with buffalo skins sewn-together. Once inside, Wolfgang regained consciousness and instantly realized the extreme pain and chill that ran through his body. He saw tongues of orange, yellow, and red as small flames flickered in the darkness, illuminating the wikiup. Wolfgang was glad to be warmed by the fire. An old woman was washing the thick, crusted blood from his wound and body. Wolfgang realized the journey to this village had taken awhile. The blood under the bandage had turned a dark brown color. The blood on the outside of the bandage had turned a blackish patina. Wolf sat on his haunches, behind the old woman, watching every move.

*   *   *

The old woman prepared the sweetly fragrant sweetgrass, as she watched Wolfgang's eyelids jerk and knew he was having a night-vision. The movements of his body told her that it was not a good dream. The smoke of the sweetgrass and tobacco would help his spiritual healing.

Her narrowed eyes followed her fingers. His skin has the pallor of a dead man, and his eyes are sunk into dark bruised cavities. His dressing is stuck to the edges of the ragged aperture in the smooth muscle on the front of his leg. A black plug of clotted blood covered the back of his leg. The skin around the wounds is hot and inflamed, and there is a faint, sickly smell of infection.

As she continued to examine him, she could see the healthy movement of his chest. The wound was bruised and swelling, but most of the bleeding had stopped. She contemplated his wound and recovery briefly. Once he is sleeping, I will make an incision and clean the wound. Later, I will sew it back together. His feeling of discomfort from too-tight skin from swelling and bruising will not last long. Seven suns at the most. The numbness will last longer. The scarring will be seen forever. Her forefinger opened his lips. The color of his gums was normal. His pulse was strong.

Semi-conscious and remembering his dead wife, the Crow tribal shaman, Dark Moon, Wolfgang knew exactly what was happening before he slept.

The administration of the medicine belongs to the gods of the spiritual world that would determine his fate. For this, the Apache shaman must sail away on the wings of a trance-on a soul flight to the rhythm of drums and rattles, to a distant realm where the pain of the ordeal and the arrows of the medicine plants worked their magic. The cure of the magic plants worked in the interplay of the mind and body among humanity, in the environment and the harmony of the universe. The sacred smoke of tobacco and sweetgrass, and finally, the sweat lodge were all used for purification.

* * *

The Medicine Woman watched the unconscious Wolfgang as his head moved back and forth, dreaming. The muscles of Wolfgang's face were contorting into a grotesque shape. A reoccurring dream had returned to haunt Wolfgang. His mind was experiencing a nightmarish hallucination that had occurred years ago, when he was bitten, by the great snake. This time the dream was even more frightening than before, He saw the slow movement of the long scaled body of the great snake glide forward, barely touching the ground. He saw it's reflected, sapphire, elliptical eyes and its steely, flat, fixed stare that burned intently into him, mesmerizing him. The snake's movements had been elegant and quick. It raised itself up, poised to strike, its mouth opened and paired, translucent fangs hinged outward as it bit him, hard and true to its mark. This was the part where he had always wakened. The conscious part of his mind, the part that knew it was a dream, waited, but it did not happen. He had a helpless feeling and felt that he was trapped in the dream. The fear became worse. He felt the hot, burning sensation of layers of pain coursing through his body, swelling it and causing his skin to turn dark. Wolfgang saw his body being torn apart by the poison. For endless hours, he saw the shadow of a woman and heard the echo of her voice as he twisted and retched.

* * *

    Wolfgang's mind gradually pulled itself up through the foggy warmth and awoke from the luminous dream. He had the fleeting sense that he had been given the answer to a question he didn't remembering asking. He tried to remember what it was. Then, he got sidetracked, as he drew a deep breath and lay quietly listening, with his eyes closed, wondering where he was. The combination of the urge to cough, the buildup of phlegm, the feeling of a scratchy throat and an irritated sinus told him he was inside a structure with a fire. He was tired, but lucid and knew someone was near him. Wolfgang felt a prick of pain and when he lifted one hand to touch the hurt place his hand was slapped away. He opened his eyes and the throbbing pain came softly, back to him. Wolfgang observed that he was in a dark, strange structure. The structure he was lying in was made in a conical shape. His eyes focused. He now noticed the interior was constructed with four posts positioned at the cardinal directions. He felt the back of his neck prickle from fear and anticipation.

    Sorceress, medicine woman or a shaman, he thought. All. He saw the fixed grin and empty eye sockets of the many smoke and soot covered skulls, mounted overhead, as if they were staring down at him.

Chapter 18

Inside the wikiup, Wolfgang was conscious, though in a state of half-delirium. He smelled the odor of wood smoke and burning sweetgrass, mixed with a strong, aromatic, camphorous odor. From somewhere in the shadows of the harsh illumination of the lodge, there came to him the soft and fast sound of a drum beating and old men's voices singing a medicine song that rose and fell with the sound of the drum. The vibration of the ground told him that feet were dancing, and there was the occasional sound of a rattle.

Pebbles inside the rattle represent souls of ancestors and spirits. Shaking the rattle is calling for their assistance!

As his head cleared, he noticed in the shadows that someone was closely observing him. He saw her outline. Wolfgang did not know who she was, but he knew what she was. His head and vision cleared and he watched the movements of a medicine woman.

She leaned forward from the shadows and moved closer to the faint, rosy glow of the small fire that radiated up and on to her face. As she drew nearer, Wolfgang could clearly see her unnerving dark eyed expression. Her eyes glittered with the shrunken reflection of the fire. From the way she sat, she was stooped and hunchbacked, from a lifetime of work. She was thin, haggard and time-scarred. A stream of orange and yellow sparks rose as a faggot cracked in two. Her eyes narrowed as she studied the flickering and fading phantom pictures formed in the fire coals. She watched the smoke turn in graceful spirals and twists before disappearing out the pointed roof. A good sign! She turned slightly and puttered among her belongings, and drew out a small container. She shook it and it rattled. Wolfgang was familiar with this ceremony. The old woman made a sweeping cast and the tiny bones skittered and jumped across a painted skin. Then came the studied interpretation.

Suddenly, she looked up, her splotchy face etched with lines and furrows and her shrewd, rheumy dark eyes were heavy-lidded and sleepy. She stared at him through gray strands of hair, and scrutinized him intently. She saw the color mount softly in his cheeks and at the base of his throat, the wariness in his eyes, and his breath quicken perceptibly.

His sky-blue eyes are bloodshot from the strain.

Wolfgang's flesh crawled. He was riveted by dangerous looking, dark eyes, deeply staring into his. The dark dots of her orbs shrank to pinpoints transfixing him. Wolfgang felt the energy when she first looked at him with her hands on her heart. He breathed in deeply and let out subtle breath. Aaaaaah.

He felt a powerful transformation, taking place within. Her powerful gaze sent energy through his body. He felt a transmission of love. An inner peace!

Wolfgang waited, patiently, as he studied her. Errant hairs poked out from under her nose and chin and her bones jutted out everywhere. He felt love emanate from her heart. He knew he would be safe, loved and nurtured. He felt his stress leave his body. Wolfgang wondered about her age.

Women often turned ancient at fifty, Wolfgang mused.

As the medicine woman heated water, Wolfgang recognized he was in good hands. Wolfgang guessed the woman with the lined face and wrinkled, sagging flesh, to be sixty. The lines on her forehead and at the sides of her mouth were deep. She looked old and frail, her hair was kinky and white and dangled to her waist. Her stoic leathery face, a nest of wrinkles, seemed one of intensity, passion, and sadness.

Her eyes penetrated into the far places of his mind. In an

instant, her deep, wild eyes became wide and shined with the joy of recognition. Through his throbbing pain, his gaze was level and steady. She slanted her eyes at him. Wolfgang heard her speak in a low, clear voice, as her hands followed her spoken words with signs.

"I saw your frightening vision. A night-vision is the shadow of something real. You have snake medicine inside you. That is good. Since the poison didn't kill you, it will keep you healthy and help you grow old. Your arrow wound will heal in time," the old woman's hands had motioned. After a period of time, she added, "I have been praying for two hands of time for you." The old woman studying Wolfgang's facial movements saw his eyes look up and to the right, as his mind flashed back to the memory of his dream, and knew what he was thinking and feeling.

Wolfgang saw her eyes briefly looked up and to the left. As she drew a picture in her head, she remained silent and in thought for a while. The old woman's eyes shone. The seriousness of a night-vision is well recognized! Then she continued, "You will have this dream for many years, but eventually it will go away. The dream means you are being transformed with greater wisdom. Every animal has a powerful spirit to communicate messages to humans. The great bear, wolf, the snake have chosen you and tested your ability to handle their power. You now have a third medicine totem you are closely associated with in your life. The snake. It has given you an increasing sensitivity to the auras of others. The more you honor your totems, the more powerful and effective they become. You must now add the shape of a snake to your war shield. Mimic them in your tribal dances." Wolfgang thought about what the shaman had said. The luminous dreams of the snake fit together with everything.

I have a snake totem!

As she placed a damp cloth on Wolfgang's forehead, the medicine woman explained, "I have been expecting you. You are the night stalker everyone calls the 'Two-legged Man-Bear.' You were the husband of the great Algonquian medicine woman and Crow shaman. In my dreams, I saw a great wolf coming and the Grandfather bear appeared to me. A large man appeared and I knew it was you, whose coming was being foretold."

"Where am I?"

"Safe." She smiled. "For the moment. I am the shaman, Wind Woman. You are in my village, in my lodge. We are what you call the Gataka. We are the most northern band of the Lipan Apache. Curly Bear is my grandson. It was he who smashed the roots of the Blue Flag plant, growing nearby, and made a poultice for your wounds." Wind Woman was silent for a time, letting him digest what she had told him.

Shaman! Holy woman! The one responsible for the well being of her tribe. The tribe's mediator, between the spirit world, and the world of humans. She evokes visions, cures the sick, the keeper and interpreter of tribal lore, responsible for success in food gathering and warfare, mused Wolfgang.

Wolfgang tried to sit up. The old woman warned, "Lie still or you will bleed more." His vision blurred and he could not bring his eyes into focus and he felt himself for a moment, on the brink of unconsciousness.

"I knew your woman, Dark Moon,"

Wolfgang's lip trembled at the memory.

Wind Woman proclaimed. "The news of her passing when the sun disappeared into a black hole in the sky, spread all across the land." Suddenly and sickeningly, Wolfgang felt the stinging pain of Dark Moon's loss. Please God, prayed Wolfgang, please give me strength to endure this. She saw from the look on his face that he still suffered her loss, and decided that she needed to tell him a little more.

The thin and frail medicine woman was silent for a time and watched, with solemn curiosity, the expression on Wolfgang's face. She recognized the deep, raw, ache in Wolfgang's spirit.

He has reacted well to the fearful and painful circumstances of his life. And, learning from them, he has chosen to go forward with his life. They have molded him, thought Wind Woman. She reflected on the past and the time she had first met Dark Moon. She recalled the words Dark Moon had spoken. The old woman smiled and continued.

She said, "Dark Moon told me one day you would come. You are like the great oak tree, whose life is a constant struggle. You are a fighter, whom, unknowingly has come to fulfill Dark Moon's prophecy of liberating our people. Dark Moon said when you are exhausted and on your knees, you struggle on bravely, never giving up. You have great strength, endurance and tremendous willpower. Your courage made her life and yours worth living. Her stories and those of many tribes reflect a man who never traveled the easy trail and refused to ask for help. You made Dark Moon's journey through life easy and pleasant. I have been watching over you. I saw you save my grandson from certain death."

Wind Woman and Wolfgang then remained silent. Wolfgang, suddenly remembering why he had been sent on this journey, said, "You must see that a runner is sent to our village and inform our chief that we have gotten our horses back and that we have punished the striped arrows, who took them."

"The message is already on the way, along with the horses. Black Shield allowed us to keep what horses we needed." "Now rest!" The medicine woman's gnarled hands were busy rolling the long, rough-edged, leaves of dried sweet-grass, into braids. She would save the braids' to burn as vanilla-scented incense during ceremonies and for medicinal purposes. Wolfgang remembered Dark Moon telling him that burning sweet-grass had therapeutic value and invoked good power. Wolfgang had seen Dark Moon and Yellow Bird Singing pick sweet grass many times. They always picked the grass before the first frost, seeking it in the meadows and low, wet prairie areas and marshes. It has a mellow, soporific effect, and is useful in helping to enter into a meditative state.

Wolfgang felt the grass' effect even now, as he remembered his loving wife. Dark Moon's hair and clothes had often smelled of vanilla. Eventually, weariness began to get the better of Wolfgang. His eyelids slowly closed and he slipped into sleep, dreaming of Dark Moon.

Wind Woman sat, braiding the long leaves and watching Wolfgang sleep. And she knew of what he dreamed.

He dreams of the woman he loves, his dead wife, the Algonquian sorceress, with the hooded eyes, Dark Moon.

Chapter 19

The old shaman sat staring into the glow listening to the crackle of the fire to attempting to predict the outcome of future events in the days ahead. She picked up a stick and tapped a burning faggot, releasing a torrent of sparks. She watched the smallest ones go out quickly as they wafted up. The larger sparks continued to glow as they were carried up by the hot air. The fire flared brighter as the faggot broke into three pieces, sending up a new wave of sparks. Then her head jerked back. She saw the image of the three hunters.

* * *

The flickering fire burnished the shrunken old medicine woman's face and deepened the shadows in the furrows of her skin, as she sat, looking at Wolfgang, with pursed lips. She studied his scarred face and body. His body reflects many wounds of man and animals. She was silent momentarily and then croaked, in an ancient voice filled with dust, "The white man's burning fever is spreading from the south, into the Great Plains, from the Spanish." She was silent for a time, in thought.

"Smallpox epidemic," thought Wolfgang.

Then she continued, "You and your friend Black Shield must perform a service for me before you leave this place. I have already sent word to warn your people to scatter and isolate themselves, and their village, from all contact, until the epidemic has past." Her beady eyes looked at the scar on his arm, her lips gave the tiniest twitch.

Its magic, that protects him from the pox.

Wind Woman, had been told by Dark Moon, about this scar and the magic it held. She had also seen this scar on some of the Spanish to the south.

"What is it you require from me and Black Shield," asked Wolfgang.

Wind Woman leaned forward, making weak, bending sounds, to look closely at Wolfgang, with her rheumy, cloudy eyes and said, " I will tell you what I require when the time comes. Now, you must sleep and heal. I will give you valerian root if you have trouble sleeping. But I think you will sleep on your own."

She sat still, deep in thought, staring into the fire. The medicine woman looked away, as she went about the process of preparing to heal Wolfgang.

A strong antiseptic is needed.

She waited until the water boiled and then sprinkled many pulped leaves to soak in the pot. Slowly, she stirred the pot. When the color was just right she pulled the pot off the fire. The medicine is strong enough. She poured out a small quantity to allow for faster cooling. To counter infection, she rinsed the wound with the lukewarm leaf tea. Wolfgang recognized the medicine woman was about to give him sage leaves. "Chew these well and then swallow them," she demanded.

Wind Woman burned aromatic sage as a healing ceremony and to reduce stress and rid him of bad airs and evil spirits. She had a good supply of the leaves that had been collected in May, June and July. The arid hillsides were covered in sagebrush and its spirit was strong medicine. She knew of its power to fight infection. To prevent the creeping sickness, she rinsed Wolfgang's red-lipped wound with a wet paste made from sage. Next, she used an alternate antiseptic derived from a shaggy carpet of gray and green lichen clusters she had collected from the open, sunny spots, atop alpine granite rocks, in the rugged mountains.

Earlier, she had made a strong cold tea from a freshly chopped stinging nettle plant. She now poured the tea into the open wound. Aiiyee! He has many wounds, from man and animal, she thought. The tea immediately began coagulating the blood and the bleeding was stopped within a matter of minutes. Drinking it would treat internal bleeding.

Next, she applied and bound a cold poultice, withdrawing the heat from the inflamed area. The poultice was made of pounded and mashed Juniper berries. It was encased in a clean cloth, on the front and back of Wolfgang's leg, to cleanse deeper skin tissue, withdrawing toxins and pus, and reduce inflammation. The medicine woman sat back, her rheumy eyes looking at the Two-Legged Man-Bear, thinking.

Later, I will crush and use the yellow oil from forty of the dark blue juniper berries, from the exposed dry slopes and add them to boiling water for a tea, and let him drink that for a period of one sun. She smiled to herself.

Juniper berries found year around are exceptionally cleansing. When he passes his water, it will smell of violets, and help reduce his wounds swelling. A very hot poultice will draw out any pus that comes with infection and will reduce the swelling and aid the healing.

Ashen faced, Wolfgang's eyes closed for a moment and then blinked open. Wolfgang told himself, firmly, he was safe and in good hands. His eyes closed again, and he surrendered to the warm, comforting sleep that came upon him. His breathing became regular and heavy as he slept deeply. The old medicine woman smiled and with well-skilled, bony fingers started working on his wound.

He won't feel a thing. I have two more remedies just in case. The Devils Club paste, to apply to his deep wound. The paste made from the plants root bark to fight infection. And, the Blue Flag root from the damp places. A decoction from boiling the Blue Flag root could be used on his wounds. A hot poultice made from the smashed roots could be used.

She eyed the hanging, fresh bunch, of yarrow herb, overhead. Its feathery leaves, crushed, were used in a poultice, as a blood-stopper, and always harvested midsummer, on a dry day, in the morning, at sunrise. She closed the wound with a bone needle and gut; she started at the mid-point of the wound and drew the edges together and tie off the gut thread. She worked outwards and quickly the wound was bound together and closed. She would watch closely for the wound to become red, swollen, and tense, in case she had to lance or open the wound and drain pus.

Wolfgang awoke, early, in the morning of the fourth day, hearing singing outside the structure. He saw the medicine woman burning juniper needles. He smelled the incense and it made him think of Dark Moon. The wounds throbbing pain had ceased. The swelling had subsided and the lacerations were closed. The torture of the stiffening wounds was finally on its way to healing. She fed him meat rich soup, thickened with powdered lichen.

"This rich soup is good for you internally," she said. He is still a little pale, but his cheeks are no longer sunken and his normal healthy color is returning.

Wolfgang saw the frail, gully-wrinkled, medicine woman smiling at him. Her eyes held a feverish glow, as the dark dots in the center shrank to pinpoints that transfixed him. He could not help but grin back at her.

She will continue to wisely doctor me with spirit ceremonies and herbal medicines, that it will be better than what the white doctors, in the east, have for treatment.

"Your wound is stitched with gut. It is now covered with honey," she said, as her faltering hands, netted with veins, moved in a slow, but smooth motion. "Your wound also looks and smells good. Now, roll to your side, so I can help you pass your water." After helping Wolfgang to pass his water, she smelled and looked at it.

The water is not cloudy. The color is clear. The smell is good.

"It is normal," her stiff hands said.

She put a small container of water by him, then broke off a pencil-sized, birch twig and stripped it and handed it to Wolfgang saying, "Chew on the tip until you fray it into a brush with soft fibers, and then scrub your teeth and rinse."

She's just like Dark Moon.

"Why are the people outside singing," inquired Wolfgang.

The medicine woman looked up at Wolfgang and smiled, "The village has assembled to sing and pray to White Painted Woman, the first to arrive on earth, and her brother, Killer of Enemies, and for you," she replied.

"Why was my wife here?" asked Wolfgang.

"Being a shaman is a constant learning process," she replied, "A shaman must communicate with others of her kind. She must always seek the knowledge of others, to heal and keep up with personal development. We are all experimenting with new and different herbs to heal the sick. We gain the power to combat spirits and heal their victims, to kill enemies and save one's own people from disease and starvation. Our ceremonies, feathers and rattles are just to catch the victim's attention. Dark Moon visited our village here, to gain knowledge and pass it on."

Wind Woman stared at the aura surrounding Wolfgang. She was pleased, yet fascinated with the energy field she saw emanating from him. She saw his strength laid out in his aura. His aura has strengthened a little. A beautiful, vivid, yellow-orange color surrounded him.

He is a determined warrior with a healthy body and mind and great self-control. His intellect enables him to master his fear and worries and inspire others. A dynamic leader! A man, with heightened mental and spiritual abilities.

As a final remedy, she boiled the roots and leaves of the agrimony flower in water and honey, for a tonic for him, to take, to sooth his emotional anxieties, tortured thoughts, and to find peace within himself. The remedy would physically help him throw himself into village activities and promote his inner peace and expel the evil dispositions in his body. It would open any obstructions of the liver, spleen, and digestive organs. Her mind at ease, she went back to her work, shredding strips of willow bark for drying. It would be used for pain, fever, and rheumatism.

* * *

In the lodge of Wind Woman, Wolfgang was resting, watching the old medicine woman checking her baskets of herbs. She never stops working, he thought to himself. She felt his eyes and looked up smiling. She didn't speak, but made a series of slight, subtle gestures with her hands in the universal language saying, "There is never enough." It is a large responsibility, taking care of people," Wolfgang's hands gestured. Wind Woman looked into his eyes. "Is there pain in your leg?" "It is only a little sore, but no." She was satisfied. "Do you feel ready to exercise it?" Wolfgang smiled. "Yes." "Good! The village needs more hunters. You will remain here with me the rest of your time here. I will enjoy your company."

Chapter 20

It was past the middle of the season the Indians knew as the Moon of Thunder or the Blood Moon. Wolfgang also remembered it as July. Wolfgang had had trouble sleeping. He had been kept awake by the roaring, of rutting buffalo bulls and the bellowing of cows nearby. A deep, guttural, muffled bellowing, rumbled across the plains for miles. He smiled, as he looked to the other side of the lodge, as the overhead skulls with their fixed grins and empty sockets stared down at him. The old medicine woman had no trouble sleeping.

Wrrooo-wrrooo-Wrrrooo,

As Wolfgang lay there listening to the distant muttering of the herd, he thought of Mouse. It is July! It is the time the small flies lay their cream-colored eggs on the whiskers of the horse's lips, under their jaws and on their forelegs. The flies trouble the horses and make them crazy at times. I must get up, and start moving around and exercising, and check Mouse.

Wolfgang got up to go out and empty his bladder, and felt the protest from his leg muscles. His leg was still weak and recovering. He could feel pain as he stretched his muscles, but knew it was time to use his legs. Something wet and cold touched his leg. His friend, Wolf who stood, looking at him, nuzzled Wolfgang. Wolfgang reached out and patted Wolf in silence.

Outside, Wolfgang noted the position of the Big Dipper, located high in the northwestern sky, the handle up, and the bowl down. The Big Dipper is the key to the night sky. The two stars at the end of the bowl, he used as pointers. His eyes followed a straight line out from the "pointers," locating the North Star. He reached down and let his fingers explore his wound. The Cheyenne arrow wound to his leg was but a neat scar. He felt ready for the saddle again, and seeing the poor state that the Apache village was in, realized the sooner he could ride, the better. He wished to properly help the people of this village.

* * *

Sitting by his fire with Curly Bear and Black Shield, Wolfgang had just finished cleaning his rifle, saying, "Burning black powder leaves a deposit "fouling" on the walls of the bore. It builds up with each shot, until no more balls can be forced down the barrel. Before this occurs, the bore must be swabbed out. The use of water is alright, but a hot piss down the barrel, is best and quicker. A thorough cleaning at night and a fresh loading in the morning is the best guarantee of quick, sure ignition, aiding accuracy."

Now, using the simple heat source of the fire, Wolfgang melted and poured molten lead into the cavity of his iron bullet mold. The lead had a low melting point. He was casting lead-ball bullets in his mold, 3/100 of an inch smaller than the actual caliber size. The lead was traded for from the French.

Wolfgang counted to three, watching the sprue freeze back into solid form. When a dimple formed on the lead surface, the lead ball was ready for the next step. He then used his sprue cutter to shear off excess lead from the top of the bullet mold and then he dumped it on a clean leather surface. He thought back and told the two warriors of the time he had spent with the Osage and the friends he had made and how valuable they had been to him and Dark Moon.

Something inside him remained of Dark Moon after her death. He felt the need to always help other deserving people. It was not logic, but something visceral. It began in the Ohio country, when he was taken by the Delaware, to Dark Moon. He remembered how they had stayed together when the frontier began to suffer, during the French and Indian War. The long, wearying years of flight through the uncharted, Indian, French, and Spanish held lands—battles, fights, and friendships forged, friends lost and always Dark Moon giving help to those in need.

Dark Moon still guides my life.

*   *   *

The small village contained approximately twenty-five or thirty lodges. Wolfgang walked through the village and talked with his hands. He noticed that there were a lot of older people and not so many warriors present. Many of the drying racks had no meat hanging for the sun to cure, their storage cases (parfleches), were empty of dried meat and pemmican.

Wolfgang noticed the women were very skilled in weaving serviceable, decorative baskets. The old women created loosely woven, gaily decorated carrying baskets that carried water, wood, or wild foods on their backs. Other women stretched skins on frames or on pegs in the ground to scrape away the flesh. The women work the hides to an even thickness with a sharp bone. Then, a mixture of fat mixed with ashes, brains and liver, was worked into the hide until it became soft for leather clothing and bedding. During the warm summer months, when buffalo hair is short, skins are taken for lodges; numerous other articles are made from soft-dressed skins or rawhide.

The women cleaned lengths of intestines to fill with meat, berries, and fat pounded together for pemmican, others, cut thin strips of meat for drying in the Sun for jerky. Wolfgang watched the older men for some time, sorting through the largest and toughest tendons collected from the leg tendons and backs of deer, elk, and buffalo and then helped them. The sinew was cut from the tendons connecting muscle to bone.

The sinew from the leg tendons would be used for backing bows and repairing cracks and splinters on the bow's back, to make them serviceable. The backstrap sinew was for arrow work, to bind nocks, to keep them from splitting, bind feathers and flint points to the arrow shaft and bow repair. Back sinews were used strictly for bow-cords, Wolfgang mused.

The women cleaned the tendons of any fat or meat, dried them and then separated the flexible fibrous strands used in making sinew. Wolfgang enjoyed talking with the men, but found it difficult to work and use his hands to talk. He found the light pounding of the thin back-strap sinew, relaxing and worked diligently to remove the protective sheath, that separated the fibers, that lie like ribbons on the outside of the flesh, along the backbone. Fibers vary in length and thickness according to the size of the animal. Those of a buffalo bull were nearly three feet long, three or four inches wide, and a quarter of an inch thick. The back sinew from a bear was not quite two feet, but was enough for two bow-cords. Wolfgang moved on, to watch another group. Older warriors worked making arrows. The wooden arrow shafts had been cut amid the cold and deep snows, during the Moon of Snows (January), and Moon of Hunger (February), when the sap was low and the wolves prowled, hungrily, outside the village. The shafts were left bundled and wrapped. During the Moon of Grass (April), when the white and bluish phlox flowers bloomed on the valley floors. The wooden shafts were stripped of bark when the shafts were determined to be dry. The shafts were straightened each day.

They were straightened with heat and sized with sandstone. Small, lethal, obsidian and flint arrowheads were knapped for deep-penetration. The arrowheads all fit inside Wolfgang's forefinger. The old warriors notched both ends and wrapped them below the nock, and fitted the small flint and obsidian arrowheads, fastening them in place with sinew. Matched right wing lead feathers from wild turkeys were cut. The arrowheads and fletching were wrapped with deer sinew. The nock was reinforced with sinew and covered with hide or pinesap glue. The entire arrow shaft and its wrappings were sealed and protected from moisture, by a hand rubbed coat of melted, whitetail deer fat.

Chapter 21

Wolfgang sat observing Mouse as he had always done since he was a colt, paying attention to what he was doing and why. Mouse always had an ear pivoted toward him and watched him. Mouse was more sensitive to his surroundings than his pasture mate's. Mouse constantly swiveled his ears, stopping his grazing to look around for danger. Mouse would continue to look at any disturbance long after the rest of the horses returned to grazing. Mouse was always focused, and sensed what was wanted. He had saved his life and given him warning countless times in the past. He was a good friend.

A few of the other horses were seen stamping their front legs, tossing their heads, or hiding their muzzles, indicating they were being irritated by flies darting at them. The troublesome flies could cause a horse to panic while being led or ridden. Wolfgang got up and walked out to Mouse. The animal's head came up, whinnied and hurriedly ran forward to greet him, slewing to a stop, with nostrils flaring and mane flying. After hugging the animal's neck, he ran his hands lovingly over Mouse, scratching his favorite places and talking to him. He found that only a few cream-colored eggs were attached to the hair shafts of Mouse's legs. Wolfgang removed them manually, with a small wood comb and sand.

* * *

The moon was in its last quarter and the stars, known to Wolfgang as the seven hunters, were in the middle of the night position. Wolfgang rode Mouse, slowly, across the prairie. He stared at the night sky, thinking.

The last quarter moon always rises at midnight. The prairie is black with buffalo in all directions, as far as the eye can see. It is the "Moaning bellowing time." Wolfgang could hear the distant bellowing of the bulls, which made the air tremble.

Wrrooo-wrrooo-wrrooo. Wrrooo-wrrooo-wrrooo.

The bull's rutting season. The herds are constantly on the move, and the meat of the cow, juicy and fat-laced. I must harvest as many young cows as possible, before the herd drifts on, to furnish meat, robes, and lodge skins. Because of the threat of being attacked by outcast bulls, there is no more exciting or dangerous time than this.

* * *

Wolfgang had remembered Curly Bear saying that the Spanish captured his people, for slaves to work in their mines, and realized that many of the villagers were hungry. Wolfgang also realized that he had a debt to repay, so he would go hunting and feed these poor people and give them hides to work. His wound had healed cleanly. Pink, dimpled, glossy scars covered the front and back of his leg. From the recovered horses, he would leave them for the tribe to become mobile again and travel well.

* * *

When the sun came up, Wolfgang had already settled on a low ridge to shoot a number of animals. His leg was still too sore to ride fast over the rough prairie. From where he lay, he could see the closest herd was very uneasy. The buffalo were intensely active and the sound of distant thunder was everywhere on the prairie. Wolfgang could hear the muffled thudding of their hooves, as bulls fought one another, head to head. The fighting bulls incited others to fight. Those bulls not fighting, moaned, tossed their shaggy heads and switched their short tails. As the sun rose in the eastern sky, the prairie came alive with the loud, impressive, roaring of aroused bulls. The sound was made by a steady, guttural, rumble and roar, as one bull elicited a response from the other bulls. Before long, all of the bulls joined, emanating a long, echoing roar.

Wolfgang was watching two large rival bulls wallow, paw and horn simultaneously, while switching their short tails, trying to attract the attention of a cow in heat, oozing mucus from her swollen vulva. Others were attacking an embankment with their short horns and some were gouging up the turf and throwing it into the air. The bulls wrinkled their faces in a grimace while curling their lips, stimulated by the scent of the cows. They urinated, often due to the tension, and were ready to attack. Many bulls were in a high emotional state. They trailed along side the cows, swinging their horns toward them, sticking out their tongues, emitting a soft purr, ending, in loud bellows, to drive away rivals. The frequent fighting incited others to fight, while the rest moaned and tossed their heads. Strangely, the mosquitoes, during this season, left Wolfgang alone. He could see that it was only the bulls that the pest went after. After watching for some time, Wolfgang decided to shoot as many of the cows as he could, before the cows ran off, taking the amorous bulls with them.

He carefully selected his .490-inch lead balls, for his 50-caliber flintlock, making sure each was slightly smaller than the diameter of the bore, so he could ram them home quickly. After dumping the powder charge into the barrel, he poured a half-inch pinch of crushed wasp nest material directly over the powder. This would give each shot consistency. Each ball would fly true. The .015-inch greased patch with the ball, made the rifle easy, and quick to load. The greased patch increased the range, accuracy, and gave the lead ball good penetration. Priming was the last component of loading and he kept his fine-grained primer handy, in a small horn, suspended from a lanyard, around his neck. Between shots, cows gathered around the dead and wounded buffalo, sniffing the blood and bellowing, as Wolfgang ran a fouling patch up and down the barrel. He carefully reloaded, making an accurate shot. He always worried about the corrosive chemical salts left in the bore and pan from black powder, after it has been ignited between shots. It was the reason for fouling.

Chapter 22

The shaman sat quietly before a small fire, attempting to communicate with the spirit world, to listen and see. She had taken a soul-loosening potion, to delve deeper into the spirit world. As the potion began to work it's magic, her pupils constricted as she studied the fire. She reached out, with the bony fingers of her veined hands, grabbed a stick and stirred the fire. The air-starved fire sent sparks wafting upward on the hot air, followed by crackling sounds from the movement of the fire.

As the potion coursed through her body, her lips moved, as her face and voice became taut. She chanted softly, twitching, and trembling, as dusk was fast overcoming the twilight. Suddenly, something deep within the shaman stirred, as she raised her arms and rolled her eyes upward, into the rising smoke. Her rhythmic chanting stopped, as a swirling, ghostlike puff of smoke appeared to open and reveal a shadow of something real. There was a far-away look in her eyes. She saw mist hovering above a small watercourse set in a distant, sandy wash, between heavily forested hills. She saw large, round tracks, round of pad and toe, and her face became sharp with anxiety. The tracks were larger than those of a lion. The tracks left the sandy wash of the creek and disappeared into the shadowed leaf-litter, under the branches of gnarled, ancient oaks. The hunter had selected the least noisy route, and moved with slow, calculated movements. Then, she saw the hunter. The wrinkles around her eyes tightened. Wind Woman shuddered.

A sinking feeling began to creep over her. The shaman in the past had performed rituals to borrow this animal's power, because it is endowed with great magic and power, a symbol of mastery over all dimensions.

El Tigre!

The cat had been roaming the riverside brush of the lowland forest. Graceful, it moved with ease, moving its ears to locate the direction of sounds. The beautiful, orange-buff, coat glowed, like gold, with solid dots, within broken rosettes, covering a compact, muscular body. The movement of the animal's short tail demonstrated its agitation. The jaguar's large, round, reddish-yellow eyes glared at two figures. A frightening grimace stood on the animal's mouth, and its curled lips displayed an impressive set of canine teeth. Unseen, unnoticed, the spotted cat's eyes clamped to mere slits. The cat started toward its intended prey in a ground hugging approach. Its short limbs, equipped with large paws, carried the beast in one fluid motion across the distance. With every step, the cat let out a faint growl, the scent of the hunt alive in its nostrils.

* * *

The shaman's vision revealed two young women, striding briskly, along a familiar mountain game trail toward their village, as the sun set. They had spent the day digging roots and were in a hurry. In one fingers time it would be dark and it was nearing the time of the new moon. The dark of the moon is when El Tigres cycle of power is the greatest. Each eye is working singly, providing greater depth of vision, magnifying images, and judgment of distance. Each night had grown darker and only the stars of the sky would light their way under the canopy of the trees. The older girl, alert to the smallest sound, felt uncomfortable. She sensed something in the stillness. There had been shifts in the stillness. She could hear the soft, even, barely perceptible steps of a four-legged animal in the shadowed undergrowth. Both women stopped along the trail, as the younger woman had to relieve herself.

The older girl waited with apprehension, telling the smaller, younger one, to hurry as she left the trail.

What is it? There it is again. Something big is moving in the brush.

The older girl waited, every sense alert, her lips open for air, her breath labored. She heard the drifting of a great bird cutting the air on silent wings, and she caught the silhouette of an owl as it glided silently by. The sweeping strokes of the raptor angled between the trees and disappeared. Then she heard the plaintive sound of the great horned owl perched nearby, and shivered in fright.

Hoo-hoo-hoo-hooooo.

Her mind knew fear. An evil omen!

Impatient and watching the sky as the sun dropped, tinting the sky with variegated shades of pinks, reds, and orange, she called out to her sister. "Hurry!" There was only the sound of the wind sweeping mournfully among the trees. Hearing no response, she called louder and with more urgency. "Come quick!" When there was no response, her heartbeat quickened. Frantic, she tearfully shouted. "Hurry sister!" Relieved, she heard the sound of her returning sister and blurted out, "Hurry!" Suddenly there was something near her that had not been before. It had come like a shadow, without sound or warning, a gliding shadow.

She was greeted with a sound that had only been described to her, but never heard, a low roar. A loud uh, uh, uh, uh, growing faster and more repetitive, until it was inaudible, but now, seemingly very close. The terrible realization of the truth crashed upon her brain. She could not determine the direction of the sound. She hesitated a moment, hushed herself, and was still as death, listening. Where is it?

She turned, in mortal panic, knowing immediately, the sound of the measured tread of soft pads deepened and became substantial to her ear, what it was that was moving swiftly towards her. She listened for the animals breathing, it weighted heavily on her. "Mother, save me," she whispered out loud to herself.

It is there!

It is the evil, hunting spirit of the wilderness known by the Indians to the south as, "The eater of us."

"Jaguar."

The big cat is known to attack from the front, rather than from behind.

Her breath was loud, punctuated by strong heartbeats. Her back was wet with fearful sweat. Her eyes were wide, showing a great deal of white, as her panic-stricken face turned in all directions trying to detect the animal. Her wild eyes, showing more white than iris. Frantically, she looked into the growing dusk for another set of eyes. She heard the methodical and stealthy sound of movement at a distance, going around the side and ahead of her. The air was thick and heady with the aroma of the animal. Then, the sound was gone again. Ever patient, the cat crouched in wait as its prey came toward him.

The great cat stood, staring at her fixedly; with its head down, looking up at its prey from under its brow's, its eyes shelved in dark shadows. A cold sweat broke out on her forehead as her legs and stomach trembled. Momentarily paralyzed in panic and the confusion of terror, but acting in self-preservation, she sobbed and dropped everything. With a strangled cry and trembling limbs she turned, quickly running and screaming in horror, as reality crashed upon her senses. Her legs stretched out in a ground-eating stride, in a terrifying, blind flight along the trail. Then, she heard the jaguar breathing harshly from her front. A ghostlike form seemed to be coming closer, moving rapidly toward her. The orange orbs of the cat's eyes and its gleaming, incredibly long white teeth seemed to float closer ahead of her, making no more noise than a shadow. Then, it screamed, as the pale claws of its hind legs, with toes spread, gave one final thrust in the dry soil.

She saw the grim reality before she could jerk in any direction. She gasped, and shrunk back. The cat's body flew through the air at her from her front, appearing suddenly, from the darkness. She screamed a blood-curdling scream as the full realization of her fate fell upon her. Before she could react, the jaguar leaped upon her. Struck from the front, she fell under the great weight, and the great claws seized her and raked her body. She saw the great teeth as they covered her head, then felt horrible pain, as the teeth bit deep. The beast's canine teeth delivered a fatal bite through the skull. The beast then released his hold and slid his teeth between the victim's vertebrae, ceasing all respiratory and motor skills, severing the spinal chord. El Tigre tore out her throat and drank and then violated her. His tail jerking as his fangs grabbed, sheared and tore the girls flesh. In seconds, the girl was dead. Her desperate cries were replaced by the blur of the animal's deadly, sharp front and hind claws, raking and slicing through her clothing, ribs, and stomach. Her quick death saved her ears from the harsh, tearing growls, the sound of teeth tearing muscle and grating on bone in the moonlight. The blood dripping from the young woman had turned into streams. Now, there was only the uneven sound of the wind, as it fought its way mournfully among the dark and ancient, gnarly oaks.

Chapter 23

Her stomach twisted with revulsion, as the shaman felt the terror, and her face reflected the horror, but her eyes did not blink once as she drank in the sight. She saw the incredible embrace, as El Tigre bit into its victim's head, neck and raked her shoulders, ribs, and once beautiful thighs. Her clothes and flesh ripped away and punctured in many places and rib bones cracked, she was soaked in blood. Slashes across her abdomen threatened to spill open and shiny gray-white tendons peeked through the gouges on her legs. The escaping blood was sucked up by the cat and some seeped into the leaf liter beneath the body. The cat ate her tongue, ears nose, jaw, neck and chest first. Then, the largely nocturnal beast consumed the shoulders and ribs. Then it opened the abdominal cavity and consumed the internal organs.

* * *

The visibly sweating and frightened shaman, with her head uplifted and only the whites of her eyes visible, had seen and heard it all, drowning out everything, even the high, rapid flutter of her heartbeat in her ears. The horrific bitterness of the vision left a palpable taste on the back of her tongue. I'm too old for this, she thought, as she took a deep labored breath and began groaning and wailing.

She called out for her assistant to bring Curly Bear to her. Wolfgang, Black Shield and Curly Bear stood before the shaman. Her piercing black eyes flashed, as she talked, and told them of her vision. Looking at Wolfgang, Wind Woman said, "You must kill yaguarete. It is the name given to it by people far to the south. It means the "beast that kills its prey with a single bound. This cat is a symbol of power. " Wind Woman handed Wolfgang the leg bone of a bear. He looked at it. A bone torch! "It is filled with animal fat and a fiber wick for use in a cave," said the Shaman.

* * *

The sun was setting and the shadows were lengthening. The slopes were losing their heat, as darkness was quickly flooding out the last of an orchid sky. Cool air was sliding down the hills. At last light they heard the gurgling of running water. Their moving eyes flicked about, never still, shifting rapidly, circling about, finally finding the tracks in wet sand along the creek, near a large pool of water that ran clean, clear, beautiful, green water. The water ran swift and deep in places over beds of gravel, where large boulders almost blocked the passage of water. The tracks were bigger than any lion track. The big round tracks were round of pad and toe marks. They decided to spend the night, where they had discovered the tracks, and built a small fire. The gloomy and somber area was overlooked by a towering rim rock formation with a grassy basin above. During the early morning, they heard a series of short, coughing roars that grew faster in volume into a series of grunting growls and then gradually grew fainter. The sound was ventriloquial in nature, making it hard to locate.

Uh, Uh. Uh, Uh, uh, uh, uh, uh.

The air and ground seemed to vibrate with the intensity and volume of the sound, making their hair stand up on their necks. The roaring of the evil, hunting spirit left them with a feeling of awe. The night was warm, but Wolfgang was sweating. They assumed the jaguar's call was about scaring game into flight or territory. It had been so many years ago, but he still remembered. The large cave, up on the Belle Fourche, when another jaguar, make its spring. The cat flying through the air with forepaws outstretched, claws extended and great canine teeth bared, in a snarling mouth. Then he heard Curly Bear.

Curly Bear whispered, "He came to investigate our fire. He often does that with hunters. He roars to frightened his prey into moving." They spent the rest of the night listening to the night sounds of birds, and the yipping and howling of coyotes.

*   *   *

In the early morning dawn, they watched, where the thermals were strongest on the east-and south-facing slopes. As the birdsong grew stronger, they had heard the footfalls in the water as the cat explored and hunted fish nearby. As the sun was painting the rim rock a rose and golden color, Wolfgang, Black Shield, and Curly Bear were watching some elk feeding on a grassy slope of a basin above them. The big trees were well spaced and the forest floor was well carpeted with grass. As the sun lit the rim rock, a flicker of movement in the sunlight caught their eye.

It was the jaguar on the high side of the slope, a heavy beast marked with deep orange-yellow spots. The three warriors decided to watch it stalking the cow on the upper edge of the herd, where the rising air carried the scent up from the elk. As the sun rose, the jaguar had waited until the wind had settled and blew mostly in one direction, before starting his stalk. The lithe, formidable jaguar came down over the rocks toward them with all the fluid grace that great cats possess. Here and there it would freeze, with only the tip of its long furry tail twitching, and then it would proceed. A cow spotted it and, almost instantly, every cow in the herd had its eyes fastened on it. The well-fed looking jaguar stopped, beautifully posed against the rocks, and turned away acting as if nothing had happened. The lead cow brought the whole herd behind and they stopped and watched. For a few minutes not an animal moved. Then they followed the lead cow trotting their way across the slope.

*   *   *

Curly Bear, looking at the high rim, pointed and stated, "El Tigre will remain well hidden in the daylight hours, laying up in cover of broken rocks or a cave until the sun goes down. In the darkness, El Tigre finds its greatest element of power."

As they climbed higher up the slope, they found a boundary scratching on a large tree and saw and smelled the cat's urine-scented scrape, and where it had sprayed on some bushes rose up to their nose in acrid waves. It was a smell that could have only belonged to the jaguar. While traversing a ledge, which led to a cave, they came across a large leaf and debris feces mound and the squared heel pads of the jaguar.

*   *   *

Inside the cave, the jaguar was lying unconcerned with the presence of the three hunters outside. The cat resting its massive head on its paws, then yawned. Then it started grooming himself. Alerted to a presence outside the cave, he rose, stretched and slinked closer to the entrance. The cat still remained deep within the shadows.

*   *   *

Then, they were at the entrance to a dark cave. Wolfgang selected an arrow and straightened it with his teeth, and knocked it to the bow. A second arrow he placed in his bow hand, feathers up and point down. The stench of the cat was strong.

From out of the stoic silence of the cave came a low growl. Wolfgang felt a faint rush of blood at his temples, feeling the full unspeakable horror of anticipation, as he lit the bone torch.

Wolfgang remembered his friend from years ago, the Ni U Konska Osage warrior, Big Bull, who attacked by a man-eater, had suffered bites, raking, and clawing. Keyed up, Wolfgang keenly remembered the consequences of what he was about to do. He took his first step, entering the threshold of the cave. With each mincing step, slowly, moved further into the cave, allowing his eyes to adjust to the poor light. He made out the huge tracks on the floor of the cave.

* * *

In an ominous, claustrophobic silence, Wolfgang slowly crept back into the unknown cave, craning his neck to all sides, alert for any motion. The dry scent of dust was bitter to his nostrils. The bone torch provided little light, but was better than nothing. As he penetrated deeper into the cave, the light that seeped in through the entrance was increasingly dim. He felt the spine chilling presence of a sinister evil spirit. Because of the rock and pebble-covered floor, his feet moved at a slow pace. He moved a foot forward only when he was sure of his footing. The hairs on his neck stiffened, aware that he was being watched. The temperature was pleasantly cool. The air inside the cave was fresh and invigorating.

Wolfgang penetrated deeper and deeper into the cave, as the hard floor under his feet became soft. A rustling sound overhead made him aware of a flock of bats above.

Bats! A distraction I cannot afford. The bat is a symbol, of facing my fear. I must trust my senses.

Wolfgang felt an overpowering dread fill him of this horrible, narrow place. He chased the fears, gathered in the dark corners of his mind, away. From deep within the cave, came another, louder, growl. He stopped. Now, there was only silence. Gradually, he became aware of a strange sound. He could feel his heart pounding. Now, he knew what the sound was. He worried because he could not see or locate the animal.

My teeth are chattering. I am afraid.

There was no noise or movement for the longest time, in the deep awful silence, which chilled him. Then, something made him start up, as he became aware of a new sound. He listened intently for a few minutes. Wolfgang realized he was listening to the harsh, rhythmic breathing of the big cat, to the front and above him on a ledge, and knew he was in great danger. The nervous cat crouched in the depths of the cave, its nose pulsing for scent.

The sound is growing slightly louder. The cat is creeping forward.

Wolfgang's eyes probed the gloomy confines of the dark cave. In the almost complete darkness, he saw an enormous, shadowed bulk move. Then, before him, he saw the shadowed outline of El Tigre in the light of the bone torch. The beast's size alone inspired awe, respect, and fear. All fell silent and tentative.

El Tigre is studying me. Calculating!

Tight lipped, he could hear its harsh breathing, and felt the claws of cold apprehension rise in him, as an abiding stillness, as the darkness closed in, embracing him. Then, through the gloom of the cave, he saw a pair of amber eyes glaring at him in the dull light of the torch and heard a low rumbling growl. Then, it snarled its defiance. Wide eyed, his pulse hammering in his ears, feeling nausea overtake him and a knot at his scapula as his stomach stirred. Filled with anxiety, he felt his heart stammering, as he tasted a bitter, metallic taste, creep up into the back of his throat, as the sick-sweet odor of fear wafted around him. Wolfgang set the bone torch on the floor of the cave, as he became aware that the cat's claws were thrusting back into the gravelly debris of the floor for its charge. A mound of muscle coming toward him in a semi-crouching position, growling at every step in a blur of paws as a headache took shape between his eyes. Wolfgang's blood ran cold. His breath became short and he felt helpless as the long, gleaming, ivory teeth floated toward him. In a massive surge of adrenaline, Wolfgang, in one motion, raised and drew the short bow and released. The turkey feathered, fletched arrow shaft, flew true and mortally hit the snarling, roaring beast. The one hundred and ninety pounds of a mule deer's worst nightmare was skewered. There was no need for the second arrow in the left hand with the bow.

* * *

Outside the cave, Curly Bear looked at Wolfgang in awe and said,

"The spirits favor you," looking deep into Wolfgang's eyes' he went on, "The spirit power of the jaguar is yours. It is part of the endless cycle. You acknowledge that one day your spirit will leave you and become part of all that has come before and what will come."

Chapter 24

Wind Woman, with her shrewd eyes, gleaming with the light of the fire beneath iron-gray brows, looked up and offered a smile to Wolfgang, Black Shield, and Curly Bear. "Listen closely, this is not a request," she said. "I am sending you three on a dangerous journey to the Spanish occupied territory, to the south, to find a Spanish camp. There are few travelers in this empty land. Journeying on your own will be fraught with danger. The Spanish camp is located in the northern part of the San Luis Valley, in what the Spanish have named, the Sangre de Cristo Mountains."

The Blood of Christ.

Wolfgang shifted uncomfortably. "Hmmmm." He wondered what he was getting into now, as his eyes opened wide and he looked up into Wind Woman's wise old face. To the small, rapt group of listening and watching men, the emotion of the shaman seemed to radiate a deep power. It illuminated her eyes, they were as bright and as lively as a young woman's, and made her voice irresistible.

Wolfgang was convinced that this path he had followed, since meeting his first wife, Dark Moon, had always been his destiny. For the first time in his life, he was free from guilt, remorse, fear, or question. He was resolute. He would carry out Wind Woman's plan.

Wind Woman went on, "It is a place where evil spirits live. High above this camp is a mine known as, the Caverna del Oro, its meaning in Spanish is the cavern of gold. It is located high up where the eagles fly, above the tree line. The high mountains there are filled with caves. You must search. The mouth of the cave is marked with a sign of an engraved, red painted cross. There are reportedly about fifteen of these caves nearby of various sizes. To all the plains tribes, this is a place of mystery, awe and death; not a place to go. This cave was found many lifetimes ago."

"Watch closely," said Wind Woman. She drew in the dirt with a stick. As Wolfgang watched, he saw a cross of four, straight-lined, pointed arrowheads, meeting at their points, with the ends of the arms consisting of indented 'V's.

Wolfgang's mind drifted back to his early days in Germany. He had been taught about this eight-pointed cross.

The Maltese Cross, a symbol of protection. The oldest order of warrior monks, that fought for Christendom and pledged to sacrifice their lives for their fellow man, had adopted the cross. The Maltese Cross was introduced, to the Order of St. John of Jerusalem, during the Christian warrior's time after they moved to the island of Malta.

The shaman, Wind Woman, was quiet for a time, thinking. She gazed intently into the smoke of her fire. She saw across the distance of the wide-open spaces of the prairie. Once again, she skewered them with her eyes and continued saying, "The wild mountains of the San Luis Valley is a place littered with our peoples corpses. It is a place where headhunting is practiced, and the white man and animals have a taste for human flesh, often killing from ambush. Animals and demons hunt and stalk and eat human flesh. It is a place where death rushes at you and men completely disappear. A place where devils and demons exist underground in the mines where they work. It is a place where dead souls go. The Spanish come north, from the southern end of the valley, from the Taos Pueblo. I am sending you three because even when your eyes are closed and your minds are unconscious, you hear every sound."

As Wolfgang listened, tightlipped, he suffered conflicting

thoughts about man-eating jaguars, lions and bears. He was excited, but wrestled with the dread of what he was hearing.

Wind Woman, looking at Wolfgang, arresting his gaze with her feverish glow, raised one bony old arm with its trembling claw-like hand, marked with the liver spots of age, and pointed an arthritic finger at him saying, "Dark Moon's prophecy to me long ago revealed the future and told of your coming. I have burnt offerings in the fire and saw the signs of your coming in my dreams and heard the rustling of the great oaks; an omen. Your life has been determined by fate, and it has taken its course. You are here. You will take my son, Curly Bear, with you. He can think like a horse and talk their language. He is capable of being accepted as their leader and can earn their respect without fear, by mirroring the horses own pattern of "talking," in order to bond. He will be useful. He belongs to the Na-a-mo called, Horse Men, whose lodge is restricted to only the bravest warriors. Horse worship! " She remained in thought for a moment, looking into Wolfgang's eyes, then said, "The successful killing of the jaguar portends a dangerous journey from the gods."

The next day, as Wind Woman stood near the three mounted warriors, she could see a lone, black raven and hear its song. It flew in a southern direction. The horizon was clear in all directions. The day was well omened, for travel. All three travelers knew Wind Woman had interpreted the signs of the bird and sky for their day's journey. Wind Woman's last words were, "Once on this path, you must pursue it to the end. Do not, feel pity for your opponent, be ruthless. Do not check your attack or drop your guard. Curly Bear has been well trained and is an educated torturer, one who knows more than just how to inflict a painful death. He can inflict more pain than any victim can bear and keep it at the desired level of intense agony for as long as possible." Wind woman had spoken rapidly, her hands following her spoken words with sign's, her facial expression emphasized her seriousness. Go carefully. Bring back our people.

* * *

Curly Bear, Black Shield, and Wolfgang made a last minute check of the contents of their buffalo-hide parfleches. The parfleche was an early French voyageur (traveler) term, widely used on the plains, to refer to a hide that had been cleaned, dehaired, and dried; the Indian equivalent of saddlebags or storage bags. Their parfleches were crammed with two weeks worth of jerked buffalo and venison. They briefly talked among themselves and decided they could make better time traveling south, on the plains, where they could easily spot hunting and war parties.

* * *

It was during the last days of the Moon of Thunder. The moon was in its first quarter. A myriad of stars filled the sky, making travel at night easy. Wolfgang, Black Shield, and Curly Bear picked out a star to follow and traveled southeast noticing the moon's points were looking unusually sharp.

There would be high winds.

* * *

The three travelers passed through a sandy valley floor, followed the high ground along the North Platte. They had seen Indian burial sites, of warriors wrapped in skins on scaffold in the distance. Wolfgang was filled with wonder and awe of the imposing range of hills, its reddish sandstone cliffs and the tree-covered flatlands. After reaching the low country, they tethered their horses to sage. They sat in a little circle, overlooking the river, staring back in the direction from which they came-their homeland. They were leaving their beautiful country. Black Shield unfastened an embroidered pouch dangling at his belt and got out pipe and tobacco, and made leisurely, but careful preparations for a smoke. Wolfgang brought forth a small glass wrapped in thin buckskin, and focused the glass upon the mixture in the bowl. A thin streak of smoke began to rise. Black Shield's eyes got large as he drew steadily upon the stem. The pipe lit, he stood and held it up to the sun. Finished with his prayer, they smoked. They gazed fondly over the landscape, which was embraced by high mountains and plains of rich grass with fat rivers fed by streams clear as crystal.

Chapter 25

They had been on the trail for a month. It was the Moon of Ripening, the end of summer. The time Wolfgang knew as August, the time when the pine nuts were ripe and the deer's antlers were full grown, but still covered with velvet. Wolfgang remembered the tribes that knew it as, the Red Moon, because it appeared reddish through any sultry haze. Wolfgang still found this terrifying, vast, emptiness of rolling, undulating plains incomprehensible. The brutal, howling, incessant, hot prairie wind that rose and fell, caused his body to dehydrate, eyes to burn and lips to crack.

The horses settled in to the long journey, picking their way through the prairie grass, sagebrush, and prairie dog holes. Now and then, in the sage, they were startled by a flushing, black-bellied sage hen or by a short, rounded, blackish tailed prairie chicken in the grasslands. As the two Crow warriors and the Apache rode across the country in the usual, slump-shouldered manner, they scanned the horizons, of every flat and ridge. They studied the folds in the sun-cured brown and gold grassland, and sighted their way from one cottonwood grove to the next. In the low ground beneath the whispering boughs of green cottonwoods groves, there was water, fuel, and shade from the burning days. Their training, since childhood, had taught them to see great distances and to interpret signs of everything happening around them. Their keen eyes and noses read the stories of the trails and tracks of animals and other riders. They watched for storms, running buffalo, prairie fires set by Indians, lightning, and always for the signs of man.

Now and then, they found grass trail markers, where grass was tied into bunches. The knotted grass tops indicated direction depending upon which way they pointed. Three such bunches indicated a message. In rocky areas, a smaller rock placed upon a larger rock marked a trail. A small rock, depending upon the side it was placed beside the trail marker indicated direction. Three rocks, placed one on top of the other indicated a message nearby. A series of broken sage bushes indicated a trail. A broken branch with the butt end to the right is placed upon the ground, indicated the trail turned right. In large grooves of cottonwood trees, they found blazes where the bark had been chipped away at eye level. Whitened Buffalo skulls, marked directions and serving as bulletin boards.

Upon the golden-grassed prairie, they sighted their way from one Cottonwood grove to the next, always sure of shade in the burning day beneath the boughs. The fluttering leaves of the cottonwoods were beginning to turn yellow, leaf-by-leaf, shimmering in the sun at the whim of the dry wind. Here they found fuel, water, and game. The riders always made camp in a protected spot near a body of water. As they entered the shade of the trees, bird song filled the air, and a flock of turkeys moved slowly away. They selected their camp and prepared for bad weather in the shelterbelt of the cottonwood grove, where their open-air cooking fire, with its orange and red flickering could not be seen. For the fire, Wolfgang gathered dry grass for tinder, small dead, dry twigs from standing deadwood for kindling, and a few oak limbs for fuel. They cooked only during the daylight always conscious of the reflection a fire would cast at night on the trees. Oak would provide a long-lasting fire, glowing coals, with few sparks and little smoke. Curly Bear went for water among the willows and hackberries, and found some horse and moccasin tracks, along the sluggish flowing creek. Curly Bear had told them it was Comanche. The sole's of the moccasins had a peculiar, straight inner side, unlike the inward curved inner sole of the Crow and the pointed tip of the Apache boot. They heard the long, hoarse triple gobble of a long beard from deep within the timber.

"Gaaarrraaoooobble-obble-obble!"

They heard the distant, extra heavy sound of a gobbler flying. "Whump-whump-whump-whump." The three warriors thought as one. "Dinner!"

*   *   *

Black Shield went hunting and quickly had a turkey-it was soon roasting over the fire, as Wolfgang and Curly Bear returned to camp and joined the successful hunter around the fire. The aroma of good food soon filled the air. As the shadows were lengthening and deepening in the waning pink and orange twilight, a pleasant coolness drifted in as the day's warmth slipped away, in the fading light of day. The three warriors immersed in their senses, sat up talking of the ring that had been around the pale yellow moon the day before. The stars had appeared bluer than normal, and in the early morning hours of the full moon going into its new phase. Its First Quarter! When the Seven Hunters, in their circle around the North Star, showed it to be about midnight, they got up and relieved their bladders. They returned to their blankets, snuggled inside and slept.

*   *   *

Wisps and swirls of mare's tails followed the next day telling confirming an incoming front of worsening weather. The birds and low flying insects had become quiet during the day. During the night, the wind direction shifted and blew from the east. A smell of a fresh breeze was blowing. When they got up during the night to make water, they saw the sky began to roil with spectral unsettling shapes of cool and stormy weather ahead.

Rain!

Their eyes watched every movement around them, smelling every waft of air, their ears and bodies picking up every vibration. "When rainmaker comes, he will help hide our trail," said Curly Bear, "We should not move. We can rest and eat. The horses can use the rest. It will hide our tracks. The coming sun and the strong prairie wind will hide all sign. The wet grass will soften and return upright hiding out back trail."

* * *

The three riders came upon the low, wide valley and bordering high bluffs of the North Platte River. From the high bluffs, above the broad valley, they saw no cottonwoods along the river, but observed a range of distant hills to the south. The riders, passing a prairie pond, saw sage grouse eating sage and grasshoppers. They listened to the soft rustle of the grass in the breeze and the cheery, warbling whistled song of the prairie dwelling meadowlark from its perch. The meadowlark helped the travelers find joy from within on their journey, and remember that every individual event is part of a greater journey of self-discovery. To the three warriors, the birds were gods. The bird's cycle of power often foretold death and could bring good or ill fortune.

Cautious, they often stopped and took in both the natural and supernatural significance of the bright yellow-breasted singer emblazoned with a bold, black "V" on its chest, as they studied the area. The silence was further broken by the staccato, incessant honking of geese overhead as they passed on their way south. The geese stirred their imaginations about searching out a new world. The high-flyers seemed to be calling to them about fulfilling their own promises to Wind Woman of their great spiritual quest.

Above the low moan of the dry wind, the faint, wispy flute-like gargling call of sandhill cranes carried through the air. "Kar-r-r-r-o-o-o-o." The sounds reminded Wolfgang, Black Shield, and Curly Bear to keep the proper focus in their lives. Black Shield broke out into singing a song of their journey as the others listened. Black Shield sang about the events of their journey and how each individual event was part of the self-discovery of a greater inward journey, and the joy of the quest itself. As they listened to the cheering song, they saw the brush and grass of the foothills give way to the sagebrush, which covered a large expanse all the way to the river.

* * *

They crossed the valley, seeing many great blue herons and evidence of the many nest, of their rookeries, in the brush. Ducks, geese, and turkeys abounded along the area of the river. They continued to ride south, across a great, grassy plain, toward the South Platte River Valley, interspersed with groves of trees. The beginning of the Great Plains started in the lowlands of the Yellowstone country, mused Wolfgang. The largest single herd of buffalo known migrated north of the Platte River area each year.

Wolfgang looking at Curly Bear asked, "How many sleeps, are there to the Arkansas River?" Wolfgang saw his friend show six fingers.

Without any hesitation, Curly Bear had replied, maybe this many sleeps. Gesturing in the universal language, Curly Bears hands had motioned, "He held his closed hands up in front of him. The palm of his right hand opened, palm outward and extended all the fingers of the right hand upward. Curly Bear touched the thumb of his right hand to the thumb of the left hand. He extended the index finger of the left hand. The other three fingers of the left hand remained closed."

Wolfgang nodded, understanding.

Seven suns!

The three travelers, responding to the mood of their horses heightened senses, became more alert. The horses, blowing and snorting through their nostrils, had picked a strange scent. The gelding's ears had heard a familiar sound. The horses wide ranging, scanning eyes detected something of interest, warning them, as they stepped with nervousness. Wolfgang and Curly Bear's attention was diverted as they saw Black Shield point to the southeast. Then, Black Shield's hands motioned as he brought his two hands together and extended his right index finger over his left hand, saying, "Sunka wakan."

Chapter 26

Sunka Wakan!
Both Wolfgang and Curly Bear knew its meaning.
Sacred Dog!

The sound of thundering hooves was rising in the distance, and the men sat in stunned reverence to the sight building before them. Feeling the heat in the wind, eyes squinting in the intense light, they stared in awe in the distance and watched the waves of swift, four-legged spirit animals. The wild horses with strong legs and backs and big bright eyes, ran through grass up to their bellies. The rainbow of colors—yellow, tan, buckskin, reddish-brown, bright red, mahogany, blue-grey—enchanted and excited the men. Many of the horses were further accented with black dorsal stripes. The show was made even more spectacular by their flowing manes and tails, which moved like the grass in the wind. Without averting his eyes, Wolfgang opened the side of his mouth and clucked through his teeth and the restless Mouse took the cue and started walking.

* * *

They had traveled fast for seven days along the front range of the Rocky Mountains, watchful for the many grizzly bears that they saw following the buffalo herds across the rolling hills and grassy prairie. Several times they had been challenged for the buffalo they had killed on their journey by pugnacious grizzlies. The grizzly bear was always ready for combat.

Alert and watchful, as they rode, Curly Bear, looked at

Wolfgang and Black Shield and signed "My people have a village east of here on the Platte River near the source of the Republican River. They often trade with the French, who follow the Platte to the Front Range."

Curly Bear's thoughts turned more serious, "According to the stories of our old people, many winters ago, Pawnee and Otoe warriors defeated Spanish soldiers on the Platte River and drove them back south. The land we enter now is the home of the tribe called the Komantcia by the Ute tribe and the Comanche language is the main spoken language of all the different tribes. The Spanish got this name from the Utes."

"I know little of New Spain or the province of Tehas," commented Wolfgang.

Curly Bear continued, "Long ago, it was forbidden for the people of this land to the south to ride horses. The Spanish made it a crime punishable by death; because they knew once mounted they would rebel against Spanish rule. It is said that the Utes, traded for horses from the Pueblos many life times ago. The San Juan Pueblos, under the Tewa shaman Pope -who refused to convert to Christianity and was flogged by the Spanish priest—was responsible for bringing horses to the tribes of the Southwest. Pope and other religious leaders revolted against the Spanish over the issue of their traditional religion, which the Spanish wanted to replace with Catholicism. During the Moon of Ripening, Pope and the Pueblo warriors attacked the Spanish missionaries, driving them from their New Mexico mission to El Paso, where they remained for 12 winters. The Pueblos took the entire Spanish herd of three thousand horses from their pastures near Santa Fe. The Utes, in turn, traded the horses to the Apaches, Shoshones, Nez Perces, Blackfeet, Crows, Kiowas, Navaho, and Comanches, who followed the buffalo," said the hands of Curly Bear.

Wolfgang knew the Moon of Ripening as the month of August. It was the height of summer and the landscape was alive as he studied it.

The land is beautiful! The ragged-looking Indian Paintbrush is still blooming on the plains and hillsides. The dense spikes were still in full bloom, coloring the landscape in scarlet red, pink, orange and white.

Curly Bear continued saying, "After the Pueblo Revolt, many horses escaped to the plains and became wild. The horse thrived and multiplied. My people say the Apache were the first to understand what we as hunters and raiders could do with the horse. But as a people, the Comanche understand the soul of the horse better than anyone else and has the skill in breeding it. Most of the horses they ride are geldings. They are very careful of what horses they castrate in their herds." Then he was silent for a time. Wolfgang and Black Shield could see he was thinking, and remained silent.

Continuing, Curly Bear said, "The Comanches are known by the Sioux as the Padoucas. They call themselves the Nermurnuh, for true human being. The Comanches were Shoshones who, on obtaining horses, split off from their parent tribe riding away from the mountains to the Great Plains. They dwell in the land between the Platte, Arkansas and Red Rivers far to the south, along the eastern side of the mountains. The Comanche are supplied with guns by the French who encourage their raids against the Spanish. During the Moon of Long Nights, in the severe winters when the Cold Maker hits and continues with strong winds, the largest herd of buffalo, antelope, elk, and deer are forced to migrate below the Arkansas River to the Canadian River area. It is there that these animals feed the Comanche who also winter there." Curly Bear paused and was silent, thinking.

Wolfgang thought about what Curly Bear had said.

The Moon of Long Nights is December.

Then Curly Bear went on, "The Comanche bitterly resent the invasion of all white men. They form what is called the

Comanche Barrier on the southern plains between the northern tribes and the Spanish. The two bands of Comanche in the north where we travel are the Kotsoteka, known as the Buffalo Eaters and the Quahadiis as the Antelopes. The Buffalo Eaters' villages are in the Canadian River Valley and the Antelopes, are in the headwaters of the Colorado, Brazos, and Red Rivers of northwest Tehas (Texas). The Kotsotekas are the main raiders of the Spanish settlements in Colorado and New Mexico. After each winter, when the grass is old enough, they raid other tribes and white settlements for horses. They have huge horse herds and are skilled horse breeders and trainers. The children are skilled horsemen because they are given a horse at age five to develop their skill, as you will see. Courage and speed in a horse is what they desire. They trade horses, hides, and captives for guns with the French and constantly war on the Apaches and Spanish. For entertainment, they will mutilate and torture to death anyone they capture. They strip your clothing, stake you out on the ground, cut off fingers, toes and private parts, then place live coals on your abdomen."

Curly Bear said, "I like their beautiful blankets."

Looking at Curly Bear, Wolfgang said, "Where do they get those blankets?"

"Comanches have attended the annual fair at the walled plaza of Pueblo de Taos since before I was born. As far back as my people can remember, mounted Apache warriors have also raided the New Mexican settlements.

"Have you been to Pueblo de Taos?" asked Black Shield.

"Once. It is a place where the lodges are massed as high as seven or eight men, surrounded by a five-sided adobe and sandstone wall. The Pueblos were built by the Anasazi people from Chaco Canyon. The plaza is split by Red Willow Creek that flows from the sacred Blue Lake behind the mountain. The Comanches trade buffalo robes and slaves for corn and Navajo blankets. The blankets are highly prized by everyone because of their water-shedding quality," Curly Bear responded. He went on saying, "The Comanches trade their captured Pawnee, Apache, and Kiowa women and children at the market in Santa Fe. This is why they are so feared. In the east, the Comanches sell my captured people to the Kitikiti'sh (Wichita), the raccoon-eyed people, who live along the Red River. They turn around and sell them to the French. The French call the elaborately tattooed Wichita 'Taovayas.' The French take my people and others to the Mississippi River landings and put them on flat boats to the slave markets in New Orleans."

Wolfgang watched his Apache friend talk with stolid indifference, but saw his friend betray himself with a barely perceptible quiver of his lip.

Black Shield said, "What does the name Komantcia mean?"

"Anyone who wants to fight me all the time," replied Curly Bear. "They are great warriors and we must avoid them at all costs."

Black Shield asked, "Who is the Comanche chief?"

"He is the arrogant Chief Cuerno Verde of the Kwahadi Comanche. They are the Antelope band, who live the farthest west, and who remain aloof from the other tribes. Chief Cuerno Verde, known as Green Horn, is the greatest and most dreaded of all Comanche chiefs. He wears a green horn on his forehead. His son carries on a murderous vendetta against all Spaniards, and his medicine man considers himself immortal," replied Curly Bear.

Both Black Shield and Curly Bear heard Wolfgang as he suddenly made a strange "Hmmm" and had that shivering sort of feeling when the hair on his neck goose bumps rose.

He nodded, turned his head looking at them, and pointed to a location far to the east. They sat on their horses, searching the skyline. They saw what looked like a dissolving thread of signal smoke twisting up into the sky. The rising column was soon gone. They could not make it out. They talked about it and agreed that it appeared that a large ball of smoke had been formed and drifted lazily upward.

Curly Bear said what they were all thinking, "One puff of smoke meant 'attention.'" Wolfgang's insides experienced a slight twinge. He had a premonition of danger. Like the others, he wondered about the smoke. Are we riding into a trap!

They continued looking around scanning the distant horizons but saw nothing. They continued on their way with an unsettled feeling of apprehension, always watching for sign of local tribesmen.

Chapter 27

Each dawn, the prairie was throbbing with life and the movement of game and bird life. It hummed and buzzed unceasingly, with a changing pitch in intensity from the songs of the multitudes of insects.

The three traveling warriors found their four directions fairly accurately. With their acquired sense of direction and using the sun as a rough guide, they continued traveling south with the rising sun on their left. By sighting landmarks and memorizing the landscape, they would be able to return by the same route or a different one. Anything that attracted their eye, they memorized: a bluff of rock, a bend in the creeks or rivers, clumps of cottonwood timber, saddle-backed hills of a ridge.

Passing a prairie knoll, the trio of riders heard a hissing of displeasure and stopped to observe. The three located a badger near one of the holes of its den. Its hole was marked by bits of fur, bones, and snake rattles. The brown and black face of the badger with its white cheeks and narrow white stripe running from the nose over its forehead to its neck and shoulders began to pop its teeth, growl and snarl at the intruders.

"This is an omen. The badger is a keeper of knowledge," commented Curly Bear. "The badger hunts day and night. He is bold and ferocious, aggressive and never surrenders. He speaks of a new story in our lives about to happen." Curly Bear contemplated his thoughts, then continued, "He is saying we must be like him on this journey. Bold!" Wolfgang looked at Black Shield, then at Curly Bear, and smiled.

* * *

Wolfgang, Black Shield and Curly Bear stopped their horses within sight of the Republican River. They dismounted and squatted in the shade of their horses, watching a familiar gathering of birds, plumes billowing upward. They recognized the circular flight pattern and wing motion of the patient hunters that seemed to float, rise and soar for long periods of time without flapping their wings. Vultures! The big, ugly birds were gathering far on the horizon. The three warriors lifted their noses and smelled a familiar wind-blown odor: a musky sweetness permeated the air. Black Shield's hands gestured as "he placed his partly closed hands close to the side of his head, palms inward, and extended his index fingers.

Wolfgang and Curly Bear nodded, understanding.

Buffalo!

They picked up a few blades of grass and dropped them to watch the direction they fell to the ground, then headed their horses into the wind toward a distant high ridge to conceal their approach.

Dismounting, they headed slowly on foot up the ridge until they saw the many different cowbirds in the air. There were blackbirds, redwings, magpies, starlings and egrets that follow the buffalo to feed on the insects stirred up in the grass and on the parasites on the buffalo. The animals also provided a snug perch for the birds on the near treeless prairie. The flatter areas allowed the many tribes of the plains to locate the herds long before seeing them due to the black cloud of birds flying above them.

In the quietness, disturbed only by the sound of birds singing and a breeze blowing through the sage and grass, they peeked over the ridge. Wolfgang, Black Shield and Curly Bear could see buffalo too numerous to count. The buffalo were active, being wary and spooking easily. Cows were issuing their subdued grunts, looking for their calves, and calves were sounding their distressed grunts looking for their mothers. Their eyes and ears paid scant attention to the steady, deep bellowing roar of rutting buffalo bulls further to the east where the land was dark with buffalo.

Aware that the buffalo's sense of smell was its main means of detecting danger, the warriors knew the animals would tear off immediately if they became aware of the three men's presence or scent.

Without turning his head, Wolfgang said aloud what they were all thinking, "A hunt has taken place."

Black Shield responded, "I do not see any signs of a village or Comanches. But, many birds circle on the distant horizon far to the southeast. We must move away from this place."

"When we get to the horses, we must ride slowly and not raise any dust, the Comanche may still have a Wolf watching the herd," said Curly Bear. After some thought, he spoke again.

"If you don't see any Comanche," Curly Bear advised, "that is when they are watching. We must watch our horses carefully. The Comanche, love to steal horses and leave you afoot."

They scanned the sky above and all around them, but there was no sign. They saw no perched eagles that might take flight and warn the distant Comanches of their presence by flying away from their location. Seeing nothing to alarm them, the men rose up on their elbows and toes and backed away and down from the ridge, looking for cover. Then they rose to their feet and scanned the area around them as they moved back down to their horses. The horses had been ridden together so long, they had become friends and were nuzzling each other as they approached.

Chapter 28

It was late afternoon and the three Crow warriors, riding south, had stopped and were resting their horses, letting them graze, while a large coyote squatted and barked at them. It watched them through a screen of sagebrush. "We have approached too close to the female's den," commented Black Shield. "She is still watchful, but will soon grow tired of them and force them away to hunt on their own."

Husband! The low sound came like a whisper on the wind, as he felt a chill at the base of his bones. He wondered if it had been his imagination. But he had heard it clearly. He felt the first trickle of unease. Wolfgang realized Dark Moon had spoken in warning. His head lifted a little, and moved like the coiled snake painted on his war shield, searching.

Black Shield shifted his weight on his horse and started watching his animal's head.

While resting the horses and letting them crop the grass, they now noticed the pricked ears and the shift of their mounts heads: lifting, lowering, and tilting, to catch the light to focus on a distant object, their nostrils flaring. Wolfgang suddenly held up his right hand and cupped it near his right ear and turned it slightly back and forth. Then his poise was motionless. Both Black Shield and Curly Bear caught the action and meaning of Wolfgang's wrist. Listen! They turned, their eyes searching everywhere. Again using sign language, Wolfgang placed the tips of his fingers over his lips, and inclined his head slightly to command silence. Both friends looked in the direction the horses were looking. Wolfgang was not sure, but thought that he had heard something barely perceptible above the wind. It had filled the lull between the gusts of the ever-present wind. The horses stood patiently, switching their tails and flipping their ears against the flies, then resumed cropping grass.

"Horses point their ears toward things that concern them," Curly Bear said, breaking the silence.

Mouse broke wind as he jerked his head up and around, looking off toward the horizon snorting loudly, pricking his ears forward in alarm and rolling his eyes as his hide rippled. Wolfgang ran his hand gently along Mouse's neck to calm him. Mouse had a knack for smelling and seeing everything that moved. Wolfgang became more alarmed. A nicker and a stamp from the other two horses told them they were about to have company. Alerted by the heightened senses of their animals, they again made a quick scan of the area nearby revealing nothing. The horses stood still with their heads erect telling their riders the horses saw a distant object. The wide-ranging eyes of the horses perceived a distant disturbance rising into the sky: a black object that did not have the steady wing beats of level crow-like flight. In the distance they heard a gravelly cough sound, it was the bird that spoke the language of the animals. Aiee, it was the unexpected surprised sound of the spirit bird.

Quork!

The Raven! He-With-The-Sun-In-His-Mouth. The symbol of dark prophecy—of death, Wolfgang thought solemnly.

"To see only one raven is lucky," commented Black Shield gently.

"It is good," said Wolfgang.

Then there was the rapid series of loud, raucous notes from a family of disturbed magpies accompanying the raven. They had been disturbed from their feeding on the backs of the elk.

Black Shield, without moving, suddenly raised his nose and pointed with it in an easterly direction. They saw the large, startled black bird fluster away. Its wings beat loudly rising into the air, as the sun reflected its deep, rich, shiny black plumage. Wolfgang and Curly Bear turned their heads and saw a herd of fast trotting cow elk coming through a distant draw. The raven has been riding on the back of an elk eating ticks. The heavy and solid elk moved into a steady run, their ungulate hooves pounding a drum beat.

"Hmmmm." Wolfgang's brow furrowed. What is it? He wondered. "The grass-eaters should still be resting and chewing their cud," commented Wolfgang, "Something is wrong!" He felt a chill, which made the hair prickle at the back of his neck whenever there was a sign of danger. Wolfgang's confidence was shaken.

To see one raven is lucky, he thought. To see two ravens meant misfortune. To see three ravens meant they would meet the devil.

The three warriors wondered if the elk were trying to run away from the biting flies and mosquitoes to seek a place in the wind more to their liking. The men knew that the misery of the insects would not abate until the time of the first frost. This was the time of year when the cows selected the choicest piece of prairie that offers the most nutrition. The cows needed the extra energy from the lush grass for nutrition to make milk for their calves, and to get through the coming winter. They instinctively scented danger and their faces showed their fear at once as they looked up. Wsh, Wsh, Wsh, came the rhythmic sound as they heard the raven fly above them and fix its eye upon them. The lone raven swept close, laid out its wings and banked, circling them, speaking in its gravelly voice.

Tok!! Tok!!

"The spirit bird is sending us a message of warning," stated Black Shield.

Wolfgang and Curly Bear, following Black Shield's example, lay flat, masking their bodies by dropping a little further over the hill and using sage to hide their heads. They took the raven's warning seriously as they continued to watch the surrounding area of the draw from which the spooked elk had appeared. Wolfgang sighed. He looked around, the immediate vicinity seemed to be clear of any enemy, but he felt little sense of relief.

Shading their eyes against the sun, they watched the skyline to get a view of the fleeing elk, knowing they can usually outrun their predators. The elk continued to maintain their strong pace for a long time. The Crow warriors took notice that the elk stopped only once and all stared back the way they had come. The Crow could hear squealing sounds as the cows and calves called to each other.

They listened to the shorter and more high-pitched sound of the calves, ee-uh, ee-uh.

The familiar sounds of the cows answered with eee-ow, eee-ow.

Then came the sharp, loud barks of alarm. Raising their large, buff-colored rump patches in warning, with their heads lifted and noses held high, the elk were off for the distant horizon at their fast bounding, distinguished gallop. They did not veer right or left and made a straight line of flight. An ominous feeling began working its way up from Wolfgang's gut, tightening at his chest, creating an awareness of trouble in him. Danger, he thought. The trio of friends was filled with unease.

"An omen," said Black Shield. "The elk have shown themselves to tell us to move faster." As they watched, the raven flew in a southerly direction following the elk. Taking a deep breath, Wolfgang turned his blond shaggy head this way and that, taking in the barren landscape, searching for something more than his blue eyes could see. Weariness filled him.

"We must go," said Curly Bear scanning the horizon.

Their horses, aware of the sound and scent, snorted and neighed. The warriors knew they were in trouble.

"It's too late," said Wolfgang. "Look," he said pointing.

Then came the murmur of drumming hooves. The sound was faint. Wolfgang felt the hot taste of acid fill the back of his throat.

The strange Indian riders came into view. They moved at an easy walk paralleling their direction at a respectful distance, keeping up with them and out of effective range of their weapons. The Indians continued to ride along making no threatening moves toward them. Then the strange Indians started shouting challenges. Wolfgang consciously straightened his back, carrying his rifle across the pommel of his saddle

Chapter 29

The large group of fierce-looking riders who were painted black and red and wearing deer antlers and buffalo horns came into view, their eager horses moving effortlessly and efficiently across the harsh landscape holding their tails and heads high, hooves spewing puffs of debris and dust. The riders pulled up their horses for a moment when they saw them. Some of the most excitable horses reared onto their hind legs and pawed the air with their fore hooves. Other horses skittered and pranced, eyes rolling nervously and tongues lolling as they twitched a heel and came on slowly reining in on line. The riders kept their mounts beyond biting and kicking distance. The horses could be heard making their soft, soprano-like whinnies in kindly fellowship, mutual understanding, and greeting. The horses rapidly filled their nostrils with air, emitting a loud snort to attract attention. The horses were already excited and continued to nervously shift their feet.

Curly Bear could see by the style of their braided hair, the fashion of their leggings, and the painted symbols on their mounts who they were. He signed, never taking his eyes from them. He held his right hand up, palm outward, index and second fingers extending upwards, in the sign of "friend." Then he extended his flat right hand with fingers pointing to the left and front, swung his hand to the right and front while turning the hand so that the thumb up and back downwards, and returned it to the first position, in the sign of "no" meaning enemy.

Again, his right hand motioned outward in a sinuous motion. Both Wolfgang and Black Shield understood the meaning of snake.

Comanche!

Wolfgang stiffened slightly as his jaw clenched, watching. He no longer felt weary of travel as he felt his muscles tense and heart rate increase. His palms felt sweaty, as salty beads of sweat were making their way down the back of his neck. His amiable expression disappeared, replaced by hardness.

They could see that the Comanches favored paints for their unusual color. The bodies of the warriors and horses were painted in the rich colors of red, vermillion and ochre. The Comanche' horses heads and tails were painted red. The warriors glittered with ornaments of silver and brass. The Comanches raised their war cry, a mighty volume of fierce, unearthly, high-keyed voices.

"A war party," Curly Bear whispered.

"How do you know," replied Wolfgang, as he began to become slightly nervous and experience a headache.

"See the long, upright coup sticks with their many trophy scalps and feathers. The more coups on the stick, the greater the warrior. Notice the feathers and scalps dangling from the bridles, spears and shields. Can you see the painted red color of their horses' heads and tails, and themselves?"

"Yes."

Bright feathers dangled from their manes and tails.

"It means war."

The war party in battle array advanced slowly on the skyline to maximize the full dramatic effect of their appearance. "They seem to be looking in our direction," said Curly Bear in a hushed voice.

"I thought as much," said Wolfgang, as he tried to focus on relaxing with deep breathing. It's hopeless. Wolfgang thought dully. There are too many. He steeled himself.

"Their name comes from the Spanish, who call them the camino ancho, meaning 'broad trail." He paused in thought, then continued, "This name is given to them because of the large extent of land they travel. The Kiowa, Shoshone, and the Ute call them the Snake People. They control almost all this southern land in order to steal horses from the Spanish and control the horse trade with the tribes to the north. They trade to horse-poor tribes and make alliances with the Kiowa, Cheyenne, and Wichita on the Red River. They also trade horses to the Americans who take them to their villages and woodland farms in Natchitoches and Can-tuc-kee."

Currency of the plains.

Breaking the brief silence, Wolfgang looked at Curly Bear asking, "So what is to be done now?"

Seeing the situation, Curly Bear began to speak slowly, "I am made to think that sooner or later it is meant for us to face them. We will try to talk if they are after us. I know their language."

Curly Bear, looking at Black Shield, said, "We must fight for our lives."

Black Shield kept his composure, looked at Wolfgang briefly and then back at Curly Bear, saying, "We have done this before."

* * *

As they watched, they saw the Comanche stop and dismount. They had large painted shields attached to their horses. They were largely bareheaded except for those with the gorgeous, fluttering bright-feathered war bonnets and buffalo-horn headdresses. Wolfgang could make out the long, V-necked, fringed shirts they wore. All were contoured to fit the body with long fringes at the elbows. Their shirts had combinations of yellow and green hues. Their moccasins were ornamented with elk teeth. The Comanche wore long hair, but most of them had it braided in two braids and wrapped in otter fur, leaving a scalp lock at the back with yellow or black feathers attached. The part in the warriors' hair was painted white, red, or yellow. Their faces were painted red, black, yellow, green and blue.

The manes and tails of the horses were decorated with the tail feathers of golden eagles. The horses' bodies were marked with red or white circles around the eyes, long stripes and speckles decorated their chest and flanks. Lightning bolts and short horizontal stripes decorated their legs and rounded hoof prints decorated the animal's butts. There were circles, palm prints and rectangles that told the story of the horse's rider's accomplishments and medicine symbols.

* * *

Wolfgang was worried. He raised his body slightly on his elbows and slid his body backwards until he was sure the disturbers could not see him. He carefully studied the terrain behind them.

Wolfgang whispered, "I don't see any sign of riders to the west."

Both Curly Bear and Black Shield now joined Wolfgang, talking at the same time saying, "We must go. They are coming this way, one of their wolves must have seen us." Their horses stood still, their ears pricked sharply forward, noses thrust out, and nostrils flared.

Quickly, Wolfgang, his heart thudding in his chest, looked at the sky and seeing the dark clouds massing on the horizon in the northwest mentally counted the days, while evaluating the terrain to the southwest and west.

The time of the new moon was just past and the phase of the moon is heading into the first quarter. There would be ample light to move until the sliver of moon and stars disappeared behind the oncoming clouds. A storm is possible. We must stay ahead of them until then.

Wolfgang, looking at both men, told them his plan, "We

must go! We can stay ahead of them until dark. We will ride fast straight south until dark. There is a distant cut in the hills to the south that turns west. When the clouds cover the moon and stars, we will change direction and enter the creek, he indicated with his hand, and change our direction and move west, hopefully losing the Comanche."

But, it was too late. The sound of drumming hooves swelled in volume.

Chapter 30

Five whooping, Comanche warriors rode forward, whipping their ponies at every jump. Over the rumble of the hooves and tremble of the ground, the group could hear the shrill, falsetto war cries of the riders and the thwack of quirts and spluttering cough of hard-breathing horses echoing across the plain. The steady slowing of the deep rumble of the horses' hooves marked their arrival. The warriors rode to within shouting distance, and with a sliding stop their open-mouthed horses' nostrils flaring, lips frothing and chests heaving, like bellows, created an aggressive atmosphere, as a pall of dust hung in the air. The Comanche's screamed and delivered loud, defiant whoops at them, letting them know they were not afraid.

Wolfgang, Black Shield and Curly Bear sat nervously within range of a bowshot from the Comanches, suspicious and ready for trouble. They felt their pulses pick up. Watching the arrogant, sullen-looking warriors curling their lips in snarling threats, Wolfgang and his friends tried to appear relaxed and confident.

Both Wolfgang and Black Shield looked at Curly Bear with questioning glances. "They are merely screaming taunts and challenging us to single combat," replied Curly Bear without expression. Wolfgang's breathing became short and shallow, as his neck and face colored.

Two warriors rode out toward them within speaking distance, their dark faces hard. They looked to be tall, sinewy, and muscular. The Comanche had a solemn dignity. They were men with dark, haughty, mean eyes. They were mounted on fine horses with Spanish-style bridles, saddles made of hide, and ropes of twisted hair. One rode slightly to the front wearing a short-sleeved vest shirt of mail and a full-length headdress. With nothing in his hands, the Comanche turned his horse to the right, the animal shifted, exhaled a loud noise through its lips, while plunging and stamping its hooves. The one riding slightly behind carried a lance, the tip pointed at them to show their intentions. Black Shield spoke low to Wolfgang without turning his head, "The tip of the lance is not pointed at the ground. Their intentions are not friendly." Wolfgang's eyes momentarily glanced down at the pistols mounted on both sides of his saddle.

The mail the Comanche wore was of a very fine mesh and light. The one wearing the mail yelled across at them while his hands gestured in the universal language. The three warriors watched with rapt attention. The two Comanche promptly reined in at a safe distance, steadied their mounts, still snorting for breath after their gallop, and watched them: their stony, dark eyes were inscrutable. Their magnificent horses stood with their heads up high, bodies stretched out, ears pricked, and tails fanned out behind them. Wolfgang's horse unsettled, skittered sideways, ears flattening, head bobbing, its heightened sense smelling the fear. There came the universal sound of nostrils drawing the air, weighing the scent.

The horses seem to sense when things aren't right, Wolfgang thought.

The lead warrior kneed his Spanish mustang, which was light golden--the color of the sun-cured grass-forward a few paces and returned the greeting. The taut face of the dark-skinned warrior had a lean intensity that looked uncompromising, indicating the violence in him. His thin mouth revealed a rigid control of his natural tendencies. He sat the sound, short-backed mount with the smooth muscles and rounded rump silently. The animal's mane and tail were cream-colored. The tough, hardy looking mustang was a beautiful, big-boned Ysabella sorrel.

Wolfgang noted, it is a mustang of great speed and agility.

The Ysabella sorrel stood square with its low set tail fanned, alert to its rider. Its concave head and convex nose raised well. The medium-sized ears were pricked, giving horse and rider a regal appearance, as it stood perched on its toes, hind legs braced, ready to charge, trembling with suspense. A beautiful animal! Wolfgang tightened one rein, cocking Mouse's head to let him focus on the Ysabella, just in case things happened too quickly.

Wolfgang watched the Comanche horse closely for it to come alive and work the bit with his tongue, indicating the rider was preparing to make a move.

The Comanche chief had an aquiline nose that gave him the regal appearance of an eagle. With narrowed, inscrutable eyes, he sat pondering the three strange warriors sitting on their horses before him side by side for what seemed an endless time, noting every detail of their outfits and taking their measure. His eyes lingered the longest on Wolfgang's scarred face-- a sign that accentuated him as a formidable warrior--his straight nose, and piercing light ice-blue eyes. A white man! Then the chief stared at the symbols on his shield. A bear dreamer! A great warrior! This warrior is big and lean, supple and quick, and has the look of a warrior who is capable of almost any physical exertion.

Wolfgang's eyes locked on the heavy-lidded dark eyes of the chief and studied them. The chief's lips twisted with bitterness, his cold and hard squinting eyes were full of suspicion and mistrust. He had seen eyes like this before and always in men who were evil and dangerous. Wolfgang felt there was something ominous in the chief's behavior, like he had an almost uncontrollable impulse to make a move of some kind. The Comanche chief's fierce expression did not change, nor did he raise his hand in greeting. Wolfgang's eyes continued to watch the Comanche. The one with the full-length war bonnet of eagle feathers remained cold, hostile, his glittering eyes holding no mercy, glaring. The two Crow and Apache looked directly into the Comanche chief's eyes staring him down.

Curly Bear felt the menace in his bones of the nearness of his ancient enemies as he touched his animal's flank and moved toward the front, two steps. He reminded himself to breath right and to take deep breaths to return to a more productive rhythm. Calm down. I must slow down my breathing. Focus! He used sign language and obvious motions very slowly and carefully without any sign of irritability to greet his hated enemy, his heart had slowed and his nerves felt steady. Curly Bear's appearance and demeanor were composed and dignified, Wolfgang mused.

Each hand sign can have several meanings, however the precise meaning of any hand sign depended upon all those that precede and follow it, and the context in which it was used.

"We come as friends."

The Comanche expelled an annoyed breath.

Wolfgang always marveled at the beauty and imagery of the use of the universal language. The hand gestures were beautifully rounded and sweeping in their rendition.

As Wolfgang watched, he heard surly grunts of amusement from behind their leader. He and Black Shield glanced uneasily from one to the other. The taut face of the Comanche leader slightly turned a stern face in an impatient gesture, motioning them to silence. The sounds stopped. The dark, deep-set eyes of the Comanche fixed upon Curly Bear.

The Comanche leader arrogantly stared at Curly Bear deep in thought on what course he should take from here. Curly Bear saw the little muscles around the Comanche's mouth twitch, indicating his decision for the moment. A silence settled between the two groups facing each other. Curly Bear's dark eyes revealed nothing. Minutes passed and no one stirred. Then the Comanche leader, looking him straight in the eye, motioned rapidly, signing, pointing his thumb at his chest, then his index finger at the Apache, curling his hand palm up, then gesturing from his mouth to Curly Bear, meaning "We talk."

After a moment the Comanche extended his right thumb and touched the center of his breast, using his hands to gesture his name, as he spoke. The movement of his hands said, "I am Cota de Malla chief of the Kotsoteka Comanches." Using his right hand, he touched his index finger with his thumb. His index finger snapped out to indicate the word "talk." He continued extending the index finger, meaning, "How are you called?" The Apache took a deep breath, his distrust was aroused. He did not like the part he was forced to play, as Black Shield and Wolfgang waited patiently.

"Curly Bear," the Apache answered.

Cota de Malla's hands paused briefly and then continued saying, "You are known to me. It is said you have counted many coup upon your enemies. Now tell me how it is that you have entered our country."

Curly Bear shrugged, hearing the contempt in the chief's flinty tone and seeing the hardness of his enemy's face, as if it really made no difference. "We are only passing through." He started to go on, but was interrupted.

"To where?"

"We do not really know. It is a place occupied by our enemy and yours, the Spanish. When we find the place, we will know it."

Wolfgang looked from face to face of the five Kotsoteka Comanche warriors; eager for something that might betray their thoughts as the Comanche men glanced at one another momentarily. He heard some grunt or nod their heads as the talk continued. He noticed the throbbing temples of Cota de Malla.

"You are not welcomed in our country," stated Cota de Malla as his hands gestured, his voice rising. "You must fight," he said as he turned away.

Wolfgang and Black Shield looked to Curly Bear, as the

Comanche turned back to his warriors. Wolfgang, Curly Bear and Black Shield could hear murmuring break out among the more distant warriors. Wolfgang immediately felt some anxiety and frustration over getting caught up in another fight where he was unable to avoid the possibility of getting hurt or killed. Risk and chance!

Chapter 31

Curly Bear, seeing his two friends looking at him for confirmation of what was said, replied, "He said that his name is Iron Armor or Cota de Malla. You can see his Spanish metal vest. I know of him. His Comanche name is Ecuercapa Guaquangas, which is derived from the Spanish term for leather jacket.
He is the youngest son of Cuerno Verde, the Chief of the Kwahadi Comanche. Cota de Malla is distinguished by his skill and valor in war. He has "Medicine power." It is what the Comanche call puha, attained in his vision quest, during his search for spiritual power. He has killed many men in battle, and wears some of their scalps on his belt for all to see. He is intelligent in political matters and without equal in military achievement." He has presented a single warrior challenge.

Curly Bear remained silent for a few moments, then his hands signed, "They have too much of a high regard for their masculine virtues."

* * *

There was one warrior who wore a buffalo-scalp bonnet. Most of the Comanche warriors wore colorful yellow and green thigh-length shirts with breastplates contoured to fit the chest. The arms of their shirts were fringed and they had belts for carrying accessories. Those that had dismounted had thigh-length, close-fitting leggings that were gartered below the knee. The flaps of their breechclouts were ornamented and hung to their knees. Eagle feathers could be seen fluttering on their leggings and shields. They were fine-looking men, tall and graceful.

Wolfgang's eyes were bright with a terrible certainty as he turned, inclined his head, and raised his eyebrows, as if to signal, "Here we go again." The stoic warrior, Black Shield, was always coldly amused by the facial expressions of Wolfgang. Curly Bear watched the two Crows as they exchanged glances.

"But first, I will teach them not to follow us too closely," stated Wolfgang.

" If you are going to shoot, kill the one with the buffalo-scalp bonnet," said Curly Bear. "He is the one who must be protected at all cost and is the one who all the other fighters must rally around. They are members of the shield group, because they carry identical war shields. The next most dangerous is the "crazy" warrior. The crazy warrior does everything opposite of the others. When the others hold back, he will attack. He is the one wearing a long war sash over his left shoulder and rolled up under his arm. They are very brave."

As they talked, a lone Comanche launched forward carrying bow, shield and a 14-foot lance. He crisscrossed his war pony back and forth in front of them, shouting insults and waving his bow over his head. Then with a keening battle cry, he broke into a gallop heading directly at them, whooping and drawing an arrow. The horse was decorated with a palm print and a circle, indicating that the rider had killed an enemy in hand-to-hand combat. The circle meant he had fought the enemy from behind a breastwork, rock, or log. The rider was galloping at full speed, as the thrumming of the horse's hooves grew louder. Suddenly, the high-pitched, blood-chilling cry of the warrior on the attack reached their ears. Before overrunning the three companions, the Comanche veered slightly away from them and then gradually turned, quickly passing in front of them.

"He is going to shoot at us," said Curly Bear.

As they watched, the young Comanche warrior leaned over to the off side of the horse, using it as a shield. The warrior used a hair halter braided into the mane of the horse at the withers, which formed a sling where he rested his elbow and supported his body. Only a little of a leg could be seen. His heel, an arm, the top of his head, and one eye were visible, peering at them. He shot two arrows at them from beneath the horse's neck. They heard the twang of the bow's release and the wisp, wisp sound of the fletching catching the air. One arrow barely missed Curly Bear and went skittering off the ground beyond them, the other stuck in the ground directly in front of Wolfgang.

Wolfgang marveled at the mass of muscle and hoofs flying at full gallop, and at the rider's agility, strength, and horsemanship. The healthy horse, breathing in a deep breath with each stride, galloped away as its rider--encumbered by his bow and quiver, shield and lance--stayed hidden until he was what he considered a safe distance away. Wolfgang picked up the osier arrow shaft that had engraved "lightening" channels and examined it. The arrow shaft was banded with red and green paint. The arrow had swallow-tailed nocks.

"He is a skilled horseman but needs to improve his shooting," said Curly Bear as he lifted his rifle and steadied it on the retreating figure. The rifle barely came to steady when it cracked and belched smoke. At the sound of the explosion, the young warrior threw his arms up into the air and toppled lifeless as the horse galloped back to the other Comanche horsemen. Curly Bear was a deadeye with a rifle, mused Wolfgang.

Two Comanche warriors were now racing toward the fallen brave. Wolfgang, Black Shield, and Curly Bear held their fire. The two Comanches racing their horses slowed their mounts as they reached their fallen comrade. They leaned down, grabbing the fallen man by the arms and lifted him up between them. It was a point of honor not to ride away and leave a dead or wounded man behind.

* * *

From the protected area where Wolfgang was laying and preparing to shoot, the wind was calm. Wolfgang checked the grass around the distant buffalo-scalp bonnet-wearing warrior on the skyline and noticed the swaying of the grass.

They all noticed the headdress had a row of eagle feathers, with breast feathers tied about the bottom of the quills that reached the waist of the wearer. They could make out magpie feathers in the back.

As he watched and waited, he gauged the wind. He needed to time his shot so that it went off between gusts. He kept his eye focused on the target and his head down on the stock after the smoke erupted from the rifle. He wanted to ensure a good follow through. The powder smoke burned in his nostrils. When the smoke had cleared, the lead Comanche warrior was on the ground twisting in pain. Wolfgang quickly reloaded and shot again. The surrounding Comanches just sat on their horses with stunned looks on their faces as they stared at their leader and the crazy warrior dead upon the ground. Wolfgang felt elation at making a good shot, but immediately felt remorse for the brave warrior.

"Let's go," he said.

Wolfgang, Black Shield, and Curly Bear set off at a measured trot.

* * *

Two days later, just as the sun had made its appearance above the horizon and long shadows still hid most of the land, Wolfgang and Black Shield saw Curly Bear rein in his horse and freeze. He stared into the distance. The only sound was the impatient stomp of the horses' hooves, their breathing and the toss of their heads now and then.

Wolfgang and his Crow companion squinted into the distance.

"There!" Black Shield indicated the direction.

Wolfgang leaned closer. Black Shield pointed with his finger toward the distant horizon. At first Wolfgang could see nothing.

"See the eagle soaring high, pushing and gliding toward the east," said Black Shield, "now look to the ground under him." The eagle dipped its wings and circled in a wide arc and flew toward them.

Wolfgang blinked to clear his eyes. He looked again and saw dark smudges on the horizon emerging from the shadows moving like ghosts as they moved out against the faintly lighter horizon. Having thought that they had lost the Comanche, Wolfgang's senses were overwhelmed by the sight. As he watched the sun rise higher in the sky, it seemed that time elapsed at a nerve-racking pace.

It was too late to flee.

The sun put the individual riders in relief and accentuated the dust the horse's hooves kicked up. A chill gripped Wolfgang's spine and his heart began to beat like a hammer. As they watched, they could see the lances and shields in silhouette. The buffalo scalp bonnet, was now worn by another warrior.

"Thank you for identifying yourself to me," muttered Wolfgang.

Their ramrods clattered as they tamped the lead balls down their barrels. Because of the dampness in the air, Wolfgang prayed that they would not have any slow ignitions or misfires.

They suddenly noticed a Comanche in the background wearing a full-feathered warbonnet: the full, eagle-feather headdress. A Comanche

A special class of war leader!

Now, they were worried. The Comanche warriors, with their hellish yells, swung their bodies from one side to the other side of their horses to avoid being struck or shot as they bore in on the three friends.

Click!. . . phfft . . .kaboom.

Wolfgang heard the gut-wrenching sound.

Hang-fire!

The delay caused his sights to drift off target.

Wolfgang knew it was now too late to reload as he dropped his rifle to the ground. As the obscuring grey smoke drifted away from Black Shield and Curly Bear's rifles they could see that two Comanche warriors had gone to their Father.

* * *

Wolfgang walked over to recover his rifle. He picked up his rifle, checked it, and saw the reason for his hang-fire. His rifle had a dirty flash channel between the primer and the main powder train. The last time he oiled his rifle he had forgotten to fire a priming pan of powder to burn away any remaining oil from the ignition source, touchhole and flash channel.

* * *

The three mounted warriors continued their journey through the short, lush grama and buffalo grass over reasonably flat ground. They camped and rested in the game filled shelterbelts of low cottonwood draws filled with water, wild plum, and chokecherry. Always, there was the hot, dry wind. The hot days were becoming cooler with light rainfall and the nights were cold. They watched for the Comanche's.

Chapter 32

They had not gone far when a lone figure appeared on the skyline to the east. As one, the three turned to face the threat. The lone Comanche warrior was crisscrossing his warhorse to get their attention, waving his bow over his head. The warrior making a high, keen cry, rode at a slow collected gallop directly forward, his horse's hooves kicking up little scatters of dust as he came, then he stopped, waiting. His horse nostrils flaring with interest, tossed its head as it sensed the tension, and nickered, the low sound carried faintly through the thin air. An overwhelming silence descended around the three nervous friends. They studied the Comanche. Wolfgang turned his head this way and that, taking in the barren landscape, while his hand briefly checked his bone-handled knife.

A band of whooping Comanche suddenly came into view and rode toward them, they made themselves small on their horses, swinging to the off side, turning, riding hidden on the other, while shouting and waving insults. The Comanche wheeled about and urged their ponies with quirts, and came steady into an easy, long-striding run. The horsemen slowed and came to a halt, maximizing the full dramatic effect of their appearance. The deep-chested and slender quick legs of the Comanche horses carried themselves proud. The proud heads of the Comanche horses lifted, their small ears pointed ahead toward them, nearly all making a quivering snort. The Comanche talked among themselves, until one made a high, wild, quavering yell.

Curly Bear rode out to confront him and talk with his hands

and in the warrior's own Comanche tongue. His horse whinnied loudly in response to the presence of the strange horse. As he approached, Curly Bear felt the wrathful gaze of the great young chief of the Kwahadi Comanche, Ecueracapa, who hated the Apaches. Where are the others?

Then came the hollow sound of hooves coming up out of a well-grassed draw, the tremble of the ground gained in strength and volume as Ecueracapa's followers fanned out in a long line.

The Kwahadi Chief had a clever, watchful face with cold eyes. His mouth was set in a firm, thin line, as he looked closely at Curly Bear, narrowing his eyes in a manner that conjured a startling menace. The Comanche held his right hand well out in front of his shoulder flat and upward and drew it back towards his face.

Come Closer!

Curly Bear edged his horse within a few yards of the Comanche.

Curly Bear, meeting his gaze, saw what was in his eyes: complete contempt. He did not have to think of the Comanche tongue. It came at once. "You have many warriors," said Curly Bear. The chief, wearing his light mail shirt, just smiled. It was not a pleasant smile, but a promise of pain to come. His hands motioned in the universal language as he spoke, his voice, stony and edged, saying, "We can overwhelm you easily this time but it will not give us any honor. We Comanche are accustomed to hand-to-hand combat with shield, tomahawk and knife. So, we will match you individually, one at a time and these three fights will decide the battle. I have spoken." Curly Bear was disgusted by the chief's venomous words.

Wolfgang was amazed at the calm, deliberate manner in which the Comanche leader had spoken; yet he had felt the venom in his voice. Ecueracapa's attention was momentarily, broken by Mouse, breaking wind, raising his tail and depositing a great load of horse apples on the ground. Another sound followed.

OooooooooOOOOOUUU!

Ecueracapa wheeled his gray gelding and stopped, hearing the long, full-throated, low bowel-shaking howl that proceeded to a shorter, higher one. A wolf. His imagination was seized with dread and terror because of the rising and falling sound of wolves. They did not howl at this time of day. The sound was spirit-lifting for Wolfgang, for his four-legged companions were advertising their presence to him and his companions.

A second low moaning cry arose, with a different pitch that lingered, piercing the silence of the open prairie. There was a distinct difference in scale and tempo. There were two different wolves! OooooOOOOOUUUU!

Black Shield's hair tingling, he knew the two wolves howled to advertise that someone was about to die.

Ecueracapa and his followers looked to the source of the sound and saw two large black wolves, their red tongues lolling out. Sitting! Watching! The sudden staring eyes of the wolves gave the Comanche a feeling of curiosity. The feeling was quickly replaced by respect and fear of these spiritual beings, who strangely howled in the light of day. The Comanche war chief turned his horse, signaling an end to their talk and rode back to his warriors. Wolfgang, Black Shield, and Curly Bear saw the Kwahadi chief talk to his warriors briefly, followed by a deep-toned haunting chant. Then came a loud chorus of bloodcurdling cries. The Comanche horses stomped at the noise and had to be held back from charging on their own.

"Ecueracapa has decided on a challenge," said Curly Bear, wondering why the wolves howled in the daylight. "Which of us is to fight," asked Wolfgang, baring his teeth. It cannot end here, Wolfgang thought fiercely, turning his blond head toward the silent horsemen and eyeing the Comanche.

"All three of us, one at a time," replied Curly Bear, "Those who live will be allowed to ride away. They give no quarter.

Comanche fight to the death." The reality of their plight sank in. Wolfgang stiffened, surprise showing on his face, as he felt a familiar smoldering in his gut. "Why?"

"Spirit power! Medicine! Adding our medicine to theirs. A warrior feels a keen satisfaction and excitement like the hunter, and takes delight in battle to gain confidence in themselves and kill without hatred."

Death is not to be avoided. To risk death is among the highest achievements to gain respect and supernatural assistance needed to succeed in war, tribal leadership, and love, Wolfgang thought.

Chapter 33

The first Comanche warrior approached on a horse whose flank was decorated with a rectangle symbolizing that the owner had led a war party.

Wolfgang resigned himself to go first. He felt a hand on his forearm and turned his eyes to see Black Shield, who had stepped forward, far too close for comfort. Black Shield looked at him intently with an ominous look. His eyes like black bottomless pits, skewered Wolfgang.

"No!" commanded Black Shield.

Wolfgang grimaced and searched Black Shield's eyes for an uncomfortable moment. He began to speak, but Black Shield raised his hand.

"Uncle," he began, using the People's term of respect for any adult male, "I am your blood brother. You have done this thing for our Crow people many times. Now you must stand aside. It is a good day to die," said Black Shield looking at Wolfgang, his eyes directly on his. His tone was firm. Wolfgang felt a deep heaviness in his heart. A Crow warrior considers it a great honor to die in battle. Wolfgang's throat constricted with a slight burning sensation. He paused and caught control of himself before continuing. His face was stern, but behind his features was sadness as his tormented eyes looked at his friend. Black Shield felt a familiar tightness in his throat, a sickness in the pit of his stomach and a giddy euphoria in his head.

"Little Brother," Wolfgang managed to say calmly as he looked into Black Shield's eyes, "You are mentally strong and have a good attitude. But remember, there is no finesse to a fight, only forceful, desperate blows for survival. Life or death is totally up to you, and you alone." After a moment, thinking, Wolfgang continued saying, "You must think as he thinks. Then, you can anticipate his intentions. And do not let your opponent see your fear. Forget your fear, it stiffens the muscles."

"I know, time slows down and pain vanishes. You have taught me well," interrupted Black Shield.

Wolfgang smiled, looking at his companion closely. He paused in thought and continued, "Remember proper footing. Keep your body balanced. Allow no advantage to your back. Do not toss your weapon. Your first distraction will be your last. They want blood."

"They shall have it!" Black Shield responded.

He rolled his head, loosening the muscles in his neck.

After some thought, Wolfgang stated, "To defang the snake, remain at a range where he cannot cut or hack you but you can strike him. Help him to lose control or drop his weapon by moving away from him when he strikes, then launch your attack at his extended arm. You cannot check your attack, you must pursue it to the end." Wolfgang nervously went on, "Remember: hit hard, hit fast, hit first."

Black Shield nodded. Wolfgang said nothing more, but exchanged a rueful grin. The young Crow turned and walked purposefully toward the Comanche warrior. Like a carnivorous beast, the Comanche's lips curled back from his teeth.

Black Shield's emotions churned as he walked forward, his spirit surged with the desire to prove himself in this challenge. He felt his mouth go dry, his nerves screaming as fear flowed through his veins. His knees shook and inside he felt sick as his stomach lurched. The Comanche malevolently drew closer, his eyes narrowed in malice. Then Black Shield was face to face with his opponent only feet apart. They glared at each other for heart-stopping moments. Black Shield stood alone, exposed, and vulnerable.

Black Shield fought to keep his emotions in check. Sweat poured as his blood surged and raced through his veins to saturate every muscle in his body. His heartbeat quickened. Black Shield's new strength was empowering his muscles with strength and speed.

The Comanche warrior had a sneer on his face as the two men stood facing each other. Black Shield dropped into his fighting crouch, shield up, weapon and body hidden. Only his eyes stared out over the top of his shield as he studied his opponent. Black Shield, now composed, felt the desire to face this challenge flare through his veins.

The Comanche warrior, lean and hard looking, gave him a withering, contemptuous look. His lower face was painted black, and the upper part of the face starting halfway up the nose was red. Yellow surrounded his eyes. With a slight grin on his thick lips, he stretched his arms toward the sky displaying his physique. He stood a full head above Black Shield. His broad, tattooed chest was scarred from other battles. He wore his hair in two braids wrapped in otter fur. A scalp lock was worn at the back with a black feather attached. The part in his hair was painted red. He wore only thigh-length, close-fitting leggings, gartered below the knee. His moccasins had large ankle flaps. His buffalo-hide shield was adorned with fluttering feathers, and a snake--his guardian spirit helper--was painted on it.

The Comanche was in a crouch his body and weapon hidden, with only his narrowed, flat black eyes visible above the shield. He stood, transfixed, his eyes weighing the Crow, looking for an opportunity to attack. He was ready to spring into an attack, or defend if the Crow struck first. For a few heartbeats, all was still as the two combatants faced each other, their emotions mirrored in each other's stare.

The two combatants shuffled about, measuring the other's defense, speed, and balance, trying to create an angle of attack. Both warriors matched each other's movements, cutting off any angle of attack. Wolfgang, Curly Bear, and the Comanche watched with rapt attention.

"His opponent is bigger," said Curly Bear.

"But Black Shield's medicine spirit is bigger and stronger. He is a strong, highly skilled opponent against anyone," said Wolfgang without taking his eyes away from the two fighters. Wolfgang swallowed down the acid climbing in his throat, "I have seen his eyes, he is focused and will absorb any pain and punishment. He changes just before a fight and becomes mean and evil. He is not intimidated and has proven his fighting ability and horsemanship. He defies death. That is why he travels with me." After some thought, feeling his pulse rate increasing with the pounding in his ears, Wolfgang continued saying, "He is a young, but proven warrior, and is in good shape and very strong. He is a warrior of the first three grades. He is entitled to wear 'The Crow.'" It is an ornament fastened around the waist and worn at the back in dances. It is a circle of feathers, with a foxtail on the left and a crow skin on the right. The "Crow," symbolizes the vision of an eagle, the power of the fox, and the cunning of the crow, he went on. Curly Bear didn't say anything. "The Lakota, Cheyenne and Arapahoe often come to bother us. Our men are constantly fighting." The emotions of anger, frustration, and uncertainty of the situation welled up and were weighing heavily on him. Wolfgang's palms were moist and clammy as nervous beads of sweat broke out on his forehead.

Black Shield slipped on the leather wrist loop of his axe. He went into his ready stance: a low crouch, feet apart, weight evenly distributed, typical of a shorter man. He kept his feet moving, his shield held well away from his body, circling cautiously.

Chapter 34

The Comanche revealed his intentions when his eyes widened and bulged. Black Shield sensed the attack was coming and prepared to shuffle to one side at the last moment. Evade the ax and get out of range of the initial attack, he thought. With sudden violence, the Comanche exploded into action. He rolled forward, screaming in the attack with rage-fueled courage, using his shield. The Comanche hoped to beat Black Shield down with his shield and then hack him with his ax, but Black Shield gave ground sidestepping to one side. Black Shield had turned him neatly with surprising ease in an explosive move and kept circling. Moving on the balls of their feet, knees slightly bent, the two circled each other slowly. Black Shield stamped his right foot, as if advancing. The Comanche flinched.

Again the Comanche lunged forward, his ax blade coming down in a great sweep making a bright sparkling arc through the air. The Comanche hammered the shield of the Crow warrior throwing him backwards. Black Shield was quick to block, and he violently twisted his shield, hoping to jerk the axe out of his opponent s hand. The impact jarred up Black Shields arm to his shoulder, despite the pain from his arm he recovered and moved into close range. Blow by blow, step by step, Black Shield was driven back. Breathing hard, his chest began to burn as he attempted to drag in air. The sound of the constant flurry of hammering blows was echoed from the thud of blows landing on the shields, as feet churned up the grass. The blows caused painful vibrations to shoot up Black Shield's arm and through his entire body. He knew that soon he would barely be able to block the savage blows.

The two warriors gasping for breath as their shoulders heaved with exertion, paused to size each other up, to see if the other was weakening. Black Shield could hear his own breathing, harsh, labored,

Watching each other warily, the Comanche quickly stepped forward and feinted. Black Shield knew he was being tested. Then, with an explosive grunt, the Comanche renewed his frenzy, launching a real attack again and forcing the Crow backwards as they locked in combat. Each blow was countered, sending jarring waves of pain up and down Black Shield's arm. As each blow struck, Black Shield's teeth locked in a wild grimace of hatred and rage.

Wolfgang's tortured eyes saw the speed of the Comanche's ax had increased significantly. The maddened, wide-eyed Comanche had a look of victory on his face, gritting his teeth and growing bolder with his attacks. Sweat plastered Black Shield's hair to his forehead. His arm muscles were straining and his shoulders heaved under the pressure of the barely blocked blows as he was driven back. Gamely, the Comanche attacked again as Black Shield leaped aside. Wolfgang and Curly Bear admired the smooth, instinctive coordination of mind and muscle of their young friend.

Black Shield's lips tightened as he formulated a plan in his mind to use his retreat as a ploy. He was backing up under the assault, but realized that he could not continue this too long, because his strength was declining with each blow and his arm was becoming numb. He was hoping to trip the relentless Comanche as he attacked.

Wolfgang was worried. He saw the Comanche was too fast and that Black Shield was breathing heavily. His chest heaved, sweat dewed his face and began to drip down his brow, and his body glistened with the effort. Still, the Comanche battered the Crow shield without respite.

Black Shield wanted the Comanche to become over confident and was conserving his energy. The watching Comanche warriors started an isolated staccato yipping that was joined by the others. Then a deep-toned, haunting chant along with high-pitched scream of sounds flowed together, gaining in strength and volume, urging their companion on, wanting a quick kill. Black Shield occasionally hit back letting the Comanche tire himself before he launched his own attack. They separated and circled each other, shuffling in and out, warily feinting, and seeking out, an angle of attack. Each combatant tried not to let the other know the level of agony being inflicted upon his own body. Both warriors were reaching the point where they could barely raise their arms to block the savage blows of the other. The Comanche stared at Black Shield's tomahawk in his hand. The little muscles around his mouth twitched. His eyes looked up furtively and wary, meeting Black Shield's for a moment and Black Shield saw fear there.

Now, with a wicked light in his eyes, Black Shield braced his feet apart ready, feinted, and his opponent attacked. Black Shield quickly moved sideways to narrow his profile and hopefully trip his opponent. He staggered and the Comanche harmlessly slipped away out of reach and circled.

Wolfgang saw the deep glow in Black Shield's stony eyes.

The attack of the opponent's tomahawks on each other's shields rained down relentlessly. Each combatant was trying to wear the other down. Caught up in the wild rage of the moment, they gritted their teeth and butted their shields forward, trying to overpower the other by pushing and shoving with their shields. Each man tried desperately to find and gain an advantage, anticipating the other's blows. The rising intensity of the high-pitched war cries of the watching Comanche were inaudible over the cacophony of the scraping and clattering of tomahawks thudding into shields as the combatants' frenzy reached a boiling point.

The Comanche fell back slowly, blocking Black Shield's blows. Suddenly, Black Shield changed the angle of his attack, breaking up the rhythm of the fight. His opponent's ax sliced down and glanced off the angle of the Crow shield. The sound of their shields was thunderous as they crashed together. For the merest moment, the Comanche's guard was down. Now! Now! Black Shield's mind screamed, and he grinned. With his war shield over his mouth his shocking, sudden war cry reverberated loudly, as he swung his axe. The Crow war cry was still hanging in the air when another reverberated off the shield as Black Shield made a rapid spin. There was a flash of red and he heard a hiss of pain. The wound sprayed Black Shield as he soared past. The Comanche, shocked and now fearful seeing his own blood, felt his spirit drain as he saw the energy in the eyes of the Crow warrior. Black Shield's tomahawk had sliced flesh and a rush of fire filled his veins. He smelled the iron odor of blood. Locking eyes with the Comanche, he tipped his head slightly to one side and grinned. The din of noise from the watching Comanche's died down. Wolfgang and Curly Bear stood transfixed, watching the battle going on in front of them.

The Comanche, breathing heavily, again, felt and saw the projected energy of the Crow warrior in his eyes. They both drew back from the melee to draw breath and take stock. For several heartbeats they stared at each other in a standoff, both of them panting. Black Shield saw that the confidence had drained out of his opponent. The Comanche noted the cold expression in Black Shield's eyes. With hate-filled eyes glaring, the Comanche's face turned to determination. Black Shield moved into a low fighting crouch, preparing for the assault that was coming. His Kwahadi opponent grunted, gritted his teeth and came at Black Shield. The sweat broke out heavily across the Comanche's forehead as he landed a ferocious barrage of blows, causing Black Shield to give ground and circle to the uphill side.

Separated briefly, they circled. Black Shield's eyes glinted angrily and he growled. The Comanche warrior bent in a fighting crouch, a sneer on his face, and stalked the Crow, cutting off any angle of attack. Black Shield panting with effort filled his lungs with air. They continued to circle. Again the Comanche, with eyes alight and nostrils flared, attacked with a flurry of snake-like strikes. They traded blows for a few moments, trying to gain advantage of the other. The Kwahadi warrior knew he was sapping the energy of his opponent and hoped to paralyze the Crow's shield arm while watching for opportunity.

Black Shield was able to intercept the strikes with his shield and remain upright. Neither man was able to get past his opponent's shield. Black Shield's arm felt the paralyzing impact and the spasmodic pain of the blows. He knew the relentless barrage was tiring his opponent as well. The beaded sweat stood out on Black Shield's face, as he put all his body weight behind the small shield, and punched it into the Comanche's face. He staggered backward across the ground.

The stunned Comanche's vision was filled with bright white sparks bursting before his eyes as blood flowed freely. He bellowed in pain, staggered back, and lowered his guard just enough.

Now, Black Shield's instincts screamed at him. Now was the time.

Scenting blood, Black Shield redoubled his effort. Using his momentum, twisting at the hips, his quick dancing feet followed giving his spinning body angle and balance during the turning movement, to maintain his center of gravity, and spin about off the warrior's right side evading his opponent's oncoming strike. Black Shield's fluid offense was lethal in accuracy and power in an instant.

Black Shield swung his ax horizontally, deeply cutting the neck of the Comanche. The blow snapped the Comanche's head to one side as it cut through flesh, covering Black Shield with a fine film of blood.

The Comanche lost his grip on his shield, staggered an involuntary step, wobbled, and toppled forward. His mouth and mind were frozen in shock and animal pain. His ax fell from his hand. The stricken warrior's whole body was eroded by pain. From his twisted mouth, blood gurgled and foamed. Warm, sticky blood gushed out of his neck. Blood splayed out and spurted from his terrible wound. His wide, bulging eyes became unfocused and slowly glazed over, giving way to the darkness. A last final breath escaped his lips as his eyelids flickered. A long, rattling sigh ended in silence as his body went limp.

Every muscle in his body tense, Black Shield still crouched behind his shield, his feet were braced apart and his tomahawk was poised, ready to strike again. Feeling the dryness of his throat and breathing heavily, he stared down at the warrior, feeling elation and relief. Black Shield bent down and took up the Comanche's shield. Although he felt exhilarated, his body and mind were exhausted. He rose and turned, walking away on visibly shaking legs back toward his friends, carrying the Comanche shield. Curly Bear and Wolfgang stared at their friend. His face was splashed with blood and there was a wild look in his eyes. The corpse still bucked and twitched as the ground darkened from the rushing blood. The bladder and bowels of the corpse stained the ground in the epilepsy of death.

* * *

Another Comanche warrior approached on a horse whose front legs were decorated with many palm prints and short horizontal lines on top of one another signifying coup marks. Each horizontal mark meant that this Comanche warrior had struck an armed enemy in combat. Each palm print meant the rider had fought and killed in hand-to-hand combat.

A tested warrior!

The thrill of bloodlust upon him, Curly Bear could feel the

blood coursing through his veins as he walked forward with the grace of a cat. His hand twitched for the hilt of his knife.

Now this young Comanche chief, Ecueracapa, and all his Kwahadi warriors will see the mistake made in this challenge.

The bravery of Black Shield had been contagious, for Curly Bear felt little fear.

"Are you prepared?" asked the concerned Wolfgang.

Dark malice glittered in Curly Bears deep-set eyes, "I am at one with my enemy," responded Curly Bear, "I think as he thinks, and know his intentions. Long ago, I learned to channel my frustrations and temper against my opponent."

Two or three paces apart, they stared at each other.

Chapter 35

With a savage grin, the Comanche warrior shifted his obsidian eyes and fixed Curly Bear with a battlefield glare. He narrowed them almost imperceptibly and stared at him from a crouching stance, twirling his knife and trying to make Curly Bear shift his eyes. Curly Bear's blank eyes stared back, unwavering, from above his shield. The silence was deafening, broken only by the wind and their collective breath.

Curly Bear noticed that the Comanche held his single-edged knife with the edge of the blade facing outward to the rear. He was using a forward grip with his thumb laid over the index finger. This gave his opponent control over the knife and would make it difficult to wrest the knife from him. With this grip the Comanche could punch, slap, stab, thrust, slash, gouge, rip, or use a pommel strike by adjusting the wrist angle.

Curly Bear crouched in a fighting position holding the fighting shield on his left arm up and back, protectively guarding his crouched body. Curly Bear feinted to the right, and as expected, his opponent moved away. They stared and circled. Curly Bear held his double-edged knife in his right hand using a reverse grip, knife forward for close inside fighting. Curly Bear's lethal reverse grip was held forward making it possible to hook, drag, stab, gouge, rip, or slash with great power. The Comanche's dark, cold, and cruel eyes signaled an attack.

The Comanche leaped forward, stabbing underhand with his large knife. Curly Bear lowered his shield and parried the stabbing strike with his shield and felt the impact back up his arm. Curly Bear lunged forward with a strike that was too short and the Comanche swayed back out of reach. Curly Bear crowded the Comanche bobbing about and stabbed his knife forward again, but the Comanche angled his shield to deflect the strike. The Comanche, hopping from one foot to the other, desperately counterattacked and made a quick thrust and slash taking a chunk of leather from the Apache's shield. It didn't take Curly Bear long to understand that the Comanche was keeping his technique simple. He was determined to maintain possession and control of his knife because he was not attempting to use any grip variations. He wanted the greater use of distance when executing his stab, thrust, and slashing technique.

Curly Bear screamed and made a swipe at the unprotected head of the Comanche, but the strike was parried. The Comanche's jaw clenched and the grip on his knife tightened. He felt his blood pressure increasing as he lunged forward, slashing the unprotected knife arm of the Apache, Curly Bear. There was a spreading smear of blood from the shallow cut across Curly Bear's upper right arm. The small cut burned. Rivulets of warm blood covered his arm. The Kwahadi warrior sneered haughtily, as he tried to curb his rising anger and not give way to his rising fury.

Cut! Curly Bear thought. I have been cut before! Curly Bear's chest began to burn as he dragged in air. He moved away and shifted his shield to the other arm and the knife to his left hand. He moved swiftly, changing his angle by sidestepping, thus removing his body from the attacker's line of strike. I only have to make contact with one good strike. And quickly, before I grow weak.

Curly Bear's blade flashed out and cut the Comanche's forearm. Curly Bear, seeing his opponent's blood, felt a hot surge of elation. His eyes widened, gleaming in anticipation upon seeing the open artery and flow of the blood. He knew his strike had rendered the limb useless. In an undercurrent of fury, Curly Bear felt the bloodlust welling up within him as he prepared to take his opponent's life. The large knife fell from the attacker's hand. The Comanche staggered back, blinking in shock, a stunned pain etched on his features. Curly Bear, feeling the adrenaline start to flow, kept close and followed up with a kick to the shield, robbing his opponent of his will to continue.

His face grim and set, Curly Bear counterattacked instantly by making a barrage of savage cuts and then battered the Comanche's shield aside and smashed his face. Curly Bear felt the force of his knee crush his opponent's balls and followed it up by throwing an elbow, as the two men pressed together. Curly Bear's elbow struck his opponents nose, and heard an audible crunch as the cartilage broke.

The blow had shattered the Comanche's nose bone. The warrior's knife dropped to the ground. There was an awful gasping sound as Curly Bear's knife tore through the Comanche's guts. Curly Bear twisted the knife and wrenched it back. The Comanche's mouth opened in an O of surprise, as his pupils dilated with shock. He could hear the watchers scream and shout defiance and support from the two sides. The Comanche collapsed forward and half way curled up writhing, shuddering in pain, and twitching in agony. A low moan emanated from the mortally wounded form.

Curly Bear leaned his head down and stared into his enemy's astonished staring eyes, seeing his own reflection in them. Curly Bear was quick, conveying no mercy, while feeling the Comanche struggle. He yanked his head back exposing his neck, and stuck the knife under the jaw at the top of the throat and shoved it upward amid the considerable noise made by the victim. The Comanche's eyes flicked wide, flicked and fluttered and came wide again. The Apache felt and heard his knife grate off the cartilage as it slid home. He listened to the final breath hissing out. Curly Bear watched his enemy bleed to death, and make a convulsive series of movements, and then nothing. The Comanche lay still in an expanding pool of his own blood. The tension in the Apaches shoulders began to ease, and he let out a long, slow breath as a small smile curled on his lips.

Wolfgang and Black Shield saw Curly Bear put his face up against his opponent's, then unleash a fierce, piercing, exhilarating battle scream with all his might. Curly Bear turned toward the watching Comanche warriors and whooped with pure joy. The fight had been fast, with the knife popping in and then being retracted, mused Wolfgang.

Curly Bear is a great knife fighter. He can smoothly cover distance while striking and evade oncoming strikes from an opponent. The Comanche seem anxious to study the moves and strategies of the fighters.

Wolfgang's teeth bared unconsciously, as he carefully watched his opponent ride forward on a horse marked with one red and one white circle around the eyes to enhance the animal's vision. Lightening bolts were painted on the horse's legs to invoke speed and power. Its butt was decorated with the palm prints of warriors killed in hand-to-hand combat.

An experienced and tested warrior!

Black Shield briefly looked at Curly Bear saying, "Watch closely, it is hard to believe how fast the two-legged man-bear is."

* * *

Black Shield and Curly Bear watched Wolfgang. Focused on his breathing, Wolfgang felt an extreme sense of calm as he stretched and rubbed his muscles thoroughly to give himself an edge. Wolfgang bared his teeth.

Chapter 36

Black Shield and Curly Bear closely watched their quiet, much scarred companion with powerful muscles rippling beneath his darkened skin revealing the latticework of visible old scars the width of a man's finger front and back. The marks of the Great Bear crisscrossed their friend's blond head and face for all to see. As Wolfgang stepped away from Black Shield and Curly Bear, both men noticed how quickly his demeanor changed. They both thought that Wolfgang seemed unnervingly calm.

Wolfgang saw two overhead passing shadows on the ground. The whirring of flat wings broke the silence. Two large birds had passed overhead. A distant, low hoarse, metallic sound came to his ears.

Tok, tok. The Norse god Odin's messengers!

Wolfgang was silent, thinking.

Wolfgang's eyes had caught the lazy flight motion of the two ravens gliding and soaring upward like a hawk on flat wings toward a near hill and disappear beyond it. Atop the hill stood a tall figure of a woman, watchful, her hair unbound, blowing in the wind. A large, attentive wolf was beside her. In the unnatural stillness, Wolfgang stood frozen, drinking in the sight of her, with a solemn expression.

Dark Moon!

Wolfgang was startled momentarily. He heard her voice say, "Fight well, husband."

The gaze of both Black Shield and Curly Bear followed the direction of Wolfgang's head, but saw nothing, and wondered about the pair of ravens.

The shapeshifters! An omen!

Black Shield and Curly Bear were both aware that with the raven, animal and human spirits intermingle and become as one. They witnessed Wolfgang's sudden fight response, as his back straightened into his full stature and his head came up. He inhaled deeply and his body swelled as his muscles became engorged with blood, stretching his muscular back. They saw his wolf-like eyes dilate and narrow. His eyes were fierce and determined. He had become the animal.

Breathing deeply, Wolfgang hastily slipped his left arm into the leather wrist loops of his shield as he approached his opponent. All the Comanche were silent, taking note of Wolfgang's shield. It denoted a warrior with grizzly bear, wolf, and snake power.

The shield design evoked spiritual protective power. The Comanche chief wondered about the snake totem. Warriors who had this totem were fast, attacked quickly, and were true to their mark.

The tracks of the great bear, wolf, and snake on the fighting shield revealed the strength and valor of the warrior with these totems. Men were uneasy and feared any warrior identified with a powerful animal spirit because they felt a kinship with bear's, as they believed they were half-man. The wolf tracks represented both the magical powers from which the man's name was derived and the magical powers ascribed to his helper, the wolf. The wolf star was a reflection of the wolf coming and going from the spirit world. The snake represented speed in changes, shifts, and agility. The Dark Moon on the shield represented the magical powers of the man's wife. Among all the plains tribes, these Bear Dreamers excelled as warriors and were known for their special abilities.

All the plains tribes had heard the tales of this white warrior. The Iroquois far to the east had called the man

"Okwaho"—the wolf—and the legendary woman "Dark Moon." Surprisingly, the eyes of the Comanche shifted to Black Shield and Curly Bear, who were suddenly aware of the presence of the two wolves staring intently at their enemies. The muttering Comanche were slightly unnerved.

* * *

Black Shield and Curly Bear were anxious to study the moves and strategy of the legendary warrior known as the two-legged man-bear. Wolfgang now became conscious of his breathing to oxygenate his cold, aching muscles as a fight-enhancing tool, to generate power in the speed of his strikes and to calm down in order to focus. Is this my time? Wolfgang wondered. If it is, God, protect my friends on the rest of this journey. And let me die well.

Wolfgang emptied his mind, seeing the light and shadows upon the land, smelling the grass, feeling the sun on his body, the wind on his body. He listened to the wind rustling the grass, tasted the dryness in the air. He felt the earth beneath his feet as he began to sway gradually, then he reached behind and deployed his heavy knife from its sheath faster than a rattlesnake could strike. Wolfgang showed it to his opponent. He held the knife up to the light and pointed it at his enemy as he squinted along its edge. The two-legged man-bear gently rocked the knife back and forth, the edge of the sharp knife appeared thin to the point of perfection. The edge was just about invisible to his eye. Wolfgang's face was a cold, calculating mask, with no emotion. He felt his heart and breathing rate accelerate, as the blood flowed to his muscles.

The Comanche's hair was braided in two braids wrapped with otter fur, leaving a scalp lock at the back with a yellow feather attached. He wore thigh-length, close-fitting leggings that were gartered below the knee. His thigh-length yellow dyed shirt contoured to fit his body, with close-fitting sleeves and short fringes at the cuffs.

The Comanche warrior had fierce, piercing black eyes that looked out from beneath a strong brow. His face was painted red from his nose and cheekbones up to his hairline, but the war paint could not hide scar tissue curving up across his chin, over his large lips, and up his cheek. A feral snarl twisted his features. The lower part of his face was painted black. He was taller and in good shape with a powerful build, broad shoulders and hard eyes. His body had strangely patterned tattoos. All these impressions burned into Wolfgang's mind's eye in a flash.

He's done this before.

Wolfgang had reached his normal rhythm of breathing. He had avoided the shallow, low breathing that led fighters to be deprived of oxygen and become tense, depriving them of speed. His right hand held the bone-handled, double-bladed knife in a hammer grip ready to strike at the arm, groin, stomach, or throat. His left arm was raised to act as a shield against any stab or thrust. Wolfgang watched the other warrior's eyes and his breathing pattern, which would telegraph his move. Wolfgang saw what he needed to see.

His opponent was a chest breather! I must remain aware of all his body movements and try to watch my enemy's chest. When his chest expands and his eyes telegraph change, it's probably a sign that he's taking a breath before striking. That's when I will try to hit him.

Their eyes met over the dully-gleaming steel as they circled and stared, weighing each other up, just as a sudden, ill wind roared over the prairie. The Comanche saw a scarred, unpainted, terrible twisted, malicious face that made him feel the urge to step back. He had never seen blue eyes. The glaring, intense, cold blue eyes and the hair the color of the dried prairie grass unsettled him. There was no expression of any kind, except for a mesmerizing stare of the snake. No fear! And, he knew he was looking at death.

Wolfgang looked into his opponent's eyes and saw his weakness and inner fear that made him vulnerable to his gaze, as he smiled. The smell of his fear was pungent. Wolfgang saw his opponent's forehead and upper lip were bedewed with the oily fear of sweat. A muscle in his opponent's right leg slightly quivered, and he knew the Comanche's stomach was tight, and his throat would be unable to swallow. It was an uncanny power that he had. Fear is my advantage over my opponent; it will stiffen his limbs, thought Wolfgang.

Wolfgang flexed his neck and rolled his shoulders moving forward, sliding his moccasins carefully forward to make sure he did not loose his footing. He stopped just within kicking range of his opponent in order to deliver a low kick for knee destruction or to use a foot sweep if the opportunity presented itself. God, Wolfgang prayed, Give me strength and courage.

Wolfgang was no longer aware of his companions. His pulse increased, as his eyes, like his mind, were trained on his opponent. He thought fervently, the first target that the Comanche warrior presents to me I will disable with a slash or thrust.

The Comanche took a deep breath, the veins enlarged in his neck, and his eyes widened and bulged, telegraphing his intent to strike as his shoulders and shield rotated. Then he skipped forward using his shield to knock Wolfgang back, pivoting and grunting with the effort of making a low, quick, futile stabbing motion that missed by a hand's width. Wolfgang's reflexes were too fast.

Black Shield looked at Curly Bear saying, "We believe a live animal, batsira'pe, exists in him and will emerge."

In a graceful dancer's whirl, Wolfgang's adrenaline had kicked in and he easily dodged and weaved, flowing away from his opponent. Black Shield and Curly Bear, watching in fascination, saw the mental transformation on Wolfgang's face and knew he did not fear death, that he was willing to embrace it. They saw the beast within surface as Wolfgang lowered his lithe body into a crouch, poised on the balls of his feet and rapped his weapon on the rim of his shield as he nodded grimly. Wolfgang was free of all human compassion and emotion.

Wolfgang noticed the Comanche was breathing in a shallow rhythm and was becoming tense. His movements will be slower. Wolfgang was aware of his opponent's speed and rhythm. It's time to pick up the pace. With a renewed frenzy, Wolfgang's opponent came in with a guttural shout of rage. Wolfgang deflected his strike with his shield, stepped forward, and snapped out his forearm, thrusting his lead shoulder in the direction of the blow for power toward his opponent's face. Wolfgang bounced lightly on his feet, alternating between right and left, with one always poised to snap out and strike. He faked in, causing his opponent to slash early, then, he struck his enemy with the rim of his shield across the jaw and nose. The Comanche was knocked backward dazed, grunting in agony at the sound of his cartilage breaking. His smashed mouth and nose began to bleed, as he was momentarily blinded seeing a blue flashing light and white stars behind his eyes. The Kwahadi warrior knew his nose was broken. He began to cough up a lot of blood as it filled his mouth. Sweat dripped from the Comanche's hair, and his shirt was stuck to his back as he staggered and gasped for breath. He snatched a deep breath, open-mouthed, his teeth stained red. The Kwahadi's spirits sank. Suddenly panic-stricken, he stared at Wolfgang as his breath came in ragged gasps. All watching saw that Wolfgang's face was fixed with a snarl, contorted into an expression of fury as the scent of the kill overtook him. Wolfgang was too fast for the younger warrior.

Wolfgang's actions were quick as the two feinted and thrust, trading blows with their shields, seeking to make a lethal strike. Panting, Wolfgang and the Comanche punched with their shields simultaneously and thrust forward with their shoulders behind their shields with their body weight, knives trying to hook around the other's shield, each missing the other. The painful impact jarred up through their arms.

Anticipating the Comanche warrior's move and using quick footwork, Wolfgang watched for the flick of the warrior's glinting knife swipe outward and blocked his savage strike as he shifted his weight on to his right foot and brought his left foot back and around changing his angle. He lightly slipped away on the side of the warrior's shield, and as the two men passed Wolfgang took a breath and let half of it out and struck as he exhaled. The edge of Wolfgang's blade had quickly lunged and swept downward sliding the knife through the exposed flesh, cutting deeply into the startled Comanche's arm.

Wolfgang recovered his balance and braced himself, then, he heard a moan from deep in his opponent's chest as his knife dropped to the ground. The Comanche's eyes shined with terror. His stunned face contorted and jerked back in a look of pain. Agony and shock were etched on his features as he felt the stinging pain of the sweat in his wound. Blood flowed freely from the strength-sapping cut. His mouth was slightly agape, while trying not to show any emotion, attempting to gain the favor of the gods, knowing his dead ancestors and the spirit world were watching.

Wolfgang went into a highly mobile ready stance: a low crouch with his feet apart and his right foot quartered behind the left, every muscle in his body tense. This position gave him instant mobility to spring into a powerful attack. Breathing heavily, his teeth clenched, eyes wide and staring madly, he evenly distributed and balanced his weight, his left arm acting as a shield held away from his body. His eyes looked over his left shoulder and above the top of his shoulder as he tried to determine his opponent's possible moves. Then he noticed the knife on the ground.

He's dropped his weapon!

Wolfgang knew that he could now safely deliver a kick without being cut. He focused on the big warrior and the position of his shield. Gritting his teeth, and generating momentum with his arms, he pivoted his foot, hips, and shoulders into the kick with a catlike movement as he bellowed his insane war cry he was not even conscious of.

"EERRRGGHHHH!"

A strike to the nose will momentarily shut down his body and cause a temporary loss of vision, thought Wolfgang.

Wolfgang's bent, supporting left leg straightened out just before his relaxed kicking leg came around. He rose lithely high into the air with his right leg cocked. As he rose off the ground, Wolfgang again let out an awful, wild animal roar.

"EERRRGGHHHH!"

As Wolfgang's bent left leg straightened out in full extension, his slightly turned right foot struck viciously in a nearly straight path. The outside of his heel made crunching contact as his foot slammed the shield, smashing the hard, wooden shield rim into his opponent's head.

The Comanche had not seen the striking foot. A grunt of pain. With a sickening, loud snap, light exploded in his head and he saw spots before his eyes, as blood gushed from his nose and split lips. The Comanche arms wide was knocked backward to the ground and sent sprawling, floundering to regain his balance. Everything went dark. His eyes rolled white and then all expression died from his face, as he went limp.

Black Shield and Curly Bear both heard the whip "crack" as Wolfgang's leg straightened out on impact and saw Wolfgang crouch over the warrior and his knife flick out penetrating the man's throat, severing his spine. Wolfgang's face and hands were splashed with blood. Those watching heard a gulping, choking sound as dark red blood spouted from his mouth and the light died from his dark eyes. They saw the Comanche's body convulse, jerk and tremble, then lay still.

Fighting for breath, Wolfgang's mouth felt bone dry, as his lips peeled back with satisfaction. He heard voices but they were faint with distance as Black Shield and Curly Bear in wild exultation started chanting their war cry. Their cries increased in volume.

Wolfgang stood staring at the watching Comanche. His opponent's lifeless eyes were now sightless, purple and flat.

Chapter 37

Disgusted and disappointed, with a grim, maniacal fury transforming his face, the Comanche chief Ecueracapa's nostrils flared, the veins in his forehead pulsing with rage. Veins stood out in his neck, and his bulbous, hard eyes were red and glittering as he shot them a venomous look, staring and gaping at the white man who had exploded so lightning-fast into action, devastating his warrior. The unflinching manner with which the two Crow and Apache had faced their opponents had brought about a profound respect among his Kwahadi band. It was not the desired effect.

The tall, straight, white warrior is shrewd and quick. His arms thick, with hard muscle. His white skin, a rich brown. He is quiet and devoid of fear, with unwavering confidence. His eyes are cold, clear, and sharp as the great cat. He always does exactly the right thing at exactly the right time.

Ecueracapa locked eyes with Wolfgang with intensity for several heartbeats. His eyes narrowed, pondering. He had to see it again and waved another warrior forward.

A sinking feeling began to creep over Wolfgang, as he growled and stepped back, his upper lip twitching, as his steely-eyes, went into a fixed stare. His heart tightened.

The warrior's lean, muscled body was hard looking and there was the look of restrained eagerness about him. His body was shiny with sweat. The pride of his stance set him apart from the other warriors. His burning black eyes had the expression of satanical fury and his face was lit with the glow of bloodlust. His lips were drawn back tight, showing his teeth.

He's coming for me, thought Wolfgang. Concentrate on the next enemy, he thought. Stay focused. Wolfgang took several deep breaths to mentally prepare and work back into a productive rhythm. It had a calming effect.

With a deep-throated, exultant battle cry, the new, large, graceful warrior came running toward Wolfgang, his bulbous eyes glittering with fury. His long, braided hair was wrapped with otter fur with a scalp lock and yellow feather at the back. He wore only a knee-length breechclout and thigh-length close-fitting leggings trimmed out with scalp locks. The part in his hair was painted yellow. Skunk tails were attached to the heels of his moccasins.

The warrior's hand came up with a tomahawk. But, the fighting madness was already upon Wolfgang. He fixed his alert eyes on his new foe as he faded backward slightly crouched, gritting his teeth and tightening his neck muscles as he grasped the oncoming warrior's wrists and flung himself backward, dragging the warrior with him in a quick, flowing, graceful move.

As Wolfgang's body made contact with the ground he continued to roll backward pulling his knees in to his waist and kicking a sharp blow with his feet into the warrior's stomach and turning him upside down. Using the warrior's forward momentum, Wolfgang sent him up and over in a blur of motion. The warrior landed flat on his back. Wolfgang, rolling over, came up on top of the warrior, straddling him, still holding the warrior's wrists. Wolfgang looked deeply into his eyes and there was a thud and an explosive gasp of breath as the blade was rammed straight into his heart. The frightened Comanche's face was stunned, his eyes opened wide. The Comanche warrior was finished. Wolfgang wrenched his blade free from ribs of the dead warrior, smelling the strong coppery odor of blood. He rose to his feet carefully, stood motionless with his blood-spattered face to the sky, his eyes and face lit up. Thank you, God. I live! You have brought me far with your purpose, he prayed. Watch over us as we continue the journey. Sweat ran down Wolfgang's face and into his eyes. The salt stung as he shifted his gaze to the distant hill. Nothing!

Black Shield's eyes widened, and pride filled his face.

Black Shield and Curly Bear stood in silence, staring at Wolfgang as he continued to stand over the fallen Comanche warrior. Stock still, Wolfgang stood and watched. He stared at the war party with a fierce expression on his face, his ice-blue eyes glittering with fury, sweeping over them, missing nothing.

* * *

The Comanche chief and his warriors with their venomous eyes staring in astonishment had never seen a real human move with the speed and deadly agility of a hungry wolf. For all who watched, it had been a fascinating lesson on distance, positioning, and muscle control.

The Comanche collected their dead, guided their horses' heads away from them and rode off. The brooding and irate Cota de Malla stopped and turned his horse and yelled at them while hand signing for a long time. His hands signing rounded and sweeping in their rendition, had been fast and accurate. His eyes turned east and he followed behind his warriors. Wolfgang watched as Cota de Malla rode away. He glared at the Kwahadi chieftain's back, enraged.

"What did he say?" Wolfgang asked Curly Bear.

"His father Cuerno Verde, also known as Green Horn, was killed by the Spanish officer Colonel Juan Bautista de Anza twelve sleeps ago near Fountain Creek, just north of Huerfano Creek along with his eldest son, four chiefs, a medicine man and ten other warriors. His father was the greatest of all Comanche Chiefs. The Comanche lost 131 people. He also said it would be wise for us not to be seen by the Comanche again." Curly Bear paused. "The Comanche are noted for revenge killing. We must remember that they know where we are, and that they will watch us, and wait."

That would make it 3 September 1779, thought Wolfgang. Wolfgang's eyes met those of both warriors and widened them, telegraphing, Let's go now!

They traveled on.

*   *   *

Black Shield, riding on Wolfgang's left, leaned forward where he could see Curly Bear on Wolfgang's right. No one said anything, but all three men had a large grin on their face.

As Wolfgang rode, he was curious. He took the Comanche shield and cut the lacing away that bound the two discs of rawhide to the wooden hoop, as the horses moved along pleasantly. He wanted to see the packing material used inside the shield that had blunted the blows of Black Shield's sharp ax. The space between the discs had been packed with the pages from Spanish and French Bibles.

I must trade for a few of these Bibles in the future.

"Most Comanches use the thickest part of the buffalo skull bone for inside their shields," said Curly Bear watching with interest.

"What is ahead?" Wolfgang asked.

Curly Bear shrugged.

"More like this. Three, four sleeps."

"And then what?"

"The river. Then we turn west."

"Let's use the moon while we can."

Black Shield, Curly Bear, and Wolfgang rode slowly across the prairie of the front range. The horse's breath made small clouds in the crisp air as they moved along pleasantly; the horses turned their heads now and then and snuffed at each other. When they were not talking, there was only the sound of the wind, and the clopping noise of the horses' hooves, whispering through the sun-cured, golden grass of the prairie. A sage grouse got up ahead of them and canted off with a lot of wing flapping and settled in the distance.

* * *

Wind Woman was sitting before her fire, listening to the crackling hiss and smelling its bittersweet tang. The fire spat, jolting her back to the present. As she huddled closer to the flames, she heard a malevolent hiss. Her eyebrows rose in surprise, someone's life was in danger. She got up, went outside, and sat in front of her lodge in the dark, casting her all-seeing eyes up to the heavens, always with awe and wonder. Home of the fearsome spirits and gods! Raising her head, the shaman smelt the air. No rain! Her eyes never still, she searched the sky. The clarity of the night air was good due to the chill in the autumn air erasing the haze of summer. She could hear the birds going south in response to the diminishing light each day. Overhead, banks of scudding clouds were passing over, and in between them the moon and stars were studded brightly all across the sky. The weather will hold. Her lips moved faintly and silently. Only when the moon is new can I see all the stars.

The shaman was filled with unease as she studied the stars filling the heavens. The dominion of the stars and their influence on the events of man was uppermost in her mind. Prepared to interpret what she saw, her search of the moon and, stars, revealed nothing. She observed the shape and color of the cloud patterns. She pondered the significance of the breeze, the air currents being full of dark possibilities, and noted the direction of the cloud movement. The cloud patterns changed as she watched them. Our future takes many shapes, and like the wind, our lives are constantly changing. The light color of the clouds revealed all was well.

She listened and watched. Then a disturbing cool breeze sprang up. The direction of the breeze was to the south. She stared into the night sky, watching and studying it, and thinking for a long time, searching for wisdom. Within a few heartbeats, she smiled with her deduction. Her prophetic abilities told her blood had been shed, but it wasn't that of her three warriors. She took up her little drum and began a rhythmic, sacred dance movement imitating the sage hen and the path of the sun entering a higher state of consciousness. The drumming vibration set the power loose on the wind. She saw the whirring flight of a sage grouse ahead of three riders. She sighed heavily. Her three warriors were still moving south.

Chapter 38

It was the Moon of Falling Leaves. It was the time that Wolfgang knew as September. Meat was fat and plentiful and the days and nights were almost equal in time. Plums were thick and ripe on the trees. Black chokecherries bent the trees with their weight, and were eaten out of hand. Large antlered animals were at the fallen trees, pushing, shoving, ripping, and goring the brush and branches, scouring their antlers clean of velvet. Soon the bucks would be rubbing the scent glands on their foreheads against small trees to warn off rivals and to attract does.

* * *

The three warriors ignored their physical discomfort. The still air smelled of autumn. There was only a whisper of wind blowing through the flag-like, loose clustered flowered grassland. The rush of the wind in their faces was intoxicating. As far as the eye could see across the plain, they could see the distinctive flag-like, loose flowers clusters of sun-scorched gramagrasses, the food of buffalo, antelope, deer, and elk that made sweet grazing. They saw the. Steam rose from their horse's dark coats, wet from the rain. The horse's heads down, nosed at the grass and browsed along, nibbling grass, as the grasshoppers flew away clacking, showing yellow wings spotted with black.

The dark prairie night was awash in moonlight as it journeyed across the night sky. The wind was cold. It was still and silent beneath the white moon, indicating fair weather, only the snuffle of their horses reached their senses. The prairie reminded Wolfgang of the ocean. The way the sunburned grass moved in the night wind heightened the illusion of waves. The fat stars, which had been brilliant and clear all night, were now fading. They sensed the Arkansas River, beyond the next fold in the land, long before they would overlook the river valley. The horses smelled it! The long, grunting calls of bulls in the rut could be heard miles away in the direction they were heading.

* * *

Cold was the day when finally the slow dawn came. A patch of gray became visible and with it the black line that separated the world from the heavens. In the morning's half-light, watching the last stars fade and hearing the birdsong increasing, the cool of the night was giving away before the early morning light of the eastern horizon. The first line of gold crept over the edge of the nearest smooth ridge, and the underbelly of the clouds lit in different shades of blue while the tops brightened in yellow and orange. The temperature began to climb. The horses lifted their heads and steadily clip-clopped along.

Wolfgang was trying to ward off the cold wind blowing down from the mountains as he paused to catch his breath. His body convulsed in a shiver as the damp, pre-dawn chill caught up with him. The three travelers interrupted the hunt of three recently weaned coyote pups forced to fend for themselves and desperate for a good meal, standing still glaring at them. Wolfgang, Black Shield, and Curly Bear laughed at the nearly full-grown juveniles with their oversized heads and big ears.

Wolfgang noticed a narrow, wavy-leafed, long-stemmed plant at the edge of the trail, where the grasslands ended and the dry bluffs began. Its white, star-like flowers were already twisting closed. His first wife, Dark Moon, the tribal shaman, had told him about them. They stopped their horses for a time and let them eat some grass. Wolfgang dismounted and kneaded his stiffened muscles to restore circulation. He looked closer at the one remaining open flower. It had a purple mid-vein. The leaves had a thin, red border.

Dark Moon called it a Soap Plant, but had said to harvest the leaves and bulb and crush them to stun or kill fish.

"What are you digging up those plants for?" enquired Black Shield, as the horses nuzzled each other.

"You see where the lowering river has isolated that body of water next to the bank of the island?"

"Yes."

"I am going to throw this crushed pulp in that deep hold and have fish to eat and their juice to drink," Wolfgang replied.

"I wish to see this magic," said Curly Bear, as they pulled the horses' heads back up from the grass and moved on.

* * *

As the sun warmed them, the sight that greeted them was most impressive. They could see the river well. It flowed out of the Rocky Mountains just to the west. Nearer to where they stood, the land dropped away and below them was the winding silver snake. Only in the ravines and on the surface of the river was the mist still clinging. They sat on their mounts, their cheeks stiff with cold. Their feet felt numb, bodies slightly stiff and cold, tired after a night in the saddle. They rubbed their muscles to restore circulation as they watched the mist rise.

Staring at the low hanging fog rising out of the bottom, they saw a rich grassland roll off to the south. Curly Bear said, "Fog in the bottom means good weather. Fog will be gone before high sun."

Black Shield answered saying, "Wind from the west, good weather."

The diffused gray and dingy light from the leaden morning sky reflected off the shimmering, swirling waters of the river and gave it a look like tarnished silver as it sparkled through the silent maze of heavily furrowed, ashy-gray tree trunks. A moving shadow on the ground caused them to look up into the sky. The Great Spirit, the messenger from heaven, and the spirit of the sun slowly glided passed overhead. The Thunderbird!

Its presence had to be of significance.

*   *   *

The three warriors knew they would soon see a new vision. As they examined the landscape, the trio realized that the movement of the river symbolized the passing of time. They could smell the familiar musky scent of the river as the mist curled off the water. They heard the sound of feeding ducks, then the roar of the multitudes of beating wings as they broke into a chorus of excited calls, lifting into the sky. Birds being the symbol of the soul, their sounds brought them emotional comfort. The sight of great flocks of turkeys flying down from their roost in the cottonwoods, made each warrior remember the turkey was the symbol of all the blessings of the earth. Its life span is twelve years; the time it takes the earth to revolves around the sun, reflecting the birds tie in honoring the life cycle of Mother earth.

Their eyes grew wide at the density of wildlife. The land was alive with movement, herds of deer, elk, antelope, and buffalo. Rapt, they watched for a long time. Lots of buffalo! They briefly watched two bulls fighting. The bulls were butting their shaggy heads and trying to take advantage of each other's exposed flanks. The deep, gruff grunts and guttural growling roar of communicating buffalo warning trespassers from their selected grazing area was constant.

Then above the prairie, winds whispered another sound. As they listened and watched, they heard a gentle, rhythmic beating on the earth. The sound gradually became a roaring sound far out on the plain, the unmistakable sound of hundreds of hooves. It was the approaching sound of wild horses. Their long graceful legs stretched in full extension, their trampling hooves shaking the ground left an unmistakable trail as they flashed across the plain.

Chapter 39

In the far distance they saw an immense herd and heard the distinctive neighing as the skittish family members sought one another. The air was full of the familiar smell of the horse. The symbol of freedom!

As if on cue, they all stated the words.

Sunka wakan!

Wolfgang knew its meaning. Sacred Dog. He was amazed by the sight and numbers of swarming game animals. These southern plains are surely the richest hunting grounds on the continent.

As they watched, they were suddenly stunned by the size of a herd of hundreds of the medicine animals with their deep-girths. They were prized for their speed, endurance, and unbelievable feats. Black Shield and Wolfgang's pulse increased and their eyes were wide at the density of horses. Curly Bear pointed to a particular large group of the herd whose coloring consisted of large patches of white and there were appaloosa, striped duns, grulla, buckskin, palomino, cremello, ysabella, and perlino.

"Pintado," said Curly Bear.

The three travelers saw many brown-and-white, reddish brown-and-white, black-and-white spotted coated horses.

Mustangs! The white-patched Spanish is horse favored by the Indians because of their coloring. It enhanced their concealment. Preferred as a warhorse because its coloring blended well with tribal war paint and they loved to paint their symbols on the white patches. The majority of war parties were to steal horses, not fight. No two of the animals were exactly alike and these sure-footed horses weren't afraid of the thundering herds of buffalo, mused Wolfgang.

Again, Curly Bear pointed out particular animals, saying, "See the spotted horses with rounded markings and white legs and white across the back between the withers and tail, and the dark heads."

They thrilled at the flowing manes of the wild-eyed Spanish mustangs that were especially prized as buffalo runners. They were running madly across the land. They studied the enduring, smooth gait of many of the high-spirited animals and saw a mighty black animal, the herd stallion. It strutted around stiff-legged, head and tail up, ears pricked forward, alert for danger in every sound. The rugged black stallion brought up the rear, its unkempt mane quivering nervously, watching for danger while snorting and stomping to keep the other stallions away. The skittish mares blew air through their nostrils, and whinnied with delight.

The three warriors could picture in their mind the twitching, black stallion's ears laid back flat, warning any challenger, his body covered with sweat and every muscle quivering. They could imagine the fighting instinct in his blazing eyes, his large, dangerous, shinning white teeth showing an ugly grin. The men wished they had time to chase and capture some of the beautiful animals. Curly Bear and Wolfgang heard the stallion's loud whistling snorting. They watched the stallion with its head held low, neck stretched out flat, as it nipped a mare's flanks that had wandered too far away from the others. They were moving toward the river, downstream approximately one-half mile below them.

"I can feel their power," said Curly Bear.

Sadly, the horse had produced a class system based on ownership of horses. There were those with and those without, mused Wolfgang.

They watched the white colored lead mare as the herd of fat and sleek mares and their colts followed her. They heard the squealing and nickering of the little ones as they stretched and arched their necks, put their heads down, kicked up their heels throwing turf high in the air, and crow-hopped around their mothers in the sheer joy of being a horse.

The three warriors mesmerized by the wonderful sight of the mysterious creatures, admired the twitching, stiffened ears and withers of the prancing, agile horses with perfect, unshod hooves and arched necks. They watched the shaggy animals nuzzling and grooming the manes and necks of their weanlings: colts and fillies that ranged 6-to-12-months old and other family members as they groomed and calmed one another and grazed.

Wolfgang estimated that most of these Spanish mustangs, with their bright intelligent eyes always scanning the surroundings, light builds, good legs, strong backs, full barrel, and sharp nervous ears, stood 14 to 15 hands high. They had black dorsal stripes.

These compact and muscular mustangs had rounded hindquarters and a low-set tail. The neck was arched and set high from the withers. The gaited animal had greater stamina than the horses of the east, Wolfgang mused.

Curly Bear pressed his gelding forward, edging his mount alongside and to the front of Black Shield and Wolfgang's geldings, his hands motioning, "We have heard recently that the Spanish claim all these wild horses as their property."

* * *

Wolfgang looked up and saw long wings. A fish hawk was circling on the air currents high above. Wolfgang pointed. As the trio watched the raptor dove, swooping at the last moment, its long legs extended to snatch a fish and disappearing into the river, completely submerged. It quickly emerged with a large fish writhing in its talons. It was barely able to fly to a perch.

"It is a good omen," said Black Shield, "Our quest will be successful."

Wolfgang smiling, looked at the clouds, and thought how they reminded him of the backs of sheep. "Clouds say fair weather." His eyes traveled over the sea of grass sparkling with dew and said, "Dew on the grass means no rain."

The river was enormous like the Yellowstone River, and did not run in just one course. The wide river flowed east over the flood plain, meandering with split channels, islands, and numerous sandbars. The upstream end of the island was strewn with debris, then a strong, dense growth of willows gave way to cottonwoods. The river was low and they were aware that the river would not rise until the winter rains set in.

"Our thoughts and actions must be like the water in the river. Our abilities must adapt to our situation, flow and change according to need," said Wolfgang.

Both Black Shield and Curly Bear sat staring at Wolfgang for long moments thinking about what he had said, and his logic. Then their attention turned back to the river.

Movement appeared.

Chapter 40

An enormous black silhouette appeared like a ghost where none had been just moments before.

Black bear!

It slowly eased along the river's bank, feeding on the plentiful berries and wild plums in the maze of tightly woven brush. The bear frequently raised its head to sniff the air. The brush from the bank opened up after about twenty yards and the interior of the island was open. As they watched, they saw it was a sow with three yearlings. The three bouncing balls frolicked in and out of the brush. Periodically, the sow would stop feeding, pause, and look around, sniffing the cool morning air with her mystical power of smell. As they watched, the sow suddenly hung up, searching for a source of danger, turned and disappeared into the heavy cover. Wolfgang, Black Shield, and Curly Bear all realized that black bears were totally unpredictable. They had all experienced potentially dangerous face-to-face encounters with this animal that was not intimidated by the presence of man. They knew that if a black bear ever got you down, it would not quit until you were dead and would often make a lone hunter its next meal.

* * *

They sat reading the steep hillside bluff angle. Deep ravines and small gullies led in and out of one another down the embankment to the river. The steeply pitched incline looked treacherous. Curly Bear edged his horse forward. Without a word, he jumped his horse forward. They watched Curly Bear lean back as his horse fought to keep its balance, its quarters almost flat on the ground. They watched the horse plunging downward, scrabbling and slipping in an avalanche of stones and earth. Down and down. Then the horse had its legs under him and was at the bottom.

* * *

The wind worried the limbs of the cottonwood trees. The large grove offered a sweet pool of restless shade amid the sound of rustling and falling of thick, yellow leaves producing a sound like a sudden gush of water.

"Listen to it," said Black Shield, breaking a long silence, speaking and using the widespread gesture language bapa'tua. "You can hear the river whispering and moaning in deep tones. I have often sat and listened to it. But, I do not understand what it is saying."

"Only the beaver and the otter understand its language," replied Curly Bear. Wolfgang remembered his friend Lone Elk saying the same thing in the moon of Grass Growing, up on Elk River when he chased the Blackfoot and their stolen horses. That was the year 1765. Fourteen years ago!

They could smell the strong tannic and balsamic aroma of the many leaves. The waters sucked at the riverbanks. Somewhere on the other side of the river two wolves howled in lonely greetings to their family. They had not seen the two wolves for a long time.

The three warriors dismounted and ran their hands down their animals' legs slowly, checking their horses' legs for cuts, heat, swollen or puffy areas, watching for signs of marked pain to the touch. They worried constantly about their animal's overstepping or kicking and dinging a ligament or tendon. Finally satisfied, they stood and conferred with each other that their animals were sound. Wolfgang, Curly Bear, and Black Shield approached a high spot on the bank of the river and stood watching into the depths of the water where they would cross.

Wolfgang and Black Shield slowly turned to the eastern horizon and prayed to the sun, the god known as "ma'sa`ka." They offered their sacred greenish-brown tobacco to the Water Spirit and their Creator with a prayer to ensure their safety upon entering the land of the Spanish. They lifted their arms to the sky. Curly Bear prayed to Ussen, the Giver of Life, for power to overcome the Spanish.

The water shelters a multitude of mystic beings, Wolfgang mused, we must always ask the Water People and the Great Spirit above to watch over us and allow safe passage when going to war.

The answering silence was deafening as they listened to the spirits.

Then, as if from a great distance, Wolfgang felt the voices and the spirits of Yellow Bird Singing and Dark Moon saying, "The Spirit Bird will watch over you."

Hearing a soft rhythmic pushing of air from the beating of wings, Wolfgang, Black Shield, and Curly Bear looked up. The mystical bird looked down on them with its glistening ebony eye and croaked once. The Spirit Bird soared upward on flat wings and flew out over the Spanish camp, turned and flew to the north. Again, The Raven! They lowered their arms.

In awe, Black Shield said, "Again he has spoken to us."

They stared in the direction it indicated. The Spanish slave camp.

The one-eyed Odin was known to shape shift as a raven, thought Wolfgang, remembering his Germanic god.

*   *   *

Looking across the river. Wolfgang, Black Shield, and

Curly Bear, splashed into the unmarked fringes of the ford riffles in the channel just after daybreak. Their horses did not hesitate a second and the water came up only to the point of the horses' hocks. It was shallow. The horses never had to swim. They paused hock-deep in the stream and drank some water as the three warriors studied the trees ahead and checked the bank for tracks. The horses stopped drinking and moved on.

As they crossed, they paid close attention to their horses' ears, depending upon their keen eyesight, because if their ears suddenly went forward they knew they had seen a deer or another horse. They rode up the shallow southern bank, bending over to study the tracks. They stopped on the bank of the river and paused, looking back over their shoulders watching and then listening to the brooding silence around them. The young trumpeter swans had learned to fly and were dabbling like ducks nearby, feeding on aquatic vegetation. Their eyes quickly sought the source of a loud rush of air. It was the riders of the wind.

Ducks!

It was the sound of wings. In the dawn's early light a passing flock of ducks alit on the surface of the river, looking for a place to sit down after flying all night. They watched another flock, with wings hooked, in an impossible vertical descent. The birds turned, sideslipping, hanging in the air, hovering and finally settling onto the water. The birds stretched, preening their flight feathers into place. It was a sight they had seen many times in their lives, but that always held them in awe. They also noticed giant, clawed footprints of a grizzly literally covering the sandy and muddy areas.

"I will be glad when the snows of Cold Maker drive the bears into hibernation in the Moon of Madness," said Black Shield thinking out loud.

November, mused Wolfgang.

The horses stood patiently, switching tails and flipping their ears against a few flies. The silence seemed deafening as they took in every detail of their surroundings. There was a vague hint of a noise in their subconscious. Then there was a startlingly broken sound of something at the edge of their hearing. It was becoming clearer. They all looked up, hearing the faint, wispy flute-like gargling sound high in the sky. They listened to the mysterious low, loud, musical raucous rattling.

Kar-r-r-o-o-o.

It was the sure sign that the days were growing shorter and that fall had arrived. The sandhill cranes were flying in their undulant lines, curving and flowing high over the landscape. Hearing the stamp of a distant deer hoof brought the three warriors back to earth. The horses snorted loudly and jerked their heads up, having a knack for seeing everything that moved. The horses were staring to the southeast, alert ears pointed forward. The three travelers turned their heads, searching into the cottonwoods. The stamp of a hoof was repeated, followed by the startled sound of a whitetail buck among the trees. The deer had caught their scent and gave a quick, loud blast of air in warning through its nose.

Whphew.

They saw his movement in the shadows and a flash of antler tines, and then the deer was gone. The silence was broken again as the three travelers heard a deep, horse rattling, cronk—cronk overhead and again looked up at the sound. They heard the familiar whir of flat wings and saw the large raven flying away from them to the southwest. The travelers turned and followed the flight of the large bird in the direction of the high Sangre de Christo Mountains. Wolfgang thought of the raven. It is the bird of the one-eyed Germanic God Odin, the inspiration for hard-bitten German warriors. The tireless raven is sent out by Odin to observe the affairs of men and provide vision. It was just another meaningful sign of their purpose.

That afternoon, their camp established out of the wind, Wolfgang harvested the upper part of chickweed plants that grew profusely in the rich, moist sandy soil of the island. Dark Moon had always told him that drinking a decoction made of the tender leaves and succulent stems acted as a tonic for tired blood and was good for salad and wrapping fish. Black Shield had found a mouse nest in an old log to use for finely shredded tinder. Curly Bear gathered the small dry twigs, and Wolfgang started the fire with his rubbing stick bow. They roasted and ate a buffalo calf. Both Black Shield and Curly Bear smiled at Wolfgang as he dug several large fish wrapped in chickweed leaves out of the embers of the fire. They looked at each other, smiling, and said, "Magic."

* * *

The travelers rested and talked about their destination, the Sangre de Cristo Mountains, and how they didn't want to attract any unwanted scrutiny or attention now that they were so close. The Blood of Christ awaited.

Chapter 41

Wolfgang, Black Shield, and Curly Bear, seeing the Spanish Peaks to the south, now turned and traveled west on the south side of the Arkansas River watching the rugged land stretching out to the distant Blue Mountains. Their eyes took in the smallest details, studying the clouds, every gust of wind, the position of the sun and its shadows, the birds and animals.

Curly Bear, pointed ahead. There was a level grassy valley before them and a faint trail leading into the range of wooded, scrub oak hills beyond. In this strange country, following the river provided a definite course.

Curly Bear warned the others of the obvious, "Following the river leads to populated areas, because it is a food, travel and water source, and observation by our enemies is likely. We must watch for checkpoints, such as occasional bodies of water, falls, cliffs, deep gorges, and tributaries to guide our return and in case of trouble. We must stop early enough to establish a secure and satisfactory campsite."

They found a number of horse droppings and dismounted. They broke the horse dung open. Maize and buffalo grass! The moisture content was only two days old and they determined they came from a nearby Mexican village because of the maize content.

* * *

The sun now rose at their backs and followed them until midday. As the day grew later, the sun became more directly ahead of them, setting in the west. Always thinking of the danger of unseen enemies, they used their wits, their minds wide awake, their eyes and ears vigilant. They watched the antelope bucks hazing does into draws and basins to hold their harems out of view to protect them from other bucks. They watched other antelope bucks giving each other long hard stares and chasing each other to keep the does in their herds. They watched one young interloper hold his ground. The herd buck, alert, stared at his challenger long and hard, then snorted, and approached the pretender, walking slow and stiff-legged with his head held low and his ears laid back toward his rival. Then the two rivals clashed and there were thrusts and counterthrusts. The herd buck gained the advantage of a piece of high ground and twisted his opponent's head and put him on the ground. The young rival was up, turned his back to flee, and was stabbed in the back by the herd buck. They watched the young rival stagger off to lick his wounds.

* * *

The dawn came slow, seeping into the east like a gray stain. It had rained. The low, gray clouds had blown across the sky to the east. The cold bit into their bones as they rode across the vast emptiness of the low rolling land that rose and fell beneath them. They tried their best to see without being seen, and hear without being heard. Always peering ahead before advancing, they used the ever-shifting plains animals, gullies and ravines, depressions between hills or the sides of hills to hide their tracks. Wolfgang rode ahead. Mouse stopped cautiously every now and then and would snort to clear his keen nose from the scent of predators that had recently crossed their path. Mouse turned this way and that from waterless, shallow or deep-sided arroyos, to stop and listen. Curly Bear looked at Wolfgang and pointed to a large, prickly and sticky looking patch. "Cholla! During the dry season, when there is little to drink, that plant is a source of water. Its red bud is sweet to eat. Its flower is yellow. We use sand to scrape the needles off the pad or burn them off. It is best after being soaked in water. The taste is a little astringent, if you are not use to it. The pad is eaten as salad. Our shaman tells us, it will prevent excessive thirst and urine flow. They are gathered at this time of year by my people." Then they were again silent. They watched and listened for a long time.

The usually quiet Curly Bear spoke and signed, "Those twin peaks are called Wah-To-Yah by most of the people."

The Indians of the area, Wolfgang thought.

After a time, Curly Bear continued saying, "It means Breasts of the Earth. The peaks are where the God Tlaloc, the rain god, the sun god, and the thunder gods make their home. The Spanish call them Los Dos Hermanos, the two Brothers."

The trio saw thin veils of smoke staining the sky as they bypassed a Mexican settlement near the junction of Fountain Creek and the river. (Find out the old name for Pueblo, Colorado) They watched the Mexicans chasing buffalo, in the distance using their swift horses and lances. "They are called ciboleros," said Curly Bear, "The Mexican buffalo hunters."

They worked their way through the small, dry, rocky hills covered with juniper and round-crowned pinyon trees up to the Sangre de Cristo Mountains. The horses were beginning to labor a little, mouths hanging open, stretching out their necks and flaring their nostrils as they climbed the hill. They slowed them to a walk. The mountains were beautiful, an area where there were no tracks of men or any sign that anyone had ever been there before. Wolfgang was in awe at this expanse of land. Its mountains, canyons, and plains evoked a deep sense of admiration in him and he knew why so many European powers were fighting to lay claim to this rich land. It was a magical place.

* * *

It was the last hour of the night as the trio of warriors made their way upward amid the strong smell of pine and subtle woods fragrances that filled the air. The darkness hung like a shroud under the lodgepole pines, opaque, impenetrable. Wolfgang could hardly see his hand before his face. Finally, the first light of dawn revealed a heavy frost and a mist rising from the canyon into a flawless sky as the stars faded. They stopped to blow the horses. They watched and listened. The silence was crystalline. There was a perfect absence of sound. The high, clean, crisp air of altitude and the lingering, sweet, fragrant scent of the mountains made the act of breathing a heady, intoxicating pleasure. It smelled like the musky aroma of the sweet-scented forest floor.

It was beautiful country of open ridges of grass, big canyons, and mist rising from the dark, damp timber. Below the gray meld of the rocky ridges there were shadows of mauve and gray with their underlying grassy slopes, scree, and rougher talus slopes. The air was clear and cool. The sun was bright. Silently, they watched from the cool, sun-dappled shade of the towering pines that encroached on the trail. They could see large, exposed, bare weathered rocks and loose shale slopes clustered around the peaks. They could clearly see the green carpet of pines layering the mountain slopes. The mountains were covered with swaths of stunning, gold-colored aspens dotting across the green-forested slopes with startling hues of red and brown. Mouse hated such breathers, and pawed and bobbed his head itching to be on the move. From below, they heard the drawn-out, wailing of an unseen cow moose.

Wuow-wuow-wuow!

* * *

Their conversation was quiet and cheerful as they rode along an exposed ridge of sage colored landscape that predominated the foothills. They felt safe, for all around them and ahead of them they were pushing a large flock of cedar waxwings. The wind was in their face as they rode uphill. They looked hard into the places it was hardest to see. Wolfgang studied the patterns of light and dark. He detected a shift of shape and stopped. He saw a disturbance in the pine needles where the ground surface had been turned up by hooves. The turned-up soil indicated where the animal had made a hard turn away from them as they approached. There was an odd highlight among a thick patch of juniper branches that broke up its shape. Then, he made out a patch of gray. He studied the thick juniper and saw the sunlight glinting in an eye. He made out the horizontal line of a back and then made out the outline, its breath visible in the cold morning air.

A deer!

There was a twitch of a disproportionately large ear swiveled rearward of a big buck, standing and waiting, trying to catch sounds from all directions. Finally, the strain was too much for the deer's nerves—he disappeared through a screen of cover over the ridge. Mouse's breath made small clouds in the crisp air as they moved on.

*   *   *

Again, they cautiously stopped to listen. Out of the edge of hearing, they heard a sound rise and fade. Again, but closer this time, the same sound came louder in answer. Time seemed to stand still as Wolfgang listened to the sound sweeping along with the breeze through the broken stands of timber. The high, shrill bugle of a great bull building toward a perfect pitch was one of the few sounds that always evoked an emotional response in Wolfgang.

A bull elk! Probably in a wallow in the spruce shade. Wolfgang eyed a distant willow seep among the alders.

And then again, the ephemeral note from somewhere below them drifted more clearly in the dawn of challenge. A high, thin, monotone, gossamer call with a slight quiver sounded from near them and died in the treetops. They talked and were mesmerized by the sight of a swarm of sharp-edged wings explode, bank sharply, then abruptly descend and continue frenetically feeding on the dark blue berries of the juniper trees around them. The going became harder as they went up the eastern slope of the mountain. They rode slowly, watching the yellow-breasted birds with the black mask and short, yellow-tipped tails feast on the bumper crop of berries that grew year around. Wolfgang's hand stretched out and stripped off several berries and popped them into his mouth to nibble to take the edge off his hunger.

Bitter! Texture of sawdust.

The knowing Curly Bear and Black Shield just smiled.

Curly Bear said, "Evidently the birds have a different opinion. If there is nothing else to eat, the berries will work magic on your stomach."

Looking at Curly Bear, Wolfgang said, "Your mother, Wind Woman, says you can talk to the horses, tell me about it."

Curly Bear began, "I rode a horse before I could walk. I grew up having only to use a soft suggestion to get a response from my horse. From when I was a child, the way I looked, smelled, and acted was always accepted by the horse." He continued, "The horses in our herd were not suspicious or afraid of me. They would not run off from me or fight me. They accepted me and I learned to communicate with them by patiently watching them, as they speak with small motions and gestures. You must penetrate a horse's mind and heart to understand him. It is a natural gift that I cannot really explain. I have never acted aggressively around these majestic animals and have always had a harmonious relationship with them. My mind has become a natural extension of their mind, body, and feet. I can ride them without saddle or bridle."

Wolfgang said, "My wife, Dark Moon, was like that."

"I know, it was she who talked to the horse and first put me on it as a baby. She was a tall woman with hooded eyes. It had always been a fantasy of mine to meet you. And now I ride with you." said Curly Bear.

Wolfgang turned his head and stared at the young, smiling Apache, as if seeing him for the first time.

Curly Bear continued, "I have heard all the stories about you."

Chapter 42

A familiar, high, shrill whistle floated through the air as they crossed an icy stream flowing through boulders, pools, and riffles, twitching and tumbling, picking up speed, and creating a roar as it crashed down steep drops and ran over smooth black rocks. Wolfgang stopped in an opening in the trees at a small overlook. They watched a small herd of elk moving down to the aspen stands to feed.

In warm weather Elk like to bed on a northeast-facing shelf in a dark spruce drainage at midday, and move to the aspens with a nearby meadow and seep to feed in early morning and late evening unless they live on the prairie.

They listened and watched. Then they heard it again. All around them the wilderness was alive with the sounds of rutting elk that ghosted through the shadows of the dark timber of lodgepole pine, fir, and spruce above. They detected the pungent scent of bull elk in the air. To pick up the aroma better they took several small sniffs, keeping their mouths open to give an extra dimension to the smell. The wind died for a moment and again they heard the unmistakable deep, raspy bugle. It was much louder. A powerful, wild sound, the bugle of a large bull elk and the constant barrage of sensual cow chirps and mews reached their alert ears. The sounds came from the thick timber just below them. The growling bugles started low, followed by a rasping pitch rise. They ascended across several octaves before breaking and dropping to a grating, harsh scream. This was followed by three deep, rough, gravel-toned grunts brought up from his stomach. The haunting call reverberated through and off the slopes.

OOooEEEeeeeeeeeeeeeeoooo, OUGH, OUGH, OUGH.

Two dueling bulls were observed moving closer and closer to each other and then going head-to-head. The gory fight lasted about five minutes. The older bull lost, limping away. The older bull also had a large gash in his neck.

Now was the time in the mountains when the cows went into fungi feeding frenzy. The elk spread out through the forest searching for the smooth, white cap that emerges in the Moon of Falling Leaves. They also heard the high-pitched squeals of cows and the slightly higher pitch of calves.

OOooEEEeeeeeeeeeeeeeoooo, OUGH, OUGH, OUGH.

Each deep, resonant bugle was immediately answered in challenge from a nearby direction by another full-throated, rut-crazed dominant bull with a shaggy neck. He sported a massive, mahogany-colored main beam thrust outward at an impressive angle rack tearing up a tree. They stopped, watched, and listened to the rasp of smooth, brown, curved tines raking against the tree. Then the air was shattered with another long, haunting raspy bugle.

OOooEEEEeeeeeeeeeeeeeeoooo, OUGH, OUGH, OUGH.

From another direction came the thin, reedy sound of an immature, spike bull trying to mimic the older bulls. The squeaky higher-pitched, blood-curdling screams of the immature bull infuriated the older bulls. The herd bulls urinated down their legs, raked limbs with their antlers, and focused their attention on protecting their cows. The young bulls whirled with a surprised grunt and vanished rather than get into a shoving match.

The clouds were rolling down the mountain, and the deer were still concentrated in the high country. Wolfgang was sensitive to his immediate surroundings. His eyes caught every movement in the forest; like the deer, his nose inspected every waft of air; his ears caught every sound and vibration.

"Thump, thump, thump."

They heard the nearby sound of heavy hooves of mule deer erupting many times from bedding areas in shale slides, deadfall patches, and rock ledges as they climbed. The mule deer had changed from their red-brown summer coats to a much thicker, soft gray coat for the winter. Wolfgang wondered about the curious deer that generally located themselves uphill from a herd of rutting elk. The wind was filled with the sweet smell of high-desert sage from the level plain below. It was just strong enough to set the pines rustling. The air was fresh and chilly and the wind blew with a cold edge that bore the promise of an early winter. They watched the drunken, crazy-flights of grouse, and listened to their drumming advertising for a mate or warning an intruder out of their territory.

Flakes of snow began falling gently. Wolfgang thought he had heard movement. Snow deadens sound! The temperature was dropping even further as the snow began to collect on the ground. A light blanket of fresh snow soon covered the ground among the old stand of spruce and the mountains felt muffled and snug. The flurries of snow would severely reduced heir visibility ahead, but would cover their back trail. Wolfgang's eyes followed a fresh set of lion tracks. As his eyes followed the tracks, he was surprised to see a gray, whiskered face frosted with white fur watching him with yellow eyes full of loathing. Aware that they had disturbed the cat's hunt, the seldom-seen lynx trotted off on gangly legs and tremendous webbed feet.

*   *   *

The next day, when the sun was one hand above the mountains, Wolfgang was aware that the light snow would soon disappear. It was a beautiful, clear, sunny day. For a moment his mind lingered on the beauty of the land. The leaves had turned a fiery red, orange and gold. The dark bodies of the deer were easy to detect against the white background. Disturbed deer ahead of them began bounding off, leaving a distinctive snow trail in which the imprints were bunched together in clusters of four.

Wolfgang turned his head, smelling an obnoxious, evil odor and observed a fresh track about the size of a wolf's. A closer look revealed five toes, not four like the wolf. The heel pad was different. It was the sign of the widely traveled, shaggy-haired, short-legged wolverine. Looking into the distance, he saw the small animal with the bushy tail and two pale brown stripes disappearing into the timber up ahead.

The first probing thrust of Cold Maker was a reminder of what lay ahead. Fall would end all too soon. Then the cold and wet season would descend upon them, gradually turning to snow. The first blizzard would come down out of the north. The dreaded long winter would be on their lodges, as they would sit wrapped and huddled in furs, trying to survive, praying for an early spring. They needed to act swiftly to free the slaves to return home and help their families prepare for winter.

Chapter 43

As they crested the trail, the sun had never shined as brightly. They looked into the heart of the mountains. The scenic, sloping valley of green felt was covered with a bright, wildflower-saturated landscape.

There, the Spanish camp sat in a short valley on a low rise. They had arrived! Black Shield reached into a small pouch and brought forth a pinch of tobacco, known to the Crow people as op ha'tskite, mixed with kinnikinic, sumac and dogwood bark, elk and buffalo dung. It was a greenish-brown tobacco linked to the spirits. In one motion of his arm, he spread the sacred supernatural medicine on the ground with the help of the wind and raised his arms, speaking to the Great Spirit, Ah-badt-dadt-deah, "Thank you. You have watched over us. You helped us cross our enemies' land. Ensure our safety as we go to war to liberate these oppressed people from the Spanish." The three warriors sat cross-legged, closed their eyes, meditating and praying upon what they saw before them. Wolfgang closed his eyes, gathered his strength, and felt a strange surge of power.

* * *

The sky was cloudless overhead and their gaze was drawn to a solitary huge, black-winged scavenger with a long tail, heavy hooked bill and curved talons. Its appearance was striking and unusual. The trio of warriors watched as it tilted from one side to the other as it flew. It soared effortlessly in wide circles, gliding gracefully on white-tipped wings held in a distinctive raised angle over the valley.

The harbinger of death.

Black Shield, Curly Bear, and Wolfgang took its presence as an omen. This spirit bird was the guardian of mysteries. It was a powerful and mystical bird, the vulture. A spirit of never-ending vigilance. Its feathers, were used by many tribes in rituals for grounding after shape-shifting ceremonies, facilitating the return to the self.

Curly Bear broke the silence, saying, "The Death Bird who faces the sun each morning and honors it by outstretching its wings. He teaches that life's suffering is temporary and necessary. That rescue is imminent."

* * *

The air was crystal-clear allowing them to see every detail below them. The valley was filled with good grass. There were many horses. There were mountains east and west, allowing the wind to funnel in from the north and rip through the camp. Beyond the immediate ridge to the west lay fold after fold of mountains, turning blue in the distance, shimmering in the afternoon haze. The compound inside the low, walled area was probably 100 meters by 200 hundred meters.

A small, shallow stream ran on the far western side of the camp. There were seven log structures in the middle of a large open area. In the center of the camp they could tell one was a stable from the horses that went back and forth from the long, low building. The building next to it was a blacksmith shop. They could see its fire and the puffs of smoke that rose when someone pumped the bellows and they could hear the sound of metal against metal coming from it.

A corral with several horses in it was located up against the blacksmith shop. Several men were leaning on the rail looking at the horses, and from the movement of their heads it was clear they were talking. Wolfgang noticed that all the best thoroughbred horses were kept there. The barking of guard dogs around the stable presented a unique problem, one Wolfgang immediately started working on.

The southern most building must have been a warehouse because nobody stayed there very long except to off load supplies into it and carry things from it to the building nearest the mine. Ladders were made in and around the building, and were carried off to the mines with loads of rope and hand-carved support logs for bracing the mineshafts.

Wolfgang located the barracks and cook shack by the sound of wood chopping. The nearer building he determined was an eating house, because it always had smoke rising from the chimney, and men came and went at times corresponding to the three daily meals. The other buildings were where men retired to at night. The one in the center of the camp was the largest, with two stories, and had two armed men posted in the daytime keeping watch.

He watched the human movement and noises of the men in the camp and located the position of the guards. The movement of the cattle outside the camp meant that the Spanish were well fed. There was a guarded horse herd on the opposite side of the camp from the cattle.

For two days, Wolfgang watched the area of the most active mine and studied the surrounding area of mysterious caverns. Wolfgang observed the light-gray rock exposures of limestone spread across the mountain in the area of the mines.

*　　*　　*

Curly Bear visited the Spanish horse pasture each night. The Apache had only one incident during those nights. A dog! A large dog! The moon was up, but winds were pushing clouds across its face. In the darkness, Curly Bear had remained motionless, stilling his breathing, and listening, while waited for the clouds to cover the moon and then use their shadows to move and crawl about. It was slow. Sniffing the air he detected the presence of an unseen dog. He closed his eyes and listened carefully. There was a slight sound. In the darkness in front of him, there was an indistinct outline at the limit of his vision.

The dog had stalked the shadows, sensing Curly Bears approach, and came close with its hackles raised. It moved forward with a lowered head to catch his scent and emitted a low growl. Curly Bear watched his eyes, tail, and body posture, and determined it didn't look threatening or afraid. Just wary! He was not happy to see it, but understood its body language and threw it some meat. The dog sniffed at it with suspicion. The dog ate it and lowered its hackles and tail. It came closer. Curly Bear fed it again. It came closer, with pleading eyes, licking and nosing, wagging its tail under his hands and whined. Curly Bear rubbed its ears and softly spoke to it. He produced another piece of meat and threw it. The dog trotted off after the morsel, and Curly Bear moved on without further incident.

*   *   *

At sunset, as the shadows lengthened Wolfgang studied the wild animals and their movement to feeding areas.

Watching Wolfgang, Black Shield asked, "What are you thinking?"

Wolfgang remained quiet and then turned to his friend and answered, "The camp is well protected, being in the open and well away from the timber. Night is the time to plan to raid them. I must pick our route down and up to the mine to avoid alerting the deer and elk with their sense of smell. If the deer and elk startle, it will alert the Spanish guards. So, I'm watching how the wild game moves, trying to take advantage of the wind. As the slopes lose their heat, the air and all its smells, drifts downhill.

Mainly, I watch the angle at which the animals hold their ears, as that tells me where the danger lies. The thermals are strongest on the east-and-south-facing slopes on sunny days and drift uphill in the daytime; therefore it is easier for the deer and elk to alert to our scent. We must be sure of our movement."

They watched quietly, together watching the last streaks of red disappear from the wide expanse of sky. They listened to the wind in the trees as the temperature began to drop, feeling the Great Spirit all around them.

OOooEEEeeeeeeeeeeeeeeooooo,Ough,Ough,Ough.

* * *

At sunrise there had been a light fall of snow during the night, and the air was sharp as Wolfgang watched the trails the deer and elk moved on from their feeding areas to their bedding areas on open hillsides that blazed with yellow light in groves of aspen. Wolfgang stared in awe at the bleak splendor before him, as every breath of the wind made the golden leaves turn and flash like the light of thousands of little mirrors. The days were growing shorter and soon the mountains, with their rugged cliffs, dominated by the pine, spruce, and aspen forest and sparkling creeks would be transformed with a sparkling mantle of brilliant white with a surprising gentleness. Then, the full richness of fall would come days later as the weather briefly warmed again. The snow would continue to build in the high country.

Wolfgang noticed one place outside the camp where the Spanish went to relieve themselves.

"We need a prisoner to tell us about the camp," said Wolfgang thinking out loud. "Curly Bear, I want you to sneak into the edge of the camp each night and acquaint yourself with the horses in the corral, so that when the time comes to free your people from the mine our plan will go easier."

"It will be done," replied Curly Bear smiling, sure of

himself.

Chapter 44

The autumn sun was slow to warm the crisp morning air when they came upon a well-used trail as they moved toward the Spanish camp. The sharply focused Curly Bear worked towards the position of the sun and stopped, pointed to some stones. Wolfgang and Black Shield immediately saw what Curly Bear was indicating to them. The low angle of the sun cast a slight shadow from three, small flat stones that had been placed one upon the other, indicating a message. Looking ahead to the farthest point along the trail, Curly Bear again pointed. The low sun angle, their good eyes, highly developed senses for tracking, and their ability to observe every detail of their surroundings allowed them to immediately see the signal stones.

All the stones in the area were lying in their natural position with their upper side washed clean, except for this one group of stones. Two dislodged stones had been placed on end resting against the other. The displaced stones and their bottom sides appeared darker against the backdrop of lighter stones. The weather had not yet washed away the soil, which clung to their bottom side. A few feet away were the impressions in the soil where the stones had originally laid.

"It is an Apache distress signal saying help is needed," Curly Bear said.

* * *

They came upon six large bundles hanging from the trees in the sun alongside the trail. As they approached, the smell told them that something was wrong. Curly Bear stopped them and squatted, looking carefully all around. Black Shield and Wolfgang followed his example.

"What is it?" inquired Wolfgang.

The hard face of the Apache alarmed Black Shield and Wolfgang.

Curly Bear rose slowly and hand signed. He extended his right hand toward them, pointed his index finger and swept it to his face. Its meaning was clear.

"Come."

Wolfgang and Black Shield followed Curly Bear to the first of the hanging bundles. They stared at the hard, dried bundles made of buffalo rawhide. Curly Bear labored to cut away a section near the top and turned the bundle so it faced Wolfgang and Black Shield. Staring at them was a face with a hideous grimace.

"This is Spanish torture. The Spaniards bend the live, upper body forward to the knees and the lower legs back to the thighs into a ball, tie it with rope, and pull it tight. Then, they wrap it tightly in a wet hide and hang it in the sun to dry. As it shrinks, the body is compressed. Bones break, and breathing ceases very gradually. Your heart may give out first. It is a hard way to die," said Curly Bear.

"Who are they? Wolfgang replied.

"Apaches."

*　　*　　*

Finally, they saw the tracks of a lone horse and rider as it came in from a side trail. They saw the fresh, distinctive "chop" marks in the ground caused by the knife-edge shaped hooves sinking into the soft soil under the weight of the horse.

They moved silently for a short distance parallel to the trail. They saw where the rider had dismounted to relieve himself.

These were the tracks of a Spaniard because the toe was turned out instead of being turned in like those of an Indian.

"This rider is just ahead of us, we will capture him. He is heading into the wind. It will mask the sound of our approach. The large trees will also mask the sound of our approach," said Wolfgang.

This is where we will get our Spanish prisoner so we can learn more about the camp.

The three warriors ran silently and hard. Without warning or audible approach, they came upon the lone rider. By the time the horse alerted him to the sound, it was too late. The sudden flutter of the Spaniard's heart and the pounding of blood in his eardrums deadened the shock of the three warriors who stopped his horse and pulled him from it. Amazement was etched upon his grey face as his horrified eyes mechanically followed their movements. The trio struck him on the head, shoulders, and back. Each man heard the impact of blows and the grunts of the other as they delivered them. The Spaniard's scalp was split and blood trickled down over his face. Strong hands swiftly bound the Spaniard's wrists, the leather cords cruelly eating into his flesh. A leather gag was wedged into his mouth and tied around the back of his head. The Spaniard was still conscious, but his head was spinning and his eyes were unfocused as they led him to his horse and away.

* * *

Curly Bear stood next to the prisoner, his face bent in a predatory grin as his cruel and relentless eyes burned deeply into the Spaniard's face. Curly Bear remained silent for a long time, staring. He saw terror in the captive's eyes and saw his lower lip twitch. Curly Bear loved to feed off the fear of his enemies. It made his heart race. It was. . . intoxicating.

Good!

Curly Bear pulled his elkhorn-handled knife from its scabbard and knelt down on one knee and put the point to the Spaniard's neck, saying, "Those slaves in the mine are my people, Spaniard."

The watching Wolfgang and Black Shield saw the dull metal and bone handle of Curly Bear's knife: The blade's edge was sharp and clean, and Curly Bear's eyes were dark pits. He showed no compassion, only hatred and a perverse sense of pleasure. Wolfgang and Black Shield knew few individuals could resist torture, especially at the hands of an experienced warrior.

Their prisoner felt cold. His thin face was sharp with anxiety. His dry mouth forced a wan smile, as his stomach lurched. The Spaniards anxiety was betrayed by a perceptible quiver of his lips. Sweat beaded on his forehead as he looked from the sharp knife to the face of the Apache warrior. Curly Bear jabbed the point of the knife further, almost breaking the skin. The smell of fear was now prevalent and pungent, as the Spaniard's right leg shivered.

In a tremulous voice he asked, "What do you want?"

Curly Bear, with a rush of euphoria, merely studied the Spaniard's face with eyes bright, almost glassy. Then, smiling, he slowly jabbed the neck again saying, "This is your opportunity to make this slow or quick. You can make it easier on yourself. Much easier." Then, for effect, Curly Bear placed the blade of the knife down on the left thumb drawing blood and held it in place, and again looked into the face of the Spaniard.

"You will give me the answers I want."

Resignation filled the Spaniard's eyes, then widened in glassy terror as he made a thin keening noise and ended in a moan, as he felt prompted by the pressure of the blade. Wolfgang and Black Shield could smell the strong odor of fear and stress from the Spaniard. His bowels released, and the ground turned wet beneath him as he lost control of his bladder.

Wolfgang's face remained expressionless, but watching intensely he saw a wild exhilaration in Curly Bear's eyes. However, his voice was as flat as the prairie and held there, unshakable.

He's enjoying this, Wolfgang mused.

With a flush of excitement, the Apache torturer drew a red line with the sharp point of his knife across the Spaniard's chest slowly as he said, "I will not give you more pain than you can endure." They heard a hiss and groan escape the mouth of the prisoner as his body bowed out to stop the knife, and then a keening wail. Sweat ran freely over the Spaniard's body as he gasped for air. His heart was palpitating, skipping irregularly, as his mind raced for a way to stop the torture. "I will keep the pain and agony at this level so you will last a long time," said Curly Bear.

As Curly Bear started to draw another line, the Spaniard spoke. "Wait." The motion of the knife stopped.

" YES. YES. I'll tell you whatever you want." He thought he was going to vomit as his heart hammered in his chest, and his mind raced. "Tell me what you want to know."

"How long have the Spanish been here," asked Curly Bear.

"Juan de Ulibarri claimed this land for the king of Spain in 1706," the Spaniard answered.

"No!" said Curly Bear, "How long have you and these others been here."

"Our group just relieved an older group a short time ago. They have gone back to Taos, our headquarters with Colonel Anza. He has ended the Comanche raids on the province. Colonel Anza and his force of 600 men went on to Santa Fe," said the Spaniard nervously.

Curly Bear said, "We see the soldiers come out of the mine with their weapons, but no slaves. Where are the slaves kept?"

"In a room off the main shaft of the mine on the right. They are chained to the wall. Most of the slaves are just chained to each other."

"Where is this room?"

"It is near the entrance on the right," he said as he felt the knife slowly cut the skin.

"How many guards are there at night?"

"Seven."

"Where are the guards located?"

"One is at the entrance. Two are at the entrance to the room to keep an eye on the slaves. The other three soldiers are sleeping with the sergeant-in-charge in the room closest to the entrance."

"Now tell me about the Comanche," demanded Curly Bear.

"The Comanche leader, Chief Cuerno Verde, was recently killed after leading a raid on Taos. Our commander, the Governor of New Mexico Lieutenant Colonel Juan Bautista de Anza, with a strong force of our soldiers and Indian allies, caught up with the raiders just a little way south of here on the east side of the Front Range. They killed Cuerno Verde, his eldest son, four other chiefs, his medicine man, and ten other Comanche out in the low country on the Cuchara River. After Juan Bautista de Anza returned from his campaign, he claimed the Comanche lost 131 warriors."

Curly Bear leveled his death stare at the Spanish prisoner.

"It will be quick, Spaniard."

Chapter 45

Wolfgang and Black Shield smiled to themselves. Their Apache friend was skilled in ruthlessness. They saw Curly Bear's face freeze in deadly concentration as he clamped a hand over the Spaniard's mouth. The Spaniard writhed and bucked, as his eyes grew wide in his startled face. Curly Bear thrust the tip of his razor-sharp knife up under his chin. The man's eyes bugged out as he emitted a slight gurgle while blood spurted from his open throat. The knife went through to the bottom of the skull into the brain and the knife twisted violently from side to side, as Curly Bear completed his grisly work. The Spaniard's feet drummed on the ground in a useless effort, then spasmed and jerked before going completely inert. The Spaniard slumped forward, his eyes frozen wide-open, staring blindly. Curly Bear relaxed his grip, removed his hand from the slack jaw, wiped the blade on the Spaniard's tunic, and put his knife away. He turned to his Crow companions and looked at them without any expression. He always felt great satisfaction at taking an enemy's life.

Then, Curly Bear, quickly glancing at the two wolves sniffing at the base of a tree for an interesting scent said, "The Spanish guards are not used to self-restraint in their movement at night and they move too quickly. They are noisy at night, making them easy to locate because of their clumsy walking, coughing, smoking, and talking habits. Their clumsy boots and lurching legs will make our efforts to locate and track the guards by sound alone easy."

They listened to the sound of the wind sweeping mournfully

around them and felt its chill, as it got colder. They watched the beauty of the autumnal sunset as it gelded the mountaintops. The Spanish camp below was already in shadows as the darkness stole up their side of the mountain. They had fasted for the day to produce a sharpening of all their senses and to have a crisp clarity of thoughts for what they had to do.

* * *

Wolfgang gazed up at the myriad of stars shining brightly, spread all across the deep blue-black sky. He checked the angle of the Big Dipper to the North Star. About three o'clock! He was long used to telling the time of night in the dark hours by the Big Dipper and its rotation around the North Star.

I like the Indian way of keeping track of the passing of the weeks in the month by the phases of the moons full, half, and new, he thought.

Looking at Curly Bear and Black Shield, Wolfgang told them of his plan, "In the land of my birth, the moon is a symbol of solitude. Each of us this night must go our own way. There are only three of us. There will be a good moon and the stars will be bright. I will take the ore mine. Curly Bear is patient, quiet, and can go among the horses without alarming them. He will get the Spanish horses and move them quietly to the meadow near the mine and tether them there for his people to ride. Black Shield, you have the night eyes of an owl. You will take care of the guards around the camp. Leave the Spaniards who are sleeping alone. Depend upon your wolf's eyes and nose to guide you in the dark to those you must silence. Bring any extra weapons you can salvage."

Wolfgang turned and pointed at a nearby mountain meadow along the trail saying, "We will all meet there before the moon goes down. We have to be on our way home before the sun rises in the east."

Wolfgang rose and put a hand on each warrior's shoulder, saying, "Embrace the darkness. Let your peripheral vision pick out movement, it is better than your primary eyesight at night. Be brave and strong. Let your fear guide you. The element of surprise is with us. Travel well. Good Luck."

Black Shield stared at his friend in the low light. He could still see the long, jagged, semicircular lines of white and pink scar tissue that stretched from his face and shoulders down to his chest. Clearly the marks of the great blond bear. Like the bear, Wolfgang is a nightwalker. Bear people are not always visible, yet they are there. Their presence is always felt.

Wolfgang was quiet as he knelt to the wolf and breathed in his familiar sweet-grass scent. The wolf's uncanny "wolf sense" told him its thoughts.

"We must go. Now!"

* * *

Curly Bear had been thinking about his preparation for this night. On the second night, I entered the pasture and moved as close to the lead mare as she would permit. The horses ran off a little way and turned warily to watch me, the intruder. They snorted and squealed now and then. They had nervously nickered and stomped the ground, nipping or kicking at a neighbor that crowded too closely. I watched how they moved.

On the third night, I saw the mare cock her inside ear at me. She was still watching me when her nostrils flared to catch more scent, sniffing inquiringly with her eyes wide. She had started to lick and chew, a sign that she was relaxing, that all was well.

She was getting curious and thinking about trusting me, thought Curly Bear. I finally got the mare to accept me.

* * *

Curly Bear had fasted and his bowels were now empty. He had bathed in the stream and had rubbed himself all over with sage and other herbs. He chewed sweet roots to make his breath pleasant.

As Black Shield, Wolfgang, and Curly Bear stood together briefly before parting, the two black wolves, sitting erect on haunches, began a low, keening howl. Gradually arching and throwing back their elongated heads, the wolves pointed their noses at the night sky and their howl reached its crescendo. The eerie, long-drawn howl was a pure hornlike sound that rose and fell. OooOOOOOOUUUU.

As the spine-chilling song floated across the mountains and valley, Curly Bear turned and faced Wolfgang. " Your brother, the wolf," "Curly Bear whispered, "Why do they howl."

Wolfgang smiling, whispered back, "The moon calls to them, don't you feel it?" Momentarily, Wolfgang stared at Curly Bear then continued, "They have announced their presence to their family, and have told them that men are about to die."

Curly Bear found looking into the haunting, intelligent eyes of the wolves breathtaking, and asked, "Who is their family?"

Wolfgang replied, "The Lipan Apache slaves in the mine."

Curly Bear, aware of the tales of the wolf's psychic abilities, stared at the two large muscular wolves and felt a slight shiver along his back and knew that for the rest of his life he would honor the wolf in his rituals. The wolf is truly the spirit of family and freedom.

* * *

Descending the mountain and unsure of their footing, the men crabbed their way down the mountain sideways on an unused game trail. In the dark, they kept their mental and physical balance, navigating over the scree and around downed trees to prevent making contact with any and all obstacles encountered. They lifted their feet high enough to step over the vegetation underfoot. The sound of dominant bulls bugling echoed off the mountain slopes in the moonlight. Their slow and silent ghostlike walk led them to the bottom without sound or incident. Moving through the brush along the creek, they moved only when natural cover sounds, like the wind rattling the leaves, owls hooting, coyotes singing, wolves howling and elk bugling, masked their movement. Then the three warriors, going their separate ways, were swallowed by shadows. Somewhere in the distance, drifting on the wind, a wolf howled and another answered.

Wolfgang knew it would be over soon.

One way or the other!

Chapter 46

Black Shield waited, listening. A crescent moon hung low in the sky. The night was alive with small sounds: the scurrying of nocturnal animals, the sudden rush of wings of night birds. The gentle wind had moved round to the east. The infrequent puffs of air brought fragments of man-made sounds of voices and laughter and the cough of a distant horse. A distant coyote barked. Others joined in. The wolf stood silently, listening, watching, and scenting. The wolf's ears, hyper-tuned for sound, and its olfactory sensitivity, able to detect even the faintest scent, guided Black Shield silently on padded paws toward a Spanish sentry. Black Shield could feel his heart beating and his palms sweating as he waited, senses probing the darkness. He systematically watched for things out of the corners of his eyes. Again the wind shifted, this time blowing straight into his face from the north.

His senses were fully alive, stretched to their limits, as he sensed a dark presence in front of him in the shadows. He froze. Wolfgang had taught Black Shield that the night was a special friend and the warrior was hidden deep within the concealing shadows. Then he heard and smelled his prey. The two guards stood nearby talking and were not alert to sense the man in the shadows.

Breathing shallowly, Black Shield stood in complete darkness between two huts, hidden where his eyes would not reflect the silver moonlight. His pupils had reacted to the absence of light and dilated to the point he could see well. He shut his eyes and concentrated on the sounds. He could hear breathing, but the breathing of one man was changing its rhythm. Black Shield froze when he heard an indrawn breath, the kind that came before a shout, but the shout never came. He waited until the breathing became normal again. It was the slow breathing of men in deep sleep on his left and on the opposite side a sleeper barely snoring inside the building. A man snorted in his sleep. Black Shield's movements were slight and painfully slow as he kept to the shadows, creeping through the darkness, his eyes scanning the walls. Stealth, he knew, required patience and care as he slipped between the houses; speed counted for little.

The wolf paused to sniff the cold night air for a scent to follow. The wind made a subtle change and Black Shield heard the sound of chatter and scattered laughter. Men were singing. He turned his head in all directions, searching for sound but again the wind changed. Sensing more than hearing movement, Black Shield inched forward, knife drawn, following the wolf. He listened to the right. Something was there. Then the shadows shifted. The wolf, with the scent of prey in its nostrils, stared with great intensity as it moved slightly ahead of its master, teeth glistening in the thin light. Their fevered eyes alight with bloodlust strained, and Black Shield could just barely make out the silhouettes of two guards now outlined by the moon and stars.

Black Shield saw a slight movement and heard a footfall. One of the guards was turning, his eyes shining with the reflection of the moon. Somewhere out in the distant darkness a wolf yipped. Then a whole pack began singing in the night. Their eerie lilting howls echoed across the mountains. The guards heard the hoot of an owl. Moments later they looked up and silhouetted against the moon they watched the magical bird of the night. An owl soared slowly and smoothly overhead on long, silent wings. It was silhouetted in silvery radiance as it clacked its beak, and vanished into the darkness. Both guards were aware of the superstition that the presence of an owl meant that someone would not live long. The darkness hid their looks of anxiety. The frightened Spaniards felt a looming presence and the first stirrings of fear as the sensation of doom closed in around them, making their breathing difficult. It was too late, they realized something was near them that had not been there before, Their eyes huge, they had only had time to open their mouths in a soundless scream as two black figures leaped out of the darkness. The shadows lunged straight at them.

Black Shield jabbed the knife straightforward through the voice box all the way to the spine. The guard immediately started, silently working his mouth spasmodically trying to scream, while drowning in his own blood. He only managed a gasp. His arms and legs felt heavy. The lungs had run out of oxygen. He could not coordinate any movement as he lost his balance. Black Shield held the body tightly to prevent any noise. He could feel the heat of the man's body, smell his scent, and hear his muffled gurgling. It was an agonizing death.

The second guard was slow to turn, but out of the corner of his eyes he saw two moving shadows detach themselves from the darkness. He was shocked to see a dark shadow bounding toward him. The guard's scream was cut short as he tried to dodge out of the way and was knocked to the ground by what he thought was a large dog.

The wolf was on him immediately. He tried to roll away, but the animal was too large and strong. The snarling, steel-like jaws tore into the arm that the guard threw up to protect his head. His arm was quickly rendered useless with the sound of teeth cracking through bones and sinew. The wolf's first lunge had been fended off but the wolf changed his angle of attack as the smell of blood drove him on. The satanic, staring eyes of a wolf was the last thing the guard saw as the wolf's jaws quickly found the unprotected soft flesh they sought. Then there was the gushing of blood. The wolf drank.

Black Shield heard the sound of the wolf swallowing and lapping blood.

"Good," he thought, "They have been taken care of."

He knelt over the lifeless shape. He peered at the whites of the eyes and then felt for the guard's carotid artery. Dead!

Black Shield entered the first hut with the sleeping men and quickly dispatched them. The pungent, salty smell of hot blood and the unmistakable odor of human urine and feces overwhelmed the room. The two shadows of man and wolf slowly came upright and disappeared, becoming one with the darkness. Only the cloying stink of death remained.

Outside the hut, the warrior engulfed himself in the shadows with his back against the wall, stopping to listen. Sensing no threat, he and the wolf moved on toward a faint glow. The wolf paused to sniff the cold night air for scent. Black Shield paused only feet away from the patch of light streaming from an open door, standing perfectly still while surveying the topography directly around him. His decision was made in a split second. He took three deep breaths and eased toward the door. He hoped the floor would not creak.

*   *   *

A shadow, with fevered eyes, passed into the room and was now dimly bathed in the light. All the night sounds were gone in the thick quiet, interior. Like a dark spirit, the shadow inched its way toward the Spaniard. As Black Shield moved away from the door, the wolf entered to watch, its body enlarged, hackles and tail raised high. The expression on the animal's broad face quickly changed: his ears were pointed forward, his lips wrinkled, and his black pupils showed radiantly, lit by the flickering glow of a small lantern that gave him an idea. His face was one of bloodlust, anticipating the kill.

The dark, beard-fringed face of the guard, wrapped in his

thoughts, began feeling an eerie sense of being watched and felt the first stirrings of a primal fear. He emitted a low laugh, trying to persuade himself that he was not alarmed.

I'm tired and letting my imagination run wild.

But, the terror still lurked in his mind. He became aware of the faint, malodorous air, smelling the scent of wood smoke, leather, and grease. The only sound was his breathing. His blood was pounding in his ears. Suddenly unnerved, he was aware someone else was in the room. He felt the hair stand up on his neck as the expression and color of his face changed. In the first moment of shock, the Spaniard was at a distinct disadvantage. Black Shield felt there was enough time—just enough as he moved forward in a blur of motion.

The Spaniard felt sudden heat on his neck, as he was pinioned by strong arms. They were locked together, their bodies entangled so closely they might have been one monstrous form. With a frantic effort, the guard fought back, feeling the pressure building on the nerve junction at the side of his neck. Black Shield gritted his teeth. Muscles bulged and veins ribboned their skin. The Spaniard's neck vertebrae did not crack. Black Shield felt his enemy gathering his strength, as the guard growled deep in his throat, lifted his shoulders and arms, and jerked his torso downward freeing himself.

The Spaniard, whirling, saw a strange, dark-complexioned warrior figure with eyes of ice staring at him as his lips pulled back in a snarl. The warrior's mouth was twisted in a semblance of a smile. The jaws of the wolf relaxed and its lips formed a happy grin as it watched its God. The white man saw the bright, glassy eyes of a predator: an evil, elemental look of fixed concentration. The Indian's nostrils flared like a predator's when scenting blood.

Black Shield hissed his hate, smelling the strong odor of fear that quickly permeated the Spaniard's clothing. He became aware of the accompanying shallow breathing, pallor, constricted pupils, and the feral look of a trapped animal.

After his initial shock, the Spaniard's face changed. Black Shield saw something sinister in the narrow, beard-stubbled face. The Spaniard's mouth assumed the shape of a smile, but the rest of his face did not join in. His venomous, piercing eyes were those of a cold killer.

In the space of a heartbeat, the Spaniard uttered some curse in his tongue as he reached for his dagger, its blade glinting hard in the candle light as it was unsheathed. Even before the movement had begun, the tall Crow warrior had pinioned the Spaniard's arm, gripping it firmly, restraining him. In a blur, Black Shield's knife impaled itself in the center of the guard's breast, fetched up against bone. The Spaniard's head snapped back in reflexive motion. Blood arced through the air. The man coughed, his eyes opened wide as he arched up, relaxed, and fell back gurgling. His lips pulled back from his teeth in a rictus of pain, as it lashed through him and he grudgingly gave up his life. A thin trickle of blood seeped from the corners of his mouth as he emitted a soft sigh of escaping air. There was a rush of blood as the sphincter let go in death.

For a long time, there was only silence as Black Shield stood listening. The putrid, acrid stench became a thick corruption in the air and clung to the roof of his mouth. Death, appalling and irreversible, mingled with the scent of the candle lantern filling the room.

Black Shield decided to go and took the lantern with him. He worked at building a number of fires. The silence was broken by the crackling of flames, and the symbol of darkness: a distant call of a hunting owl. Four booming notes, the last descending. The fires were soon licking hungrily upward through the carefully stacked fuel. The moon was already setting, and while it was still bright enough to see by he could go faster returning to the mountain meadow.

*   *   *

Behind Black Shield, the night reflected the wavering yellow flames that danced and flickered with coiling and rolling plumes of gray and black smoke rising burnishing the night. The wind-driven fire wraiths wavered and glided silently in a warm glow as the fire greedily consumed the buildings, screams and black ash filling the sky. Silhouetted running and shouting men raced around a cluster of buildings in an eye-stinging haze looking for signs of life. A gust of wind hit him with the smell of charred flesh. Dogs barked in the distance.

Chapter 47

The Spanish horses not in use were loosely herded in a large pasture and allowed to graze freely. Curly Bear found the matriarch, the dominant mare leader. The buckskin-colored mare was responsible for moving the herd and determining where they went. Curly Bear liked the way she carried her shapely head and the manner with which her neck tapered from her well-placed shoulders. Her gait was one of graceful, conscious pride and her ribs were well rounded, her tail arched. She had a white blaze on her forehead.

She's mine, he thought.

As Curly Bear watched, the mare stood motionless, trembling, and taking long, suspicious up-wind sniffs. She raised one foot and put it down. The herd stood uneasily, ears pricked, nostrils quivering full of the man smell. It was time to go. Curly Bear would return and let her grow used to him.

I must study each horse and locate the slender, fine-boned horses with spiral hair whorls above the eyes. These are the animals that are high-strung, flighty and nervous. These horses already have confidence in man. There is no need for them to use their teeth or hoofs in our getting acquainted.

Luckily, there were none that Curly Bear could see.

These Spanish have good horses. None of these are slow horses. I must bond with the matriarch. When the time comes to take the horses, they must be familiar with my sounds, movement, and smell so that they will not be frightened. I must not hurry their conditioning. Be patient.

Curly Bear stood unmoving, watching her. At last, Curly

Bear smiled as the mare lowered her head and began to walk. She started slowly walking around him, getting closer. Now she is curious.

The mare had made the decision to get close and see what would happen. Curly Bear took his eyes off the mare, turned his back on her, slumped his shoulders, and lowered his head in friendly submission. Curly Bear could hear the slow cautious approach of the mare behind him. Then Curly Bear felt the animal's close presence. Time passed slowly and then he felt her hot breath on his neck.

Inwardly, Curly Bear smiled. He turned, standing where the mare could see him with both eyes and they breathed into each other's nostrils. He rubbed the horse's neck and laid his face against her ear, whispering secret, chest-deep sounds hunh, un-hunh, until he was sure the mare was completely calm. He finished by saying, "You're safe with me." Curly Bear's hands had an acute sense of touch. He gently scratched the extremely sensitive skin on the withers, knowing horses responded rapidly to skin stimuli. He momentarily watched the eyes and ears of the mare and knew what was in her heart. Then he left.

* * *

The next night, Curly Bear appeared again in the pasture with the rising of the moon. Luckily, the horse herd was again near the gate of the pasture. He waited nearby for about two fingers of time to see if anything looked strange. There was a guard. He heard him clear his throat and knew exactly where he was as he saw the guard's breath mingle with the cool night air.

* * *

Curly Bear kept his feet low in the long grass to remain as silent as possible. The ground was soft so any sound would be dull. He moved with an almost imperceptible slowness through the grass inching his way toward the guard. When Curly Bear was two arm-lengths away he stopped. He drew his long-bladed butcher's knife from its leather sheath. A horse snuffled. He waited and listened for another sound from the horses. None came. Good! Curly Bear's piercing eyes darted from side to side to make sure the Spaniard was alone. No one. The guard leaned his rifle against a tree and fumbled with his pants. He's going to make water. Curly Bear waited until the guard was concentrating and enjoying his piss, watching the steam rise from his stream. Curly Bear moved directly behind the man and placed his empty hand under the man's chin to shut off any noise or call the guard might try to make. Curly Bear swiftly drove his knife low into the kidney. The man grunted. Then he quickly opened his windpipe with an audible hiss of air.

* * *

As Curly Bear opened the gate, the horses were startled by his presence and wheeled away in flight from him. Curly Bear stopped in his tracks to keep the horses from panic and retreated as he walked the gate around and secured it open. The rigid-backed horses, with ears pinned, emitted a frosty snort, stopping at a safe distance, their senses suspecting his movement and smell. They turned and looked at him with dark eyes, pricked ears, and flagging tails. Curly Bear entered the large pasture gate and again the horses started to move away. Curly Bear, talking in horse, made an insistent nicker that a mare would use to bring her foal back to her.

The herd stopped moving away from him and Curly Bear kept his distance and waited for the mare to come to him. The mare, no longer frightened of Curly Bear, approached slowly. He made no sudden move that might startle the horse and cause it to run. He wanted her to smell him. Then it happened.

She smells me!

She snorted and acknowledged his presence. Then she walked up without fear and stood still and allowed him to breath into her velvet nostrils. He stroked her neck. The mare pushed at him, blowing warm air against his face.

"Good girl!"

Curly Bear now had the feeling of "being at one with the horse." He continued talking softly to her, soothing her with hands and voice, as he put the light leather halter around the lead mare's neck, continuing to talk to her and letting her smell his breath as he gently rubbed her. Curly Bear rotated the loop one complete turn so when the lead was pulled the pressure was transferred from the nose loop to the neck loop and would not tighten up on the nose loop.

Curly Bear mounted the mare as quick as a panther. He waited for a time, watching and listening, then touched his heels and clucked at her to go, leaned forward and stroked her neck. The mare felt good under him. Horse and rider felt and shared a common sensation by the close contact of their bodies. Several horses were already showing their impatience by stomping their hooves, switching their tails, shuddering, and blowing their lips.

A horse can't sneak quietly, but it's time to move.

Together, Curly Bear and the mare moved in slowly on the shifting herd, aware of their breaking point.

A horse's breaking point is its withers. I must focus on the whole horse herd as one animal.

Curly Bear guided the mare from the herd's blind spot behind them, to the side to slow their movement. There was no way to hide the clop sound of the horses' well-conditioned hooves on the hard ground. As he angled toward them, he talked quietly to the herd. The horses, now looking at him with their right eyes, pointed their ears at the gate.

That's good! Now walk the herd toward the gate and slowly away.

Curly Bear slowly moved forward, applying a little pressure to the horses and they veered into a walk to the right, toward the gate.

Watch the whole herd. Don't focus on one animal.

Now Curly Bear maneuvered the mare behind the herd into the animals' blind spot, a position at the tail end of the herd to push them forward. Curly Bear felt the swell of the mare's body and saw the pinning of her ears as she moved toward the rear of the last animal that meant, Move your butt.

Curly Bear looked ahead, paying attention to the turn of the horse's head. He moved up on the side and the lead animals turned their head and eye's to the right and veered right. Good! As the herd started to move too fast, he moved forward slowly and angled toward them to slow them into an easy canter. Now they are moving more quietly, but some were breaking wind with each stride. He moved forward again to slow them down. That's it! He moved the herd to the prearranged mountain pasture and stopped them by riding forward. He quietly went about catching a good number of horses and put them on a loose tether to hold the rest of the herd, letting most of the animals graze until his people joined him. The matriarch began to lick and chew, a sign that she was relaxing. The herd began to graze, some gently snickering as they cropped the grass. He turned and stared at the Spanish camp as flames illuminated the nighttime sky with a red-and-orange hue. Curly Bear crept back into the shadows. Watching. Waiting.

Chapter 48

All around, Wolfgang could sense the shadows of the nearby mountains, darker even than the night, as he stood still as a phantom in the shadow-pool at the foot of a great tree. He shivered slightly under the lash of the night wind. It steadily strengthened, keening mournfully as it assaulted the mountain, as if the imprisoned spirits in the cave were calling to be set free. He leaned back with his eyes closed, breathing in deeply, letting the night fill him. The cold, damp, breeze tasted clean and fresh in his lungs. Remaining motionless, he did not look directly toward the cave, but to the sides and above it. A trick learned long ago.

The position of the Seven Hunters told that the night was more than half over. A crack of light in the Spanish camp was growing brighter. He closed one eye, wanting to keep his night vision as much as possible, while concentrating his ears on hearing. Sound carries much further at night! He heard a low-voiced remark from one of the guards. The gaping black stone mouth of an opening loomed ahead with its engraved and red-painted Maltese Cross overhead. Thick, oily smoke curled from the bright orange, crackling, flickering flames of burning brands that illuminated the entrance from just inside the cave, casting their glow upon the walls. Wolfgang noticed the black silhouettes of the guards as they flitted back and forth outside the mine entrance, casting grotesquely elongated shadows. The two guards stayed within the circle of light, often staring into it. That was a mistake; it destroyed their night vision.

OoooOOOOOUUU!

The two Spanish guards froze and stared into the dark as they listened to the mournful, wavering notes of eerie howling wafting on the cool breeze. The untamed music of two wolves had startled them. The Spaniards stared into the dark from where the sound had originated but saw nothing. Putting on a brave front, both guards laughed nervously. The sound had sent shivers up their spines. The shadows of the mountains and tremendous trees seemed to press in closer upon the two lonely figures as their blood ran cold and terror descended upon them.

Wolfgang felt calm, yet at the same time was filled with an excitement and exhilaration. I must silently approach in a slow stepping stealth. Get as close as we can, before wolf and I attack. Sound carries well at night, and rapid footfalls will alert sensitive ears to danger. The low ground approach will completely consume my profile. I am invisible in the deep shadows of trees and large rocks even on a bright night.

He momentarily felt a kinship with his father's ancestors who lived in the sheltered, deep spruce and fir forest valleys among the limestone and granite plateaus of the Harz Mountains between the Weser and Elbe Rivers of northern Germany. His father's people were descended from the Germanic Harii tribe, who were traditionally night fighters. He remembered his father's stories about warriors with an innate savagery. The Harii were a ghostly army of warriors who caused panic among their enemies by painting themselves black, carrying black shields, and attacking late at night. Wolfgang raised his head and uttered a long-drawn quavering wolf howl.

Inside the mine, the Spanish guards stood still as they heard the sound of two wolves. The downcast and traumatized Apache slaves lifted their heads at the sound and listened to the woeful presage that rent through the night. They believed the howl of a wolf portends bad things. They remained quiet for a time, and then started whispering among themselves.

The Apaches knew the wolf as a symbol of loyalty and

spirit, and that his cycle of power was at night. Their sense of family is strong and loyal unto death, and they live by carefully defined rules and rituals. Suddenly, they were all aware.

An omen!

*   *   *

The black mouth on the mine loomed in front of Wolfgang as he came in, downwind of the guards. Merging with his surroundings, he melded his outline into the front of a broad tree to hide his form, his eyes empty except for the shrunken reflection of the moon. His eyes swept back and forth, catching the available light reflecting off the bare surface of rocks, as he kept the guards between himself and the skylight. A large log and low stonewalls formed a defensive fort to the front of the mine. His companion, the wolf, paused to sniff the cold night air for a scent to follow.

Uff! warned Wolfgang, speaking to the wolf as he twitched his nose at him. The wolf understood its meaning. Bad. The wary wolf pricked its ears as its black fur fluffed up in excitement. It raised its muzzle to take a long, deep snuff of the air to catch the guard's smell and swiveled one ear at Wolfgang and back at the guards. The wolf raised its nose and wrinkled its dilating nostrils as it bared its teeth. It had located the Spanish scent! The wolf curled his lips, tasting the air, smelling his prey.

Imperceptibly, the wolf tensed its shoulders, raised it hackles stiffly, and extended its bushy tail. These actions marked its mood in threat to its prey. The wolf laid its black-tipped ears down and briefly wrinkled his lips baring his fangs in a snarl as his gestures told Wolfgang he understood. The wolf, with mysterious and terrible certainty, tilted its head and looked up at Wolfgang. Its ghostly amber eyes, catching the light, looked back at the guards and his body leaned against Wolfgang.

Wolfgang knelt down and put his forehead against the

wolf's, making sounds of wolf talk, then he licked and snuffled him. Wolfgang could detect only the slightest muffled growl and rumbling sound coming from his friend as the wolf started to posture and signaled his aggression The black wolf looked up at his God and felt his heart beating more rapidly. A shiver went down his spine and a deeper low growl started building deep in his throat as he enlarged his body, pointed his ears, and raised his hackles and tail.

A distant bull elk bugled his challenge and was quickly answered by another bull, the wolf gave Wolfgang an impatient nose nudge. Wolfgang worried that the guards might see the reflection of their eyes in the light and the visible mist of his and the wolf's breath as it mingled with the cold air. Wolfgang waited until both guards looked toward the light. When they turned their eyes towards the dark, they would not adjust to darkness quickly, a mistake that would cost their lives. The moon slid behind the clouds, plunging the area into darkness.

Let's go!

*   *   *

The wind in this high, wild place sounded like a wailing phantom tearing at the two guards as they listened to the squealing sound of the bull elk bugling. The glinting eyes of the guard on the far side went wide and startled for a moment. His entire body prickled: each nerve felt the imminence of some poised threat. He stared out into the night, hearing faint footsteps and then a wraithlike figure formed. The footsteps drew nearer. A shadow-like form moved forward from the dark trees. It became more defined, moving with purpose.

The sound was the padding sound and scrabbling of clawed feet, as a face swelled from the darkness just as the moon peered through the clouds. He watched disbelievingly for a heartbeat. His mouth started to open.

A demon!

AAAGGHH!

A low growl rose to a full-throated roar as the grotesque head of the wolf came flying out of the dark with jaws parted to reveal sharp, pointed teeth. The mewling guard was knocked over. The wolf's long snout and teeth quickly found the soft, hot flesh of the throat. The guard squirmed for breath, his eyes got very large, rolled and bulged as his voice turned into a gurgle. Blood began to pour from his nostrils; he tasted salt at the back of his throat. Blood silently sprayed through the night air as the wolf, with one mighty tear, ripped his throat out, almost tearing his head off.

As the other guard turned to help his friend, he felt cold steel at his throat. His eyes widened in horror and his mouth opened in the rictus of death, as the blade bit deep into his flesh. No sound came out. With a single stroke he had slit the guards throat, the line extended up under the ear to catch the carotid artery. A large spurt of blood shot into the air and then a sheet of blood covered his chest as he slammed into the ground while the night stalker kicked him away from the entrance. A foul odor filled the air as the bodies purged themselves.

Some distance away, a flicker of light blossomed at the far side of the Spanish camp. The fire below in the camp was growing and flickering more strongly, as Wolfgang extinguished the wall-mounted torch in the cave.

*   *   *

As Wolfgang squinted into the near darkness of the mine, at the limit of his vision there was a flickering orange bloom casting long and wavering shadows by a guttering wall-mounted torch. The flame leaned toward the entrance indicating to Wolfgang that there was another source of air coming from somewhere. It was as if the cave were breathing. He heard the sound of moaning not far away, saw a growing glow coming his way, and then detected the sound of voices that were growing louder.

He looked down the tunnel of timber supports standing along the wall and overhead. He realized that this was a natural cave but there were plenty of telltale marks of the miner's pick. From what he could see the tunnel went straight into the mountain. He saw thick-cut mine braces stacked against the wall and quickly moved toward them to take cover. Behind the braces he cast a quick glance down the torch-lit tunnel and saw the silhouettes on the cave walls of two approaching Spaniards coming his way. They were walking at an unhurried pace and were almost upon him, still unaware of his existence. He clenched his teeth, intent on killing quickly. With the prospects of freeing so many slaves, Wolfgang's adrenaline was flowing. He was suddenly eager and anticipated the fight. His blood felt like fire flowing through his veins as his instincts to fight and kill had taken over. Wolfgang stepped forward into the yellow light of the wall-mounted torch and leaned forward.

Chapter 49

By the time the Spaniard heard the feral growl in the wolf's throat it was too late. Reacting to the wolf's snarl, the nearest guard whirled to face the beast. As his head snapped to the side, he felt cold steel under his chin moving across his throat. The blade cut deep through flesh and muscle and finally hit bone. There was a dreadful pause and a puzzled expression spread across his face as he turned and stared into the face of the Night Stalker, his blue eyes lit with battle rage. There was a rush of blood and Wolfgang stepped back. Pleased with the quick work he'd made of the guards, he looked around at the walls of the natural cave. It was a centuries-old limestone cave, carved by the running ground water. He flared his nostrils and caught a heavy, nearby human scent. He knew they were close, invisible to the eye. Waiting!

* * *

The great wolf raised its nose, wrinkled its snout, and ceased breathing, baring its fore-teeth while sampling the air. Wolfgang noticed the wolf curling his lips and knew it was testing the air. It smelled the familiar odor of death and fear.
The wolf, richly endowed with smell and hearing, cautiously continued moving forward deeper into the cave on its large and well-padded feet, smelling more humans and hearing the faint sound of breathing nearby.

As they sat in their captive misery, the Apache slaves had heard the sound of a scuffle, and then silence. They were startled by the sudden appearance of the long-legged traveler who appeared from the gloom. It was the large broad head of a black wolf. It briefly stared at them with its head tilted aside, bowing its neck, its black pupils enlarging with emotion in the "full wolf greeting" from around the corner as it edged forward. Then its manner changed, moving its head high as it stuck its chest out. The wolf's enlarged amber eyes and narrowed black pupils were lighted by fierce anger. The watching Apache saw the wolf turn its head, enlarged its body, pointing its stiffly erect ears forward, baring its teeth and stiffening its legs, making direct and hypnotic eye contact with the lone Spanish soldier in the room. In a threatening manner, it growled its dominance. An uneasy air hung over the room.

A chill ran up the guard's spine causing him to tremble, his face a mask of surprise and fear, his heart beating faster and faster, while he finally managed to control himself. Now, the guard advanced slowly toward the wolf intending to kill it with a long dagger. The wolf, lips drawn back revealing pale gums, smiled a gruesome and ferocious smile.

The Apache saw the guard's eyes change from their cold expression to one of fear as he stared into the terrible, hypnotic eyes of the wolf. The eyes seemed to flicker and glow in the light of the cave. Suddenly, the wolf glanced back as a white warrior appeared through the entrance, the light of the wall-mounted torch flickering eerily on his face. The guard, startled by this sudden appearance, backed up, clenching his jaw. The tall white warrior had a long scar on his face and a determined look in his eyes. His heavily muscled and much scarred body stood relaxed with a suggestion of tension like a set trap. Wolfgang's gaze was briefly drawn inexorably toward the downcast men and women. He felt the bitter taste of bile rise in his throat.

God, who would believe it!

Most of the Apache registered a surprised awareness of his presence. Then their eyes widened, their jaws hung slack with realization, others locked in despair, fatalism, and fear, staring into a distance he knew too well. It started with a murmur, the whispering swelled, washing over the room. All knew it was the white warrior with the sign of the great bear marking his body. He was tall and lean and hard looking, his expression cold and remote.

The Apache noticed that his ice cold, glittering eyes were endlessly searching from side to side and forward, checking every item and person in view, missing nothing. Wolfgang saw the naked dead stacked in rotting piles, and the living chained by the neck to the wall. The prison slaves saw something terrifying in his eyes. His eyes were full of concentration and hell-fire ranged the room. His brows wrinkled upon seeing the Apache slaves, but his eyes revealed his anger.

Wolfgang's ominous, dead-serious face stared at them with clear blue eyes that had an excited glint. With a swift glance, his eyes caught their warning and followed it. There stood another Spaniard with well-defined muscle and bone, who had serious eyes and prominent features that suggested he was no stranger to heartless cruelty. A chill crept up the back of the Spaniard's neck, and his skin fairly crawled in dread, as he noticed the unsettling blue eyes of the German warrior, apparently measuring his mettle with his gaze. They were almost unblinking, hard and empty, the eyes of a man who was no stranger to violence. He suddenly realized that the presence of this strange looking warrior meant he was alone, without help.

Doomed!

He started staring wildly, his eyes flew uncontrollably about the room, shaking with fear, chilled and unnerved and smiling the dark bitter smile of one who is without hope.

Wolfgang was not sure the Spaniard would understand, but he would tell him anyway, he mused. In an accented voice speaking French, Wolfgang said, "The Maltese Cross is your symbol of protection. You are supposed to be willing to lay down your life for your fellow man. The white man has divided their land and limited their freedom. You have enslaved, tortured, and murdered these people. You have treated them more like animals than human beings. You do not value human life and dignity. You sold your conscience for gold and glory. Now you will find God."

Wolfgang saw from the look in the Spaniard's eyes that he had understood, and knew that mercy was not to be given. Wolfgang had seen the calculating cruelty of the Spaniard's eyes. The wolf's eyes glowed with bloodlust. A low growl grew in volume deep in its throat as its drooling jaws snapped, baring its fangs. The Spaniard, nearly unable to breath, knew he had no option but to fight. He emitted a loud piercing wail "Yaaaaaa," and reached for his spear. Turning his terrified face and frantic eyes fully to Wolfgang, he desperately attempted to raise his arm to the throwing position and align it on the center of Wolfgang's chest for an instant kill.

*   *   *

The Apaches watched the sure, deft movement of Wolfgang's hand. The tomahawk came into his hand with a practiced ease as his fingers closed around the grip. Wolfgang's eyes remained fastened on the guard. With an instinctive coordination of mind and muscle, they watched the smooth motion as his axe went up, his arm went forward, and his fingers opened, the axe swiftly flying through the air. The axe spun end over end. Wolfgang watched the expression of fear on the guard's face.

They heard an explosive gasp, as his tomahawk struck between the breasts of the guard's chest, followed by a gasping cry of pain and agony. The guard's eyes never left those of Wolfgang's as he staggered backwards and collapsed against the wall behind him. His body hit the wall with a thud and then the floor, his eyes still riveted on Wolfgang. The watching Apaches saw Wolfgang bend and pull a long thin blade from his moccasin boot and move toward the Spaniard. The knife tip pierced his eyeball and went into his brain. The Spaniard relaxed, and his good eye dilated was blind in death. Wolfgang watched him die.

I don't feel a thing!

Yes, I do feel something he mused—pride!

The Apaches had seen the blur of the thrown ax and knew that the competent, skillful movement was the effect of long and hard use. The spirits of the enslaved Apaches soared. Wolfgang took a deep breath, turned and faced them. His face was hard and his eyes were deep and dark.

The unsettled Wolfgang drew a deep breath and let it ease out slowly. Here were the people with shattered martial spirits, lost honor, shells of their former selves, ill from the lack of good food, without any rights--slaves, just property of the Spanish to do with as they saw fit. His hands gestured in the universal language, saying, "I have been sent by the Lipan shaman, Wind Woman, to free and help you return to your village." He heard a brief cry of triumph from the slaves as they realized they were free.

* * *

The eyes of the Apache slaves had watched in awe and disbelief at the incredible speed of the tall man. His hands had been like a blur. In their mind-numbing slowness they knew that they would talk around the fires for many winters about this dangerous, tall, raw-boned "White man" with shoulder-length blond hair. The one with the light of triumph in his eyes who fought so quickly and brutally. He wore the markings of a Crow Warrior.

The Apache slaves just looked at each other and smiled tightly. They knew that this warrior was the legend spoken of over so many winter fires. Some stories had called him the two-legged man-bear. Other stories referred to him as the "Night Stalker." All of them knew from stories that his presence is announced by a great wolf.

Wolfgang looked at the Apache slaves. They looked tired. We are all tired, he thought. If only we could rest.

"Aiee!" exclaimed one Apache softly. "It is over!"

The movement of Wolfgang's hands assured the Apache saying, "You are not dead yet." Wolfgang stood looking at them silently.

Wolfgang extended his right hand and swept it toward his face signing, "Come!"

"Come. We must go," he signed.

Bodies were slow to respond, but the freed men helped each other and dragged themselves forward toward the entrance to freedom.

Chapter 50

The autumn night was uncomfortably cool as Wolfgang took one last look at the Spanish outpost far below, momentarily hypnotized by the dancing orange flames that were spreading and consuming the entire area. The fires had broken through some of the roofs of the buildings, and the loud, horrible wrenching of splintering wood of buildings collapsing inward could be plainly heard. The smoke carrying burning embers slithered across the night sky.

Wolfgang turned away and glanced at the deep blue-black of the sky and noted the position of the Great Bear easily. The native people pictured The Seven Stars as a bowl, the bear, and the three handle stars as a trio of braves stalking the beast. At this time of year the seven stars of the Big Dipper were found low on the northern horizon. Finding it, the two stars at the end of the bowl served as his pointers. He spread his hand to achieve a straight line out from the pointers and found the North Star to guide him home. For centuries this fixed star had helped people navigate.

The hand is a useful tool for estimating distances in the sky. This time of year the stars are not so bright, but it is a clear night and there is no full moon. The intense light from a full moon would obliterate nearly every star.

* * *

Wolfgang was glad that he was away from the mountains and out on the prairie so that the Big Dipper, sitting low on the northern horizon in its Autumn position, would not be obscured by the large trees. Using the bright stars to guide their path, Wolfgang and the others tracked steadily east, to the campsite on the Arkansas River. A quick glance to the eastern horizon told him that the Great Bear and its seven hunters were growing pale in the pre-dawn sky and light would be coming soon. The velvety blackness was fading in the east to a small gray line along the horizon as Wolfgang led the Apaches away toward the old campsite on the river.

That ancient star, the brightest star in the eastern sky known as the Morning Star, could be seen close to the horizon.

Venus!

With its jewel-like quality of a brilliant dazzling diamond-white star, Venus made Wolfgang think of his first wife, Dark Moon. By the time the sun was marking noon, he and his companions were nearing the river. After they rested the Apaches at the river and rebuilt their strength with the good food and hunting near the Arkansas River, he thought that they would have no trouble when the time came to head north. At this time of year, with clear weather and the sun getting lower in the sky each day, a stick in the ground would cast its shadow due north at high noon. Even if the clouds obscured the stars at night, he had the star that does not move fixed and aligned with the terrain.

* * *

It was a beautiful morning. Wolfgang paused and glanced up. The sun had come up bathing the grass and wild flowers in golden radiance, drying the dew. Bright sunlight poured across the land. The sky had a few sheep-like clouds, its only inhabitants the vultures and eagles. To the east, the desolate landscape stretched into infinity. In places the magnificent colored prairie was shrouded in shadows from passing overhead clouds. Wolfgang looked back at the mountains. They had descended from a high point on the prairie and Wolfgang saw that the mountains and prairie were alive with an abundance of flowers at this time of year. There were strong yellows with accents of brown, white, blue, and cottonwood gold. Nearby were incandescent reds, maple scarlets, yellows, and oranges in combinations that varied with the type of trees.

Wolfgang thought of Dark Moon and then of Wind Woman and her prediction.

Our journey would be dangerous, but we would return safely. Dreams are powerful revelations, offering guidance and predicting future events.

In the distance Wolfgang and some of the others heard a high-pitched scream. Wolfgang saw the light-colored belly and throat of a mountain lion standing over its kill. Its black-bracketed nose and yellow eyes were directed at them, watching. It bounded off using its tail like a rudder as it turned sharply and disappeared from sight. To the north was a herd of mule deer watching. A sea of life swirled all about, as chipmunks scampered to and fro seeking food while small birds flitted about in the undergrowth. High above the gently waving prairie grass, a bald eagle circled, waiting. Wolfgang inhaled deeply, enjoying the fragrance of the nearby juniper, cedar, and sage. It was good to be alive.

*   *   *

Wolfgang worried about a strong Spanish force following them. Burdened with so many people, they made slow time. A good tracker could cut their trail and determine the number of people by the deeper impressions left by the horses. The number of riders could be determined by boxing the stride of the horses by eye and counting the tracks within. They could estimate the time that had elapsed since their passage by the discoloration of the grass. Breaking off a few stems, a tracker could determine the approximate amount of natural liquid still left in the crushed grass. But to the best Wolfgang could determine, they were not being followed. He had kept a good eye on the antelope, wild horses, and buffalo behind them and they were not being disturbed.

* * *

The Crow warrior Black Shield was happy. He was starting back toward the Absaroka homeland. The sun was making a low circle on the southern horizon from the southeast to the southwest. It was time for the skies to become cloudy and the rains to come. Each time it rained and cleared up, the weather would be a little colder. The autumn colors were already painting the hillsides with splashes of orange, yellow, and red in contrast to the darker colors of cedar, spruce, and pine in the distant mountains. He wanted the group to be well on their way before the snows piled high and the ravines filled with deep drifts.

Curly Bear did not look too happy. Looking at Curly Bear, Wolfgang asked, "What is wrong?"

"We are riding back through Comanche country. It is now almost the time of the Comanche Moon when these warriors ride out on their night killing raids in the generous light of the full moon. The raiders will not return to their villages until the Moon of Madness." replied Curly Bear.

The Comanche Moon is the time when the great yellow harvest moon shines. Two years out of three, the harvest moon occurs about 23 September, or the full moon closest to the autumnal equinox. But sometimes it occurs in October. "During the "pre-rut moon, when the bucks seek the old does entering estrus." Wolfgang mused.

If there are no clouds, the light from the moon is good enough to travel six days before the full moon to four days after the full moon. The moon would rise later, at least three fingers of time, each evening than it did the night before. But it would take the moon eight fingers of time to be high enough to shoot well.

* * *

The days on the prairie were still warm but the nights were cool. They could see the first light snows of autumn sitting on the changing colors of the distant mountains. In the blue sky, they could see uniform lines of migrating geese and barely hear their honking and cackling cries as they hurried southward.

Chapter 51

Feeling Dark Moon's guidance, Wolfgang busied himself the next few days treating the wounded and dying. He instructed warriors to dig Blue Flag roots from colonies of the plants in the damp marshes along the stream. He used a decoction made from boiling the roots to treat the many wounds. He used the mashed root as a poultice to treat sores and wounds. Wolfgang remembered that Dark Moon administered blue flag internally to treat stomach problems, dropsy, chronic vomiting, heartburn, liver and gall bladder ailments, sinus problems, colic, and even migraines. Masticated root hair was dipped into water, and the resultant juice dripped into the ear to treat earache. During September and October, chokecherries were abundant in the stream valleys of the foothills and were collected and used for soups. Dried chokecherries were pounded and used in pemmican. The inner bark was used for colds, sore throats, and respiratory infections. Like children, they sucked on the sweet inner bark of cottonwood trees, which was plentiful in the river valley. Wolfgang saw that the Apache had found and collected great quantities of cactus pads, which they handled with willow tongs and were burning off the large and small needles. They ate them raw and cooked. Curly Bear brought Wolfgang a rounded, plump red object to taste and eat. "This fruit from the Cholla cactus plant, is called a 'Tunas.' " Wolfgang ate it and his eyes smiled at Curly Bear. When he quite chewing he said, "It is juicy and sweet. I will have more."

* * *

The captured horses were herded up and divided among the survivors, along with captured weapons. A hunt was organized and they killed a number of fat, older buffalo cows that had stored up thick slabs of fat along their backs. The singing of a gentle breeze through the thick cottonwoods was a constant murmur, as Wolfgang, Black Shield, and Curly Bear had kindled a number of fires to smoke the meat. The meat from buffalo cows is at its best in the fall. Fall on the plains is the period of intensive hunting to secure winter meat supplies and all the warriors knew they must return home as soon as possible to help their families and villages. They ate the organ meat first, starting with the adrenal glands. They sliced the adrenal glands thinly and made sure everyone had some. Everyone ate it raw to sustain health. They scooped out the half-fermented, half-digested grass and herbs taken from the buffalo guts, and distributed some to everyone. The femur bones were broke open for the delicate marrow. The marrow from the lower leg was soft, with a creamy flavor. The boss ribs were the warriors, special meat. Thin strips of lean meat were hung in the open on racks for the sun to cure for their journey.

Wolfgang had tossed a pinch of tobacco into each fire saying a small prayer to honor the spirits. "Thank you!" he murmured half aloud to the everywhere spirit. Black shield tossed a handful of sweet grass and sage, on the fire creating a musky smoke to keep the evil spirits away. Among the giant cottonwoods along the Arkansas River, the elders among the Apaches sat in a circle around a fire.

"What are they doing," Wolfgang asked Curly Bear.

"They are praying to the gods. They are thanking the gods for their freedom and for success in killing the buffalo," answered Curly Bear.

As Wolfgang watched, he heard deep voices quavering a strange, staccato tune intoning their prayers. The sound was powerful and weird. They painted their faces and hands with a reddish-brown ochre. The oldest member drew a pipe and lit it, and blew smoke toward the four corners of the earth, toward sky and ground, and prayed.

All-powerful sun, he began, have pity on us and give us the power to hunt your buffalo and feed all your children gathered here and safely guide us through the dangers ahead. Our bodies are weak.

The Apache elders went on praying and singing for a long time as the younger men organized and prepared for another hunt in preparation for continuing their journey. They had seen no sign of pursuit by the Spanish. Their brush with death in the Spanish mine had made life beautiful again.

All was well.

It felt too good to be true.

It was.

* * *

Days later, under a pale sky of feathery clouds that reminded Wolfgang of mares' tails, their preparations were almost ready to continue their homeward journey.

Storm coming!

The drumming sound of hooves in the distance told of an Apache scout returning. He galloped toward them, zigzagging his animal as he approached to signal that the enemy had been sighted. He brought his horse to a halt before Wolfgang, and pointed behind, the way he had come from, saying in a loud voice.

"Comanches on dahl!"

He says, "The Comanches are coming," said Curly Bear.

Wolfgang asked, "How many?"

"There are about sixty Comanches well beyond the first ridge."

"Are they coming in this direction?"

"They are coming from the northeast, directly this way.
"Did they see you?"
"Yes."
"Did they chase you?"
"No. They are following at a walk"
"Do they know you are here?"
"Yes, and they will soon be in sight."
"I was watching their scout watching you and when I followed him, I came upon the large war party."
"How much time do we have before they are here," asked Wolfgang.
"We have one hand of time."

Wolfgang raised the flat of his hand to the sky and judged where the position of the sun would be in relation to the horizon when the Comanche arrived.

It looks bad, thought Wolfgang. Everyone was looking at him, waiting. He looked all around the skyline. There was nothing yet to be seen. Wolfgang paused momentarily trying to think clearly, then said, "Now, let us plan quickly just what we shall do when they come, it will only take one finger of time. That is enough." Wolfgang looked at his Crow friend.

"Black Shield, what say you?"

Black Shield looked up and said, "We must not let them know that we are many, or that we are expecting them."

Everyone, then looking at Wolfgang, waited silently, anxious for his words. Wolfgang looked at Curly Bear.

"I am sure they will come down the open bottom to approach the camp. Build up two cooking fires and start cooking a deer. Have some of your people grouped around the fires and pretend we are unaware. Have the rest of them mounted and hidden back in the timber. I will stay with the hidden warriors; we will have the captured rifles. We will hide ourselves along the edge of the timber. We will let them attack us. We will let them get as close as we can so we cannot miss. As soon as they are close in, we will fire with one group and then the other will rush out and fall upon them. Tell those with rifles not to fire until I have fired twice. This pause while I reload will make them think we are unprepared. Curly Bear, you and Black Shield lead the charge with the horses, but not until after we have fired. Those without weapons must stay behind those with weapons and take them from the fallen Comanche as fast as they can. There! I have spoken."

Everyone agreed that the quick plan was good.

Chapter 52

While the Crow and Apache waited uneasily, they checked their equipment. Another Apache scout came in and told that their enemy was not far out on the prairie, riding at a trot and heading straight for their bottom. Wolfgang checked the fit of the cock to the lock, and the flint in the jaws of the cock for quick lock time. He made sure old priming powder was replaced and the touchhole picked.

Hearing a rhythmic wsh, wsh, wsh, overhead, Wolfgang looked up ahead, and saw a rich shiny black. The raven! The Spirit Bird! The bird's flight stirred his imagination. The bird is a visible sign of invisible forces. Wolfgang remembered years ago when the raven had talked to Dark Moon during an elk hunt.

He-With-The-Sun-In-His-Mouth. The symbol of dark prophecy—of death.

The lone bird was soaring in the air over the brush. Nothing else. The raven flew over him and fixed a beady, glistening, ebony eye down upon him.

Quork!

The raven spoke to me. It foretells death.

The bird had given him a warning sense. Truly the raven was a messenger of the great spiritual realm. It has brought magic into my life. Wind Woman foretold it.

Black Shield, Curly Bear, and the Apaches were all in the brush and timber, waiting, hidden. Those sitting around the fire pretended they were unaware of an approaching enemy.

No one would move until Wolfgang fired. Wolfgang saw birds fly up from the willows downstream, and at the same time saw the first distant horses and riders through the brush. He stood upright behind the massive trunk of a large cottonwood tree, his rifle pointed up. Wolfgang, with only his head turned to watch with his peripheral vision, watched the nearest leading enemy warrior still walking his horse. Wolfgang's thoughts were racing. He saw the first Comanche. He had a prominent nose and his mouth was thick-lipped and brutal. He had a red painted face and wore a buffalo-scalp bonnet with ermine side fringes and a drooping bunch of magpie feathers set at the rear center of the cap. A warrior who feels worthy and wants to become a war leader must prove himself, so he wears the magpie feathers. The wily bird reflects great intelligence and the warrior wants to advance his knowledge.

The Comanche were getting close; their ponies lifted a cloud of dust, their unshod hooves thudding softly. The murmur of the river had masked the sound of their horse's hooves until they were close. Back in the dark timber, the Apaches placed their hands on their horses nostrils to prevent them from nickering at the other horses should they feel moved to do so. The Comanche came at a slow but steady pace, moving with great care, ears alert for any sound, eyes constantly seeking, searching. Several times the Comanche paused to listen but heard only the soft wind blowing through the trees. The Comanche saw the normal movement of the birds and came on at a near silent walk, their horses stepping delicately.

Wolfgang could make out their snake-like column of men, with their long-tailed headdresses of eagle feathers streaming in the wind, their horses were painted and their beautiful clothes were the colors of the rainbow. As they got closer, he saw the glittering of their dark eyes and long hair--glistening, feathered warriors, with spears and shields. Almost every man carried a fine shield. They appeared confident and powerful.

Wolfgang waited and watched, as a strange, deep glow glinted in his eyes. He realized that any moment they would see the immobile forms hidden in the shadows of the timber. He could feel his heart beating as he sucked in air to fill his lungs to calm himself. The first Comanche suddenly reined in his horse about 30 feet away. Wolfgang instinctively knew that the warrior sensed that something was wrong. The cottonwood is forever pruning itself of dead wood, and the falling of leaves and quantities of punky twigs made the warrior nervous. His head darted in movement like a small bird as if searching for a predator. Then the warrior peered uneasily into the surrounding gloom, noticing the melodious chorus of birdsong was absent. An eeriness prevailed. A warning.

* * *

Back in the timber and screened by a dense growth of willows, the anxious Apache horses had been quiet with nothing but an occasional whicker and grunt. A tail swished here and there at an odd persistent fly, but otherwise the horses were motionless. Now, they were pawing the ground, some were dancing on their toes, some siding with arched necks, and others were snorting and stamping, jerking their necks in anticipation.

Curly Bear and Black Shield, knowing that death may be but a short time away, said their goodbyes to their equine friends. They put their hands to their geldings' faces and put their noses to their mounts' muzzles and gently blew, as one horse to another. They mounted, looked at each other momentarily, edged their mounts up alongside each other, and grasped each other's arm. There was no use talking. The rhythmic pounding of their hearts filled their ears. The tension was great as their bodies felt the tremors shaking their limbs. Their eyes silently said to each other it was time to go, and they squeezed their legs just a fraction, pressing their geldings forward. The horses responded well with a faint champing. They began to slowly walk forward with a dull thump and thud of hoofs. Then they went into a trot. The soft thrumming of hoofs filled the air, as the many horses snorting and blowing began throwing their heads hopeful of a gallop.

Chapter 53

Wolfgang's eyes checked his rifle. The frizzen was clean. Old priming powder had been replaced. Damp powder was always a risk. The half pan of primer was pushed away from the touchhole to ensure faster ignition. The touchhole had been pricked clean. God, watch over us, he prayed.

Wolfgang turned, stepped out, and leveled his rifle--lining up the blue front sight with the thin swipe of yellow along the top of the rear sight, centered the front blade in the rear notch-- and fired. He focused on the front sight. The long sighting plane and balance of his rifle made shooting from the offhand position extremely accurate. The Comanche's startled at the sound but urged their horses on as they lowered their spears, ready to thrust.

The deep-grooved rifling makes the tight-patched round balls rotate and fly accurately and allows room for the fouling to be pushed out of the way.

Wolfgang's ears filled with the familiar sound of the clacking of steel on flint drawing sparks. Then, the flash of fire on the side of the rifle, the loud thundering roar of the ignition of black powder, reached Wolfgang's ears. The rifle hammered back into his shoulder. Suddenly, the air was full of dirty white sulphurous smoke. The smoke billowed and hung in the air, obliterating the target. The sound was music to his ears. His eyes were momentarily stunned, and his nostrils filled with the smell of sulfur. The impact of his shot had driven his target backward as the rider's horse took fright and jumped ahead to one side. With blood bursting brightly from the corners of his mouth, the rider tumbled into the air from the saddle, landed, remained in an awkward heap. The sound of the dead warrior's head striking a rock carried over the prairie. There was a chorus of shouts from the Comanche as their dark shafts filled the air. The lone, riderless horse galloped a short distance. It stopped, then continued on through the camp with the other Comanche horses.

A quick second shot with a flintlock required a life-threatening series of loading movements, sounds, and a time lapse of about 20 seconds.

The Comanche rider had no time to react. Intent on the attack, he was caught by surprise as the head and neck of his mount dropped away and the ground heaved up. The Comanche rider followed the line of his mount's fall, over its back and neck and vanished under his horse's crashing body. With flailing legs, the animal rolled skyward up above him and came down on the rider with crushing force and slid to a stop. The Comanche horse, with a hole through her chest, a broken neck and back, was already dead, with a crushed chest the barely conscious rider lay still with his mouth open. The Comanche's confusion deepened as the air filled with the sound of savage war cries, screams, and labored breathing as horses and warriors crashed to the ground. Others struggled with their wounded mounts.

Wolfgang stared at the crumpled forms. To improve his rate of fire, he had several balls in his mouth and a powder measurer—the tip of a cow horn hollowed out—tethered to a lace above the powder horn. He measured and poured down the bore, spit a ball into it, and tamped it down. The priming, with the small powder horn and its fine grains, took less thought and time. He bumped his rifle near the side plate with his hand to make a little priming powder seep into the touchhole. An arrow made an odd fluttering noise as it went past his ear. Another cut the air past him as the Comanche screamed their defiance with blood-chilling war cries. Wolfgang heard a weird ululating sound and knew that only raw courage would determine the outcome.

By the time the powder and patched round ball were rammed down and the flintlock primed for the next shot, the next leading warrior was upon Wolfgang. Sweat trickled down his brow and stung his eyes. The flint and steel turned the black powder into fire and smoke again. He didn't miss. The air filled with the nauseous stench of sulfur.

* * *

Hidden in the willows, some horses skittered and danced with their eyes rolling excitedly and tongues lolling, while other horses quivered in anticipation. "Now! Charge!" Yelled Curly Bear and Black Shield. Wolfgang had given the signal with his shot. With their eyes narrowed in malice and their lips curled back from their teeth, they squeezed their horses' flanks. The animals gathered their quarters and were leaping and crashing though the timber, charging upon the remaining mounted Comanche. With loud whooping and the clatter of hoofs, the riders thundered upon the tree line, their shrill war cries rose as they rode directly into the open flank of the Comanche. The air was thick with the drumming of hooves and a deep sonorous chant to the shrill ululation of the charge—high-pitched frenzy of the blood squeals. The fierce-faced Apache and Crow riders with their eyes hard and heads held low, leaned close to the necks of their mounts presenting a low profile.

As the rumble of hoofs grew louder and louder, the chorus of war cries was rising like a song as riders urged their mounts forward faster. He heard the thrumming of bowstrings. The air was darkened and filled with the soft buzz of arrows, as shafts drove deep into the mounts, making them stagger sideways from the shock of impact. Startled Comanche warriors toppled from their mounts, feathered shafts protruded from their bodies, their eyes crazy with fear and pain. Horses screamed.

Then came the clatter of impact as the two sides crashed together with a shock. They were locked in individual combat, horse against horse, rider against rider; empty guns were used like clubs, bow-men were in such close quarters that they could not fit an arrow. Knives and axes bit deep into flesh as men tussled in brutal encounters.

The air filled with the high-pitched whinny and shrieks of terrified, mortally struck horses with arrows buried in their hides, shuddering, staggering, and finally lowering their necks and convulsing. Other horses suffering less mortal wounds, went out of control, bucked in pain, struck out with their front feet, spun in circles, and ran into other horses in their terror. Their lungs still laboring, they drew their lips back as blood slobbered from their open mouths, as they were swaying and falling.

There were the shrieks of the wounded and dying men. Two arrows struck a Comanche rider knocking the wind from him. He fell without a sound, blood bubbling from his lips. Another, with a spray of blood and up-flung arms, tumbled backwards off the horse with a piercing yell of agony.

Pathetic whinnies were heard everywhere. Comanche horses, with arrow shafts jutting out of their sides, rumps, and bellies became frightened and panicked. Terrified, riderless bloody horses struck by arrows and in excruciating pain fell and were flailing their hooves. Horses screamed in pain, trying to nip at their wounds. Wounded horses, bleeding from wounds, made small nervous steps sideways, became enraged, mad with pain, kicked out with their front and back feet, plunged up and down, spun in circles, fighting for breath while barging into their companions running off.

Many dying beasts reared, stumbled, then their front quarters collapsing, went down, eyes white, teeth bared, whimpering. Dying horses began thrashing their heads and beating their hooves, as warriors shouted and fought to regain their footing, trying to avoid the deadly death throes of the prostrate animals. Many horses galloped away dripping blood.

Amid the sound of labored breathing, the warriors of both sides were desperately attempting to escape the blades of their opponents. Many received bow slaps to their heads, knife thrusts and axe blows to their bodies. From the confusion of battle, the air filled with the swelling sound of surprised cries and grunts as men struck blows on shields, inflicting pain as they landed. Warriors who had been knocked on the head pitched and dropped from the back of their horses, dead and dying. One downed warrior lay pinned beneath his screaming horse as its hoofs lashed the air as it tried to regain its footing. The wild snorts and whinnying cries of agony from wounded, rearing, and bucking terrified horses and the noise of screaming men swelled in volume. A terrified horse ran dragging its guts. The sharp musty stench of horses filled the air.

Chapter 54

Curly Bear momentarily halted after a successful engagement with an enemy, clicked his tongue, and urged his mount forward. He rode directly for two enemies that turned their mounts toward him. He felt the wind and heard the soft whirr of a passing arrow. Curly Bear shivered as a feral snarl twisted his features. A surge of excitement swept over him as he guided his horse into his nearest opponent, but he was too close and missed. The other warrior was almost upon him as he completed a backhand swing and struck the one on his right with his tomahawk. The warrior fell. Another arrow whirred close by. Then he was through their line, bent low over the flying mane of his galloping horse. Now, he came upright, set his mount on her haunches, and turned. He guided his horse up on the unguarded side of a Comanche and cleaved the dismounted warrior's skull in two. The Comanche fell, his body twitching, his head bubbling blood. Curly Bear twisted and wrenched his tomahawk back ready to attack again.

Briefly, Curly Bear saw the flittering feathers from a spear. He focused on a Comanche who rode down an Apache on foot and drove a hunting spear through his broad back. The stone head of the shaft entered the warrior's upper back and came out the lower part of the chest cavity. His legs gave way and his eyes bulged with a surprised look on his face as the force of the impact drove him forward. The large shaft cut through a lung, diaphragm and intestines. His face an ugly mask of pain, he croaked hoarsely as he weakly clutched for the shaft while blood spilled from his mouth before he went limp. Curly Bear's horse responded to the pressure of his legs, and with its cat-like movement turned in a circle and quickly rode down and into another warrior and dismounted him by colliding his horse into the side of the enemy's horse.

*   *   *

Black Shield clubbed a Comanche from his horse on his first pass and narrowly missed being hit with an arrow as he went by another black-painted Comanche. Black Shield turned his gelding quickly to make another run. His gelding squealed with agony at the impact of an arrow in its neck. Black Shield reached over and broke the point off with his right hand and then yanked the protruding feathered shaft from his horse's neck. He became alarmed as the gelding became unsteady on its feet and he jumped from the animal's back as it dropped to its knees. Its hocks settled, it rolled over on its right side, its front hooves thrashing at the ground. Slowly, its body became stilled with weakness and its breathing became shallow. Black Shield then saw a feathered shaft protruding from behind the ribs in the animal's vital organs, as it struggled for breath. Men were dying, but all Black Shield thought about was the noble animal, his companion. He snapped off the shaft with a sharp splintering crack as the horse lay dying, pumping its lifeblood out on the ground. He hated the quick thought that soon the coyotes, vultures, crows and maggots would tear his friend apart and feed upon it. Already a flight of distant vultures were patrolling and gathering.

Black Shield saw the still-mounted Comanche just as he brained an Apache in the head with his war club. The sound was like the bursting of a ripe pumpkin as the club struck his head. The Apache tumbled backward, and struck the ground with a loud thump.

Black Shield's nostrils flared and his eyes went wild and

wide as he let out a terrifying animal roar of a war cry and ran toward him, his chest and legs straining with every fiber of his strength. As all the Comanche started breaking off the attack and scattering, amid the deafening storm of noise Black Shield unhorsed a Comanche. The Comanche rolled, recovered, and stared wildly. Open-mouthed and snatching for a deep breath with animal instinct, his face fixed in a snarl and he gave a defiant war cry as he attacked, with ferocity and courage the two warriors slammed their shields forward and grappled, feinting and thrusting, seeking to deliver a fatal blow to an exposed body part.

Men thrown from their crippled horses lay on their sides, some horses bucked on the ground, nostrils flaring in pain as their chests heaved. The acrid odor of horseflesh filled the air. An unhorsed Comanche warrior gave an explosive grunt, arched his back, and threw his arms back from a well-aimed arrow that protruded from his chest.

With a fanatical savagery, the Apaches screamed with a deafening exultation as they were now attempting to run down and destroy their panic-stricken enemies who were slowed by their wounds, by crushing them under their horses. The Apache blades flashed and glinted as they hacked and stabbed with spears and war clubs as men with livid red streaks and oozing blood, breathed heavily and drained of strength, with only thin, rhythmic rasping of breath stiffened and fell to the ground, as fingers and body spasmed.

* * *

Seeing a cloud of dust and hearing the clattering of hoofs disappearing in the distance, Wolfgang found Mouse and with a wild leap was on the back of the horse. He whirled Mouse around and bent low over the horse's neck. He ascended the cliff overlooking the river and gave chase to a fleeing Comanche. He pressed his legs into Mouse's flanks and the animal responded into a gallop. He closed steadily. Hearing the swift beginning of pursuit behind him, the Comanche looked back and realized his danger. The rumble of hoofs grew louder and louder. He turned his head again and realized the solitary rider was gaining steadily as he whipped his horse. The Comanche's horse was losing speed, he quickly slowed his struggling animal and brought it up on its haunches to a sliding stop and turned. Now, Wolfgang saw the Comanche present a shield and lance to him and with the slightest motion urge his horse forward a few steps. He stopped and adjusted his shield and lance. The two warriors regarded each other; in the background the unnatural silence of the men behind them there was only the blustery sounds of the wind in the grass. Wolfgang took notice of the way the eagle feathers in his hair and on the lance and shield swayed, twirled, and fluttered in the wind. He confirmed the wind by checking the sway of the grass. Wolfgang's mouth was dry. He spoke to Mouse, saying, "This is a brave man, Mouse. Now he is listening to the wind and talking to his Creator, listening to what his Creator has to say. All those feathers are for brave deeds."

Wolfgang felt a presence and looked behind himself. There at a good distance away, were Black Shield and Curly Bear sitting motionless on their horses, watching.

Wolfgang turned back and saw the Comanche with his head up, hearing him singing his death song.

"He has decided," said Wolfgang, "Now, I wish I had not followed." Then very clearly, Wolfgang heard the voice of Dark Moon say, "To show mercy is the mark of a great warrior." The hair on Wolfgang's neck stood up, he looked all about him, his eyes searching. She had spoken to him. She is still here. Watching! Wolfgang sat his mount looking at his watching enemy.

Wolfgang waved his hand outward saying, "Go". He looked down at Mouse whose head was cocked, watching him, as if asking a question, his inside ear turned and locked on him. He looked deeply into his eyes and rubbed Mouse's neck. Wolfgang took a deep breath, saying to his friend, "It is time for us to go home. No more." Mouse whickered, as if in response.

The mounted Curly Bear watching at a distance, turned to Black Shield and said, " A Comanche who captures a live enemy warrior will torture him to death. It is what they do. It is what I would do." Without taking his eyes off the Two-legged Man-Bear, Black Shield responded, "It has been seen before. He is a great warrior. There will be much to tell in stories around the fires when we return."

Chapter 55

Yellow Bird Singing was alone high in the Bear Lodge Mountains while collecting the appearing black Chaga from the live, old-growth trees with the creamy, white bark. Wolfgang had told her this tree was called birch. The old trees were white with black, fissured bark at the bottom. The rough, dry fungus-type growth had the appearance of dull charred wood on the outside. She thought of Dark Moon now in the spirit world and worried about her friend Stars Come Out. Dark Moon had taught her the use of the bark and growths on the trees. The bark and chaga provided relief from pain, a restorative tonic, to stanch bleeding, prevent infection and acted as a blood purifier. She crushed or shredded it for use in extracts and powder for use in teas internally, mainly for stomach complaints. Dark Moon had taught her to cut the trunk of the tree as a covering for a lodge, roll it into a tapered stick to burn to keep away mosquitoes. She could dry birch bark in the sun, grind it, boil it in water, then seep and strain it to use on wounds and skin conditions. As she worked, the black marks on the trees where the deer had browsed the twigs in the winter were visible.

Yellow Bird Singing was thinking of Dark Moon when a slight breeze caught her hair as she saw a vision of the Two-Legged Man-Bear. She clearly saw Wolfgang watching an enemy chief painted black and crimson for war kneeling on an open plain singing his death song. She heard the words of Dark Moon speaking to her husband. She saw Wolfgang sign to his enemy to go, sparing him. The Two-Legged Man-Bear was alive!

Yellow Bird Singing packed up her belongings, remembering the sadness that radiated from the forlorn eyes of Stars Come Out. She knew she must hurry back toward the village. She had a long way to go. Wolfgang had been gone a long time. Many of the Crow people thought he was dead. She had but one thought, to get to the lodge of Stars Come Out as quickly as possible. Stars Come Out was suffering terrible pain from Wolfgang's absence. She suffered the overwhelming fear of the loss of the man she loved. Her anxiety had gotten worse as time went by to an intense discomfort on the point of panic. Her friend had started some time ago complaining to her of being miserable and sleepless. Lately she had been suffering dizziness, rapid heartbeat, chest pains, and shortness of breath over her husband. Stars Come Out lately had begun to think she was dying. The look of concern from one sympathetic woman in the village had sent Stars Come Out into a full-fledged panic attack. Yellow Bird Singing had done her best to get her friend to relax, without any effect. The saddened look on the face of Stars Come Out had been overwhelming to see.

* * *

Stars Come Out looked at Yellow Bird Singing's smiling face, as she said, "The Two-Legged Man-Bear will return when the buffalo hair is longest for robes, bedding, and winter clothing and darkest in color." She felt a choking in her throat and knew he would return in the Moon of Madness. Wolfgang called it November! She gasped, to catch her breath. He is Alive! Stars Come Out stroked her arm over and over. She was suddenly so very tired, as the tears came to her eyes.

* * *

It was the Moon of Madness and the people of the village

were hungry for fresh meat. The people of the village observed a buffalo skull with its nose pointed at Yellow Bird Singing's lodge and heard her dancing, singing and rattling inside during the day. She had begun a buffalo-calling ceremony. They saw her taking buffalo chips into her lodge where she had drawn buffalo tracks and placed them on a drawn trail. The people heard her bellowing successively in imitation of bulls, cows and calves.

Yellow Bird Singing sequestered herself in her lodge. She used her supernatural blessings to charm the buffalo near to the village by tying a bundle of buffalo hair and fat to her backrest in her lodge upon which she sang dream-songs at night, calling to them to come.

At the end of two days, Yellow Bird Singing emerged from her lodge and told the men to gather singers and commence a Bull Dance and for the women to do likewise and perform the cow dance. The painted dancers wore buffalo hair anklets. Their eyes were daubed with azure and vermilion. Their bodies were painted black, white, and red and covered with complete buffalo hides. The women wore owl and raven feathers in their buffalo hats. With the beat of the drums, the warriors stamped, jerked wildly, and bent deeply while pantomiming their call to the buffalo, their songs rising and falling with feeling.

The people of the village gathered to watch the ceremony and to blend their voices in high-pitched yelps as they watched the dancers stamp, grunt and bellow in imitation of a buffalo herd. The two-man "hoop-and-javelin game" that had the power to attract buffalo, was played to charm the buffalo to return.

* * *

The sun had just gone down behind the northern most point of the Bear Lodge Mountains. A young herder named Magpie watching the village horses stopped in his rounds. He and his horse jerked alert. Magpie watched his mount's ears and eyes. His horse twitched his ears to danger and his eyes rolled white. Nervous, he muttered his surprise under his breath, then gritted his teeth, reached up and laid his hand on the soft muzzle to keep her still.

From the direction of the badlands came sound. The faint, heavy rumbling and clattering of hoofs. Then the faint beat of hoofs died out. Magpie's experienced eye watched the nearby mares. The horse herd was only mildly alarmed at the sound and only a few mares stamped their foot, snorted a gauzy white mist, or raised their heads and ears. Mares are the most alert! He could see no one and hoped no one saw him. He suddenly remembered his friend Kicking Horse who was killed in the last horse raid by the Cheyenne.

Poised like an animal, his eyes opened wide at the faint sound of approaching horses from the south. The sound was gone. He suffered a sudden premonition of danger, as he nocked an arrow to his short bow. He sat his horse quietly, listening and watching. Then the sound came again. Now he was sure, detecting the vibration and sound of approaching horses.

A familiar voice accompanied by a dark, bear-like figure appeared suddenly as fear gripped the young man as he raised his weapon.

"Magpie, it is I, the Two-Legged Man-Bear."

Magpie immediately recognized the voice and warrior in the dark. The batsira'pe. The white warrior that harbors the great bear inside his body. Magpie's body shook with fear as the dark figure approached. "I will tell our Chief that Magpie is alert." Wolfgang approached Magpie and said, "It is good to be home. Now go and alert the ak`i'sate, the village police and the Chief that Wolfgang and Black Shield have returned with our lost horses and many others." Magpie rode for the village.

* * *

Stars Come Out heard women on the other side of the dance begin to sing in tremolo and trill their tongues and slowly the drums came to a stop. She saw the tall figure on the other side of the fire. Stars Come Out could sense the intensity of being watched. She turned her head slightly, and in the flickering light saw the piercing blue eyes of a smiling blackened face staring at her in silence from the other side of the fire. Her body began to shiver. She took a deep breath to control her quivering body as her heart started pounding. Her tearing eyes opened wide in shock and her mouth hung slack. She felt lightheaded as she took a deep breath, then smiled, tucking her trembling lips in toward her teeth, in acknowledgement. Her victorious Two-Legged Man-Bear was home!

Wolfgang stood looking into his wife's wet eyes and felt a surge rush through his body.

"Woman," he said, "I love you."

Stars Come Out could not talk, her throat was too tight as her body continued to tremble. He pulled her to him and clutched her in his arms, their bodies woven as one. His nostrils flared at the sweet scent of his wife. Tears came to his eyes and he felt her love and pulsing heat flow into him. Their lips met and fire raced through their bodies. He felt the bulge of new life in her stomach.

"She is pregnant!"

The sound of the singing and trilling of tongues grew louder. The beat of the drums slowly picked up.

End

About the Author

Charles A. McDonald was born into a ranching family, the Rocking H, in Northern California. He graduated from the Erv Malnarich Outfitters and Guide School in Montana and spent four years in the Idaho wilderness working as a wrangler, fishing and hunting guide. He has a B.S. in history from Chaminade College of Honolulu. He is a life member of the Special Forces Association and Military Order of the Purple Heart. After attending the basic and advanced VIP and Executive Protection School at the North Mountain Pines Training Center at Berryville, Virginia, he worked as a Personal Protection Specialist (PPS). McDonald has contributed a dozen articles to The Pennsylvania Outdoor Times, Bowhunting News, Instinctive Archer and The Journal of U.S. Military Special Operations.